ANISE

DEAD
LATE

Two hearts. One choice. And the clock is ticking.

DEAD LATE
ANISE EDEN

TANGLED TREE PUBLISHING

DEAD LATE
THINGS UNSEEN
BOOK 3

ANISE EDEN

TANGLED TREE PUBLISHING

ALSO BY ANISE EDEN

Things Unseen Series

Dead Sound

Dead Keen

Dead Late

DEAD LATE © 2024 BY ANISE EDEN

All rights reserved. No part of this book may be used or reproduced in any written, electronic, recorded, or photocopied format without the express permission from the author or publisher as allowed under the terms and conditions with which it was purchased or as strictly permitted by applicable copyright law. Any unauthorized distribution, circulation or use of this text may be a direct infringement of the author's rights, and those responsible may be liable in law accordingly. Thank you for respecting the work of this author.

Dead Late is a work of fiction. All names, characters, events and places found therein are either from the author's imagination or used fictitiously. Any similarity to persons alive or dead, actual events, locations, or organizations is entirely coincidental and not intended by the author.

For information, contact the publisher, Tangled Tree Publishing.

WWW.TANGLEDTREEPUBLISHING.COM

EDITING: HOT TREE EDITING

COVER DESIGNER: BOOKSMITH DESIGNS

EBOOK ISBN: 978-1-923252-06-6

PAPERBACK ISBN: 978-1-923252-07-3

Dedicated to my dear friend Rosanna Leo.
Thank you for sharing your brilliant creative gifts,
your generous friendship, and your beautiful heart.

PROLOGUE
KAYLA

"Kayla! Kayla!"

She heard the singsong voices calling her name in the distance, the way her mother used to call her into the house when the night grew dark and the streetlights came on. But these were the voices of her new friends, the ones she had met while studying abroad in Ireland. Did they think she was playing a game with them, maybe hide-and-seek?

She didn't answer. This was no game to the girl walking in front of her, the silver buckles on her tall black boots nearly submerged as she slogged ahead through the water.

She must be freezing in that getup, Kayla thought as she followed, wondering why the girl had worn a tank top, miniskirt, and thin tights on a near-freezing night like this. Kayla was quite cold herself, now that she thought about it. Her soaked baggy sweatpants clung to her legs, slowing her down as flecks of moonlight danced on the water around her.

The girl before her forged on as though driven by some wild internal engine. Kayla struggled to keep up, the gentle rushing sound of the river flowing punctuated by the sloshing noise of her legs pushing through the currents. Slowing as they approached the pedestrian bridge near the college gates, the girl glanced back over her shoulder with wild eyes.

It was those eyes, desperate and pained, that had compelled Kayla to follow her in the first place.

Kayla and her friends had been walking home from a volleyball game, following the River Lee along the Western Road. Kayla had fallen a little behind as usual, slowing down to admire the night sky, when she spotted the girl waving to her from the water's edge. When Kayla called out and asked what was wrong, the girl had only beckoned more frantically, so she had quickly climbed over the iron fence, clinging to a low-hanging tree branch as she half stepped, half slid down the earthen bank.

Could someone be hurt or drowning? But when Kayla got closer, before she could even ask, the girl turned and waded into the river. Whatever was happening, clearly there was no time to lose. Kayla kept calling after her, but she didn't reply, just plowed ahead.

Minutes passed, but Kayla couldn't say how many. It was a fight, tearing her feet away from underwater plants and holding up her arms to keep tree branches from smacking her in the face. Eventually, the earthen bank covered with trees and plants gave way to a dark stone wall as the water grew slightly deeper, covering Kayla's knees. By the time they reached the bridge, they had come some distance, and she was growing more and more worried about what they might find.

Finally, the girl stopped. Breathless, Kayla caught up to her. With an outstretched arm and a solemn expression, the girl pointed ahead toward the pillar of the bridge, just at the waterline. Still silent, she motioned for Kayla to go before her.

Kayla trudged around the girl and waded up to the spot she had indicated. She looked around but didn't see anything unexpected, so she turned back to ask the girl what she was meant to see.

But the girl was no longer there. Somehow, she was gone, disappeared.

Kayla spun around in the water, thrashing to keep her balance as she searched. Had the girl fallen under the surface? But the water was shallow, and there was enough light that Kayla would have spotted her.

The girl was nowhere to be found.

Where had she gone, then? There was no way the girl could have scaled the ten-foot stone wall along the riverbank, and certainly not in just a few seconds. Kayla's eyes scoured the water around her once again but turned up nothing. What was happening?

As she rested her hand against the cold concrete of the pillar, the realization dropped into her heart like a stone. *Oh no, not this again,* Kayla thought, shuddering with cold and casting her eyes heavenward. *Please, not now! Not here!*

Although she knew in her heart the girl wouldn't answer, Kayla called out yet again. "Hello? Is anyone there?" Met with silence, she could only shake her head as she turned back to the spot the girl had indicated. Kayla must have been brought out here for a reason, and she would be damned if she was going to end up soaked and frozen for nothing.

She pulled her phone out of her jacket pocket, turned on the flashlight, and shone it all around the pillar. There still appeared to be nothing out of the ordinary.

Then, suddenly, she spotted an object just under the water's surface. It appeared to be wedged into a crack between the stone wall and the bridge's pillar. With her flashlight trained on the object, she leaned down for a closer look.

"Kayla? Where are you?" Her friends' voices were louder now; they were close. She needed to find what the girl had been pointing out before they arrived. Her friends would no doubt insist on getting her out of the river immediately. But she couldn't stop searching, not now.

With her free hand, Kayla reached into the bitter cold of the water. The object was soft and dark and as black as the night sky. She grasped it gently and tugged. When it didn't budge, she tugged again, a bit more firmly. This time, the object gave way, and she pulled it free. As she held it up in front of her, the breath rushed out of her lungs, like the air in a pin-stuck balloon.

"Kayla, what are you doing down there?"

Her friends had won the game of hide-and-seek. They peered down at her from the bridge, their worried voices shouting.

But Kayla was frozen in place. She couldn't move, couldn't tear her eyes away from the tiny, limp blackbird cradled in her palm. As its yellow beak and wet, iridescent feathers shone in the moonlight, Kayla peered at the cloth crest clutched in its tiny claws. The fabric was torn at the edges, but in white embroidery on a red background, she could see the letter *M* and the image of a tall ship sailing between two towers.

This has to be it, she thought, seeing nothing else in the water. Pocketing her phone, Kayla called up to the bridge, "I'm okay!"

"Grab hold," one of her friends yelled seconds before an orange foam ring splashed into the water next to her and began to drift downstream.

Kayla cradled the bird against her chest with one hand and grabbed the white rope tied around the foam ring with the other.

"The water's only three feet deep," she called out. But her friends' expressions of relief switched back to confusion when she asked, "Hey, does anyone have a plastic bag?"

CHAPTER 1
NEVE

"This is so magical."

It was like being inside a living painting. Ancient standing stones encircled us, some upright, some leaning or fallen on their sides, all mottled gray with moss and lichen. Clouds swept across the sky like pieces of pulled cotton, filtering the golden October sunlight as it touched the rolling hills, which glowed shades of fluorescent green. Dark hedgerows thick with the yellow flowers of furze bushes wrapped themselves around the fields as scattered clusters of sheep dotted the countryside. I took a deep breath, inhaling the crisp scent of fresh air and wild things growing.

"You always say that about bacon."

Con's Irish brogue curved around his teasing words, the deep resonance of his voice drawing my gaze back to the man I loved. His rough-hewn features mirrored the rugged landscape as his hefty frame dwarfed our small folding table. I was touched; he had dressed up a bit for our picnic in a button-down shirt and slacks. A new wool overcoat was draped around his shoulders. The sling cradling his left arm was the only visible reminder of our recent misadventures.

I lifted a strip of crispy brown bacon to my lips and tried to bite into it seductively, but it crumbled instantly. Shards scattered across my plate. "Am I wrong?"

"You're right, of course." Con chose a piece for himself, neatly breaking it into small pieces before popping one into his mouth.

Pointing one of my salty shards at him, I said, "I thought this was called '*streaky* bacon' here. What you all call 'bacon' looks more like sliced ham to me."

"Right again." Con looked off into the distance as though contemplating a deep philosophical point. "Living in the US, I must have lost touch with my roots."

"What better place to get back in touch?" I swept my hand out toward the large stones surrounding us.

To thank us for helping his fiancée, and in a nod to my fascination with stone circles, Con's brother, Eamonn, had arranged this special meal for us. With permission from the farmer who owned the land, he had come out early that morning, setting up while their mother cooked us a full Irish breakfast. She'd included "streaky bacon" for my benefit, since Con told her how much I loved it. Then Eamonn had packed us and the food into his truck and brought us to an astonishingly well-preserved ancient site not far from their family home in Kilshannig.

At first, I had just walked around in awe, admiring the stones and asking repeatedly if it was okay to touch them. Con assured me it was, and Eamonn took a few pictures of us standing in the stone circle with our "pop-up restaurant" before leaving us to our meal.

"This type of thing was never my 'roots.'" Con gave the standing stones a dubious glance. "I've never had the same veneration you do for things like stone circles—or anything else, for that matter."

It was true, Con had an aversion toward anything to do with spirituality or religion, ancient or otherwise. Not that I blamed him; he had his reasons. For one thing, as a doctor, he witnessed more suffering than most, leading him to ask difficult questions. The answers religion had to offer, he deemed unsatisfactory. He had been raised Catholic, and the horrific child abuse scandals involving the Church that had broken in recent years had further eroded his faith.

But while Con might have a troubled relationship with the divine, I knew there were plenty of other things he held in deep reverence. "That's simply not true."

He leaned back, eyebrow raised. "Name one."

I began ticking them off on my fingers. "Let's see…. Being a doctor and giving the best care to your patients; your family; your friends; loyalty; protecting the vulnerable…."

Con tossed his head back. "Ah, Jaysus," he exclaimed, running a hand over his face. "That whack on the head you took must have been more serious than we thought!"

At that, I laughed, but not fully. Although my head injury had been accidental, reminders of what we had been through recently still sobered me. I must not have hidden my reaction very well, because Con reached across the table, enveloping my hand in his.

"I'm sorry, Neve. I shouldn't have joked about that."

"Oh, please!" I forced a smile. "Of *course* you should joke about it. *Please* joke about it. I don't think I could stand it otherwise."

"A black sense of humor, is it?" He nodded slowly. "So *that's* why you didn't object to Eamonn calling me 'Slingblade'!"

"You did nearly stab him at dinner the other night."

"Well, it *is* a bit awkward," he grumbled, picking up a knife with his bandaged arm and waving it around.

I laughed for real then. Con always seemed to know how to bring me back from the dark edges of my mind—just one of the many things I treasured about him.

We had only been dating for a little over a month, but we'd worked together at Capitol Hill General for two years before that, and in that time, Con had become my best friend. When our romance finally blossomed, it felt easy and natural, so much so that I'd agreed to accompany him to Ireland on a prolonged "first date."

He had wanted me to meet his family and see his home country, and those aspects of our trip had been wonderful. But our first two weeks had also held an unfortunate echo of the dangers we'd recently escaped in Washington, DC. In the process of helping Eamonn's fiancée with a difficult mental health problem, we had tangled with her ex-boyfriend. The man, who Con had since dubbed "Mad Max," had turned out to be the criminal leader of a nouveau Bronze Age cult and had tried to drown us both in a sea cave near Galway. Con had then taken a bullet bringing him to justice, so I had spent the last week trying to nurse him back to health—not an easy task when, like many doctors, he was a horrible patient, refusing pain meds and overexerting himself.

Everything was about to get much better, though. A week away in Cork City awaited us—on the White House's dime, no less, and requiring just two days' effort on our part. While studying abroad there, President Duran's goddaughter, Kayla, had begun to experience a psychiatric issue with possible endocrine system involvement. Since that was Con's treatment specialty, and since as a psychotherapist, I could potentially be of support, we had been asked to check in on her. It still felt surreal to me that the president of the United States knew who we were now, let alone that he had asked us for a favor. But Con seemed to take everything in stride—cult leaders and world leaders alike. In any event, we were happy to help, and it was a small price to pay for a free vacation.

And I was beyond excited by the prospect of spending a week in a hotel suite alone with Con. We hadn't been physically intimate yet—not for lack of desire, God knew, but rather due to chaos and circumstances. But while the idea of finally "crossing the naked Rubicon," as Con put it, filled me with a heady mix of longing and anticipation, truth be told, I was also a bit nervous. First of all, it had been years since I'd disrobed in front of a man for the first time, so that was terrifying.

Then there were the scars on my abdomen, though they weren't as noticeable since it had been over two months since the attack. Con had already seen those wounds; he went with me to the emergency room when it happened. But the scars remained jagged, ugly reminders of how I had failed my patient, who had been in the midst of an acute psychotic episode. He was suffering from delusions and believed that by stabbing me, he was saving me. Somehow, though, during our session, I'd missed all the warning signs—until it was too late. Ever since the incident, I'd been white knuckling my way through anxiety and panic attacks. I even avoided looking at my scars in the mirror, so the idea of baring them....

The thing was, I knew Con would find a way to make me feel comfortable. I had confided in him that when the time came, I would probably be nervous about undressing in front of him. But in truth, I'd never trusted anyone so completely to take care of my feelings. Plus, he did have a talent for kissing me in a way that made scars, nerves, and everything else fly right out of my head. I just needed to find a way to get over that initial anxiety hump.

I hadn't figured out how to do that yet, though. So it had come as no small relief to me when the doctor treating Con's gunshot wound had ordered him to refrain from "strenuous physical activity" for several more days so his shoulder would heal properly. He had argued with her, but his doctor's orders remained firm, and she threatened not to sign the "fitness to travel" form for Con's insurance if his follow-up exam revealed any signs that he hadn't stuck to the plan.

I viewed the forced delay as an opportunity for us to get comfortable with each other in ways we could only do by sharing a space twenty-four seven. Surely my self-consciousness would ebb away as we fell in sync with each other's habits and rhythms.

"What's going on in that head of yours?" he asked.

"What?" I blinked myself back into the present moment. "Why?"

"You look flushed."

Dammit, I thought as I realized heat was pricking my cheeks. Suddenly, the sun broke through the clouds and hit my eyes like a laser beam. I squeezed my lids shut and threw a hand up to block the blade of light slicing through the sky. "Ow, that's so bright!"

"Not any brighter than usual, I promise." Con repositioned himself so his body cast a protective shadow across my face. "But since the Irish sun is in hiding much of the time, your eyes get unused to it. When it does sneak out from under the clouds, it can be blinding." He peered across the table. "But you were blushing before the sun assaulted you."

"Was I?" Unwilling to divulge what I had actually been thinking about, I pivoted. "I guess I was just wondering if this is weird for you."

"Meaning?" His brow furrowed as he laid down his fork, reached across the table, and took my hand.

"Having a picnic in a stone circle. I mean, to me, it couldn't be more perfect, but for you, doesn't it feel a bit… touristy?"

Con began to stroke the back of my hand with his thumb, a gesture I always found softly hypnotizing. "If doing this scratches your 'touristy' itch and saves me having to attend a medieval feast at Bunratty Castle," he quipped, "then it's also perfect for me."

"Oh, we're totally doing that too," I cooed.

Con pulled his hand back and picked up his napkin, wiping bits of bacon from the corners of his mouth. "You know I'm happy to do whatever touristy things you like. But be aware that each one will cost you."

"Oh, really?" I grinned. "I can't wait to hear this. How much will it cost me?"

"One extra day per event."

"One extra day of what?"

"One extra day in my bed—once I finally get you there, that is." The playful glint in his eyes didn't disguise the dark hunger beneath, or the intensity of his conviction.

Heat swirled through my body as my own hunger stirred. But while Con lacked reverence for stone circles, there was no way I was going to indulge in such titillating conversation while sitting in the middle of a sacred site, no matter how much fire was rising in my veins.

Clearing my throat, I shifted in my chair. "Eat your streaky bacon."

"Don't worry." He winked as he picked up another piece of bacon and saluted me with it. "I'll make sure you're left wanting to engage in *endless* tourist activities."

I had no doubt he would. Con was a man of his word. And in an instant, my relief at our forced delay in intimacy transformed into sharp frustration. I crunched down on another crispy slice with undue force.

THE SECRET SERVICE SENT A BLACK SUV TO TAKE US from Con's parents' house into Cork City. It dropped us at the white-pillared entrance of the Hotel Gairdín, an elegant three-story brick building near the university where Con's endocrinology conference was being held. His attendance at the conference was a cover the Secret Service had devised. Apparently, Kayla had made it clear that while studying abroad, she didn't want to be "checked up on," so the White House wanted to make it look like our presence in Cork was purely coincidental. I was alone in believing the young woman would see right through our ruse.

The surrounding trees and gardens made the hotel feel as if it were far from the city, in another, more peaceful world. As we stepped into the lobby, we were embraced by old-school luxury, from the shining dark wood paneling and wide central staircase to the grand piano and crystal chandeliers. The interior design blended minimalism with the ornate in shades of gray, green, and ivory, creating a calming atmosphere. As soft piano music soothed my nerves, I inhaled subtle scents of leaves and lilies. This atmosphere was a wonderful counterpoint to the stressful situations we'd encountered lately—the perfect place to get away from it all.

The doorman took charge of our bags, and the concierge walked us upstairs. I hoped Con was listening as she described the amenities, because I was completely distracted by the gorgeous details all around us. In every nook, velvet couches and leather armchairs curled around antique coffee tables. Black-and-white photographs of famous visitors hung on the walls, and the buttery soft carpet seemed to soak up any excess sound.

We were led into an enormous two-room suite. I had to fold my hands together to keep from running my fingers over the gray-and-silver-damask wallpaper and sumptuous brocade fabric covering the bed. There was a huge balcony that gave us a sweeping view of the city. I couldn't wait to sit out there with Con and look at the stars.

He was discussing the TV remote with the concierge as I wandered into our bathroom of marble and mirrors with walls tiled in a snakeskin design.

When I spotted the deep tub, I nearly moaned, imagining how it would feel to sink down into some steaming hot water and allow the tension to melt right out of me.

As I came back out into the room, the concierge placed a small envelope on the dresser.

"I'll leave your keys here," she said with a smile. "Your bags will be up shortly. Is there anything else I can do for you before I go?"

Con turned to me. "You need anything, love?"

I wondered how long it would take before I stopped swooning whenever he called me "love"— especially in front of other people. Smiling like a fool, I said, "I'm good, thanks."

Con nodded and walked the concierge to the door. "We're grand. Thanks so much."

He had nearly shut the door when our bags arrived. As the doorman unloaded the cart, Con stood next to me, slid his good arm around my waist, and murmured, "It seems there's a conspiracy to keep us from being alone together."

"Hmm." I stroked my chin. "Orchestrated by your doctor in Galway, no doubt."

"I wouldn't be surprised," he said, eyeing the doorman suspiciously. Then he pulled out a few bills and handed them to the man as he departed, carefully arranging the Do Not Disturb sign on the outside door handle before flipping the lock.

Something about the way he looked at me set my heart racing—along with my nerves. "Um," I said, gesturing toward the bags, "we should probably unpack a little bit. You know, before we get too… tired."

Con approached, his eyebrows rising slowly. "Tired?"

"Mm-hmm," I managed to say as he stopped just in front of me, mere inches separating us. He nearly touched my cheek but dropped his fingers instead to brush a strand of hair back off my shoulder. I leaned my face toward the warmth of his hand, but he pulled away.

Con's eyes glowed like banked coals, full of heat that was contained for the moment, if barely.

"Good idea," he said, the vibration of his voice dancing across my skin. "Let's unpack. Then we can decide what to do for dinner."

He stepped back away from me, leaving my knees wobbly. I swallowed hard. "I vote for room service."

Con gave me a puckish wink. "Excellent idea."

Unpacking took longer than expected with Con having the use of only one arm. We were ready for a rest when it was done. The room service menu was full of mouthwatering options, but, paralyzed by choice and knowing we had the rest of the week to experiment, we both opted for the steak. As I hung up from ordering, Con's phone shocked us both by ringing. We'd only replaced our lost US phones the day before and were unused to the new ringtones. Besides, we weren't expecting any calls, since everyone we knew was aware we were on vacation.

Con looked at the screen. "It's Rosanna," he said in mild surprise. Not only was she our mutual friend, but Rosanna was the nurse manager on the psychiatry unit at our hospital. It was unspoken that he needed to answer—she wouldn't call unless it was important, and it might be work related.

"I'll put her on speaker," Con said as he pressed the green button. "Lolly, is that you?" he asked, using his personal nickname for Rosanna. Short for "lollygagging," it was meant to be an ironic description of the hardest-working person we knew.

Her voice shouted across the line. "Tell me you didn't get shot!"

Con and I stared at each other, mouths open. I watched the conflict play out across his face. He couldn't tell her he hadn't been shot, because he had. But admitting the truth would clearly upset her. After a pause, he said, "Well—"

Before he got another syllable out, the questions began. "Oh my God, you *did* get shot? Are you okay? What the hell happened?"

"I'm fine, and I'm here with Neve, by the way. You're on speakerphone."

"Neve! Are *you* okay?"

"Yes, I'm fine." I tried to sound chipper to assuage her worry. "How are you?"

"Never mind about me! It's so good to hear your voices. I've been worried sick. Now, tell me what's going on!"

"Nothing worth worrying about," Con reassured. "It was only a .22, and it went straight through."

"Don't you dare tell me not to worry," she ordered, her voice rising. "Imagine how I felt when I came in today to a voicemail message from Human Resources asking me to call them back and discuss what accommodations you might need when you returned to work due to your gunshot wound!"

Between the three of us, we worked out that the hospital that treated Con in Galway had called his primary care physician at Capitol Hill General to get his medical history. When it came to gossip, our hospital was worse than a small town, so it hadn't been long before HR got wind of his situation. They in turn reached out to Rosanna to set up his return to work.

But Con hadn't planned on telling anyone in DC what happened, so he was ill prepared for an onslaught of questions. He scrambled to explain that he was shot while freeing a friend of the family who had been kidnapped. Con kept the more bizarre details about Mad Max and his cult to a minimum, emphasizing that everyone was safe and the culprits were now in jail.

Rosanna was one of the few people who knew we'd recently gotten caught up in some intrigue back home. For her protection, we had lied and told her we were helping the FBI solve a hospital-related case. In reality, we'd been helping a patient stop Brickhaven, a sinister DC think tank, from assassinating the president. Still, Rosanna knew the purpose of our trip to Ireland was to rest and recover. Never had we anticipated that taking a vacation would land us in even greater peril.

Just when I thought the interrogation was over, Con volunteered, "In truth, I might have been worse off if Neve hadn't clocked the shooter in the head with a lamp."

He smiled as I flapped my hands, mouthing,

"Why?" Then I was on the spot, answering a whole new round of questions.

Once I convinced Rosanna I hadn't been hurt, she accepted Con's apologies for putting himself in harm's way, for allowing me to be anywhere near a dangerous situation, and for not calling her himself to tell her what had happened. She also expressed grudging admiration that I'd had the chutzpah to knock the shooter out.

It felt awkward to accept praise for something I still felt somewhat guilty about, so I seized the opportunity to change the subject. "I have some good news, if it helps. I spoke to Dr. Mohinder yesterday, and she confirmed there's no ovarian cancer."

"Oh, Neve, that's fantastic!" Rosanna exclaimed. "I mean, not that I thought it *was* cancer. It's just...."

"No, I know what you mean," I said. "I was relieved too."

"Do you need any more surgery?"

"Only to have the tumors removed," I explained, "but it's not urgent. They're not a problem right now, so it can wait until I get home."

"Oh, that's good to hear. I'm glad you don't have to cut your vacation short." After a pause, she added, "The whole thing's wild, isn't it?"

"You're not kidding." I knew what she meant. We

had talked before about how bizarre the situation was. If I hadn't been stabbed by my patient, my teratoma tumors might not have been found early, possibly leading to ovarian torsion or even encephalitis, which could be fatal. So, in a way, getting stabbed might have saved my life.

There was even more to the story now, though, and part of me longed to talk to Rosanna about it. Since coming to Ireland, I'd learned that the biopsy surgery had also led to the discovery of several other issues, including severe endometriosis with multiple complications. In a follow-up video appointment, Dr. Mohinder had reassured me that none of the issues they found were life-threatening. They would be life-*altering*, though. She had tried to be as gentle as possible in delivering that part of the prognosis, talking about more tests that could be run, etc. But when pressed, Dr. Mohinder had admitted that she agreed with the surgeon's initial impression: "Infertility almost certain in this case."

That had come as a shock. It certainly wasn't something I'd been expecting to hear at thirty-three years of age. In truth, I was still processing the news. Con had been incredibly supportive, as always. He was there when I got the test results, and he sat right next to me when I called to break the news to my parents. They had been wonderful and reassuring, expressing concern only for my well-being. Mom and Dad had always gone out of their way to let me know they supported my choices, including whether to have children. They'd told me that after years of trying, having me was miracle enough for them. Still, I knew how much joy grandchildren would bring them, and I was their only child. At the very least, my health news meant that the usual path to becoming grandparents was now closed to them.

I tried to ignore the cold stone forming in the pit of my stomach. Telling my parents had taken so much out of me emotionally, I hadn't felt ready to tell anyone else yet. I had decided to wait until I got home and, in the meantime, try not to think about it too much. I had underestimated Rosanna's "friend intuition," however.

"All right, what else is going on?" she asked. "And don't tell me 'nothing.' Neve, you're not still blaming yourself for getting stabbed, are you? Because we all know that's ridiculous."

"No." I ignored a skeptical look from Con, who was still working to convince me that the incident hadn't been my fault. Fortunately, though, Rosanna bought my denial.

"Well, that's a relief. What is it, then? I know you

two well enough to know when you're hiding something."

It was only when I felt Con's hand give mine a comforting squeeze that I realized I'd frozen up. "All right, all right, fine," he said. "We *are* hiding something." After pausing for dramatic effect, he confessed, "I got arrested and spent the night in jail."

"You did *what*?"

Relieved to have the spotlight on Con again, I sat back and closed my eyes while he gave Rosanna the short version of his run-in with the law. Again minimizing the bizarre details, Con blamed his arrest on mistaken identity when in reality, Mad Max had framed him. Luckily, a call to Agent Banai, our contact in the Secret Service, had secured Con's release—in exchange for our favor for the president. Thus, our trip to Cork.

Still, his story served as an effective distraction. After Con finished telling it, Rosanna asked if we planned to have any fun at all while in Ireland. "What part of the word 'vacation' do you two not understand?"

"As a matter of fact, we're in Cork City right now." Con didn't mention that while here, we'd be meeting the president's goddaughter, and he would be presenting at a medical conference. Neither Con nor I liked keeping things from Rosanna, but we had signed nondisclosure agreements with the White House and promised to be discreet. At least Con could be fully honest when he said, "I'm confident no trouble will find us here."

Rosanna made a clucking noise. "The way things have gone for you two lately, you'd better knock on wood."

I knocked on the table loudly enough for her to hear. "Done! We're staying in the most gorgeous hotel I've ever seen, and Con's going to take me to the seaside."

Rosanna approved of that plan. Finally, we said our goodbyes, and I promised to take plenty of pictures.

After we hung up, I said softly, "Thanks for doing that."

Con turned toward me. "Doing what?"

"You know, jumping in with your sordid tale of incarceration." I suppressed a grin. "You really took a bullet for me there."

A smile slowly spread across his face. "You should know, I find that black sense of humor of yours irresistible." Con pushed himself up and walked over, standing behind my chair. I shivered with pleasure as he brushed my hair back from my ear, then leaned down and softly kissed my neck. "It's going to get you in serious trouble someday."

With a blissful sigh, I asked, "Is today that day?"

There was a knock at the door. "Room service!" a woman's voice called softly from outside.

I laughed out loud when Con growled like an angry dog.

"Time will tell," he muttered. "But first, steak."

CHAPTER 2
NEVE

I FLUFFED THE PILLOW AGGRESSIVELY. TINY GOOSE down feathers escaped the Egyptian cotton pillowcase and floated around my head. I paused, trying not to inhale any as they captured the morning sunlight flowing in from the window.

Other people dreamed about having a vacation like ours. They saved for ages. The fact that Con had taken off while I was still asleep that morning, leaving behind only a note, was hardly worthy of complaint. Still, it had turned my mood melancholy. It seemed that Con was now the center of my world, my touchstone. I knew he was just trying to be thoughtful by not waking me, but I needed those moments with him—the "Good morning," the soft kisses, the hugs goodbye. I needed *him*. My mood wasn't helped by disappointment that the night before, not only had we refrained from "strenuous physical activity," but there was hardly any amorous activity at all.

Not that I was complaining about that after-dinner kiss out on the balcony. We had stepped out to look at the lights of the city and found the constellation Orion hanging in the sky just outside our room. Con pretended he didn't remember why it was significant and asked me to repeat the story of how I used to pray to Orion as a girl, asking the mythological Greek hunter to bring me the man of my dreams.

He had then stepped in front of me and, with effort, lifted both his good arm and his injured one to cradle my face in his hands. He pointed out that one of Orion's shoulders was lower than the other and speculated that the man in the stars also had an arm in a sling. Con said he reckoned that was a sign that *he* was the answer to my prayers and our relationship was divinely ordained, whether I liked it or not.

Tilting my face toward his, I rose up onto my toes to make what I liked perfectly clear. Con's warm lips and rough, demanding tongue proceeded to light up every single one of my nerve endings until I felt like a human glow stick, cracked open and burning bright.

His heart must have been pumping as hard as mine, though, because it pumped too much blood into his wounded knee and shoulder. The pain forced him to pull away, wincing. When he tried to swoop in and devour me further, I ducked, tucking myself under his good arm so he could use me as a crutch as I encouraged him to come inside and lie down. If I needed any further proof of how much he needed to rest, Con provided it by not arguing with me for once.

He was only a week into his recovery, so his exhaustion was understandable. Why *I* was so worn out, I had no idea, but after I took the long bath I'd promised myself, fatigue covered me like a weighted blanket.

To enjoy some closeness, at least, we had planned to sleep in the same bed. But once Con got situated with his bad knee elevated and his arm in a good position, there wasn't much room left. I was afraid I'd either kick his leg or roll over on his arm in my sleep, so I stayed in the adjoining room—and regretted for the rest of the night that I couldn't reach over and feel him next to me.

Now, I flopped backward onto Con's bed and made the delightful discovery that it still smelled like him. The mattress was also seductively comfortable. Turning my head, I let the soft pillowcase caress my cheek. I pulled Con's note out of my fluffy hotel robe pocket and reread it.

Gone to the conference. Enjoy room service. Don't go far and keep your phone with you. I'll call soon.

Con

I decided that taking his advice and treating myself to room service again could only improve my mood. An hour later, I sat damp-haired in my robe, savoring the best eggs Benedict I'd ever tasted, when my phone began vibrating. *Con.*

I swiped up to answer. "Hi."

There was a slight pause. "What's wrong?"

"Nothing." But he'd already picked up something in my voice; it was too late to deny it. "It's silly. It's just… you left without saying good morning."

"I did," he murmured. "You looked too peaceful. Besides, you needed the rest."

He was one to talk about needing rest. Con hadn't had a solid night's sleep since leaving the hospital. "But you said before, you didn't want to let me out of your sight."

"Oh, I haven't. I put a camera in the room. I'm watching you right now. You're rolling your eyes."

Mid–eye roll, I laughed. "Please, we both know you're not that tech savvy."

"Fair point." The same way he knew I'd be rolling

my eyes, I knew he would be rubbing his hand across his chin. "So, what's next?"

"I called Kayla. We're still on for lunch."

Besides the fact that she was studying Irish folklore, all I knew about Kayla was that she must be an incredibly kind young woman. I couldn't imagine any other reason why a twenty-year-old on her study-abroad year would agree to hang out with two alleged "friends" of her godfather's, who she must suspect had been sent to check up on her.

But there was a catch in Con's voice that I recognized. "Are *you* okay?" Between his shoulder wound and the additional wrenching his already-bad knee had endured when the gunshot dropped him to the ground, I knew his pain level was heightened. I also knew he'd been avoiding pain medications, not wanting them to cloud his head.

"I'm grand."

Experience had taught me that "grand" could mean anything. I would only know the truth of the matter when I laid eyes on him. "Where should I meet you?"

"It's up to you. You can meet us at the restaurant or come to the university, and we can go over together."

"University, please." The sooner I got to see him, the better.

"Okay, then. The next session finishes in an hour. I'll text you the address. Meet me in the main lobby at one o'clock?"

"Perfect!"

"The front desk will arrange a taxi for you—on the room, of course. If you leave a bit early, you can ask them to take you around the city, give you a sense of places you might like to visit later."

"Oh, that's a good idea. I'll call down and arrange it."

There was a pause, and then Con cleared his throat. "Listen, Neve, I have no idea what to say to a college girl. I fear she'll see right through me. She'd be much more likely to talk to you. Maybe I can just introduce the two of you—"

"Nice try!" I said, grinning. "First of all, of course she'll see right through you; she already has, I'm betting. Second, President Duran needs *your* expertise on her case, remember? I'm just coming along to grease the wheels."

"Don't be ridiculous. I won't be able to do what he's asked unless she agrees to let me look at her medical records, and to get her consent, I'll be relying on you wholly and entirely."

"Like I said, no guarantees, but I'll do my best."

"You're a godsend, you know that?" I could hear the smile in his voice. "I'll owe you one, you know. Or two. Possibly three."

"I'll be plotting ways to collect."

His voice was slightly rougher as he replied, "I certainly hope so."

Goose bumps flitted across my skin. Innocent words, but his tone was anything but. "Go back and do… whatever endocrinologists do at conferences."

A low chuckle came across the line. "See you at one o'clock."

"You'd better!" I didn't know what that was supposed to mean, but as usual, he had me flustered.

After hanging up, I let myself fall onto his bed face down and breathed in his scent.

My taxi driver, Thomas, took me on a lovely ride through Cork City, where for the first time, I was able to get a good look at our new temporary home. It had been dark when we arrived the previous evening, so I had only seen shadows of the now busy, colorful streets. Now the day was bright and dry, giving us a clear view of our surroundings.

As we crossed multiple bridges, Thomas explained that the River Lee branched out in several places across the city. He took me down Patrick's Street and the Grand Parade, wide silver-and-white boulevards lined with flagship retail stores and intriguing restaurants. The sounds of buskers added to the rich atmosphere, along with sculptures and painted murals in various styles.

Thomas had lived in Cork for sixty years and was happy to fill me in on a bit of history. While some buildings remained in the city from the medieval period, most of the architecture dated from the eighteenth century onward. I couldn't wait to do some sightseeing and get a better feel for the place.

Eventually, Thomas pulled to a stop in front of a soaring, modern steel-and-glass structure at the end of a circular drive. "Now!"

It took me a moment to understand that his one-word declaration was a full sentence. "This is the place?"

He peered at me in the rearview mirror. "Not what you were expecting?"

"I guess I had some preconceived notions," I admitted. "I was picturing old stone buildings with slate roofs, covered in climbing ivy."

"Oh, there are plenty of those on campus as well,"

Thomas said with a smile. "Get your man to take you on a tour."

"I think I will, thanks! And I certainly wish your wife a speedy recovery." Along the way, he'd told me about her recent knee replacement. "Thanks so much for the ride. I appreciate—oh no!" Too late, I realized I didn't have any euros on me. "I'm so sorry, I don't have anything for a tip. I can ask the hotel to add it on for you."

"No need. Tips are always appreciated, of course, but not expected. Don't let any greedy beggars tell you otherwise."

"All right, if you're sure."

"I'm sure." Thomas handed me his business card. "Enjoy your conference and call me if you get stuck."

"Thank you again!" I resolved to use his services again during our stay and give him an extra-large tip next time.

A wide stone staircase led up to the main doors of the building. Some students with backpacks slung over their shoulders were gathered out front, talking and laughing, while others bustled off in all directions. Meanwhile, a crowd of people in suits and dresses was filing out the doors and onto the patio—conference attendees, I guessed.

As I stepped through the glass doors into the

lobby, my heart gave a small jump at the sight of Con walking toward me. It wasn't fair, really, how handsome he looked. Con hadn't packed a suit when we came to Ireland, not thinking he'd need one, so we'd gone out and bought him one the day before. He looked dashing in it. The fact that his arm was in a sling only added a sense of rugged intrigue to his whole look. It had been hard enough to find him clothes off the rack, between his height, his rugby-player shoulders, and the extra room needed in the leg to accommodate his knee brace. But the assistants at the menswear store in Mallow knew what they were doing and had sorted him out in no time, picking out a few new shirts and ties and a pair of dress shoes for him as well.

It was one thing to watch Con try things on in the shop and yet another to see him here, fully dressed and looking at me like I was the sun just rising, bringing him life-giving warmth after a cold, hard night.

"God, it's good to see you," he murmured, cupping my elbow as he leaned in and kissed my cheek. He lingered there just long enough to inhale deeply. "Hmm." His eyebrows rose as he pulled back and asked, "New perfume?"

"Just the hotel toiletries, but they do smell good. Citrusy."

He hummed his approval, but in the next moment, a man with the purposeful-yet-relaxed gait of a politician walked up and laid his hand on Con's shoulder.

"I was wondering where you were hiding—and now I see why!" Then the man extended his hand to me. "Bob Davies."

"Neve Keane." Bob's American accent had caught me slightly off guard, although it shouldn't have. Con had told me it was a major international conference, after all.

As I shook his hand, I took in his broad smile, impossibly white teeth, and "soft power" suit. He gave off strong DC vibes.

Con's face was expressionless in a way I could tell was taking a lot of effort, and when he blinked, his eyes closed for just a beat longer than usual. From this, I took that he wasn't crazy about Bob, but the man hadn't done anything to earn his hatred either.

"Neve was kind enough to accompany me on my visit to Ireland," Con explained. "Neve, Bob is the head of endocrinology at Georgetown."

"Nice to meet you." DC, then; I had guessed correctly. "Are you enjoying the conference so far?"

"A pleasure to meet you as well," Bob said

smoothly. "It has been excellent, I have to say. Exceeded my expectations. But what I'm really looking forward to is Con's presentation this afternoon. An outstanding last-minute addition to the lineup. Psychiatry—*that* should liven things up!"

"Is that right?" I gave Con an elbow nudge. "In that case, you have to let me come."

Con gave me an exasperated look as he said, "I would advise you to lower your expectations, Bob."

"This guy!" Bob laughed and clapped Con on the back, apparently oblivious to the sling he was wearing. "Neve, you look familiar. Have we met before?"

"It's possible. I'm a social worker on the psychiatry unit at Capitol Hill General."

"Ah, that's it, then," Bob said. "I've swung through a few times for meetings and must have seen you there." He wore the cautiously playful smile of someone who was considering flirting but was prepared to pull back if rebuffed.

Bob didn't see the look Con shot him. I did, though, and I could tell Bob was now skating dangerously close to "hatred" territory.

Con touched my arm. "Neve, are you ready for lunch?"

"You're not leaving!" Bob frowned like he'd just

lost a bundle on a bet. "I thought the three of us could join—"

"Not today." Con moved closer to me, brushed a strand of hair from my shoulder, and slid his arm tightly around my waist. "I promised Neve a nice meal out, and I just got a text. Our taxi's outside."

Bob finally seemed to get the hint. His eyebrows waggled like he sensed the romance in the air and couldn't be more delighted about it. "Oh, I understand. No problem." He winked at me, and I had to suppress a shudder. "You'll join me and some colleagues for a drink tonight, though? Both of you, of course?"

When Con didn't refuse right away, I knew he was conflicted. Since it appeared he was barely tolerating Davies, there must be some other reason he wanted to go. Maybe he was expected to participate in post-conference socializing.

I decided to save him from having to make an awkward decision. "Of course, we'd love to come!"

"Fabulous!" Bob flashed me a thousand-watt smile. "I'll see you then, Neve. In the meantime, you two enjoy yourselves."

"Thanks," I called back as Con steered me out the glass doors.

"Sorry about that," he muttered. "Davies is like a bad penny. He turns up every goddamned place."

"Not your favorite person, then?"

"Bit more of a gobshite than I remembered," Con murmured. "If he looks at you like that again…."

"I don't think you have to worry," I said, grinning. "I'm pretty sure he got the message. So did everyone else in a ten-foot radius."

"Only ten?" He stopped in his tracks, drew me to him, and placed a gentle kiss on the corner of my mouth. "How about now?"

"Mmm" was all I managed to say as my knees weakened. Conscious that we were in a crowded public place, I leaned in just close enough to breathe in his rich, sharp scent.

As we made our way slowly down the steps outside, I could tell by Con's movements that his leg was paining him. I fought back the urge to suggest he return to the hotel and get some rest. Con had agreed to go to this conference and to meet with Kayla, so right now, he needed my support. I could insist on fussing over him later.

When we reached the sidewalk, he asked, "Do you really want to go out with us tonight? I'm presenting, so it would be bad form if I didn't show my face. You know I always prefer to have you with me, but I fully understand if you'd rather not spend your time drinking with a boring bunch of endocrinologists."

"What do you call a bunch of endocrinologists, anyway?" I asked. "A 'gland'?"

Scowling, he said, "If you leave me alone with Davies for too long, it might turn out to be a 'murder.'"

I grinned as Con waved to our driver. "In that case, I'd better join you. I'd rather spend the evening drinking with a 'gland' than rescuing you from jail again."

As he opened the car door for me, Con murmured in my ear, "Hearing you talk of glands and jail brings to mind beds and handcuffs. Maybe we should skip lunch and go straight to the hotel."

Oh, that we could.... But I knew he didn't mean it. We had to meet Kayla, and later, Con had to return to the conference. I couldn't wait until our favor for the president was over and done with so we could return to the "romantic getaway" portion of our vacation.

"I think I'd be safer with Davies," I teased, spinning away from him and diving into the back seat as Con laughed.

CHAPTER 3
NEVE

THE RESTAURANT AT THE HOTEL DABRONA TOOK MY breath away. It was an enormous space with floor-to-ceiling windows that overlooked the river. Light, bright, and decorated in pastels, it had the feel of a tropical resort. The air even smelled faintly of vanilla and coconuts. Couches and overstuffed armchairs surrounded low wicker tables amid an explosion of flowers and plants.

Con let the hostess know we were expecting a third guest, and she led us to a table next to the wall of windows. We decided to take the armchairs and give Kayla the couch. Con's sister, Una, had informed us that we had a habit of unconsciously touching all the time. She found it charming, but our goal was to make Kayla feel comfortable around us, not scandalize the poor girl.

While we waited for our coffees to arrive, the hostess brought over a young woman with a delicate nose ring and dramatic cat-eye makeup. She wore her bright blue curls in high pigtails. With an easy smile, she radiated effervescence.

"Hi! You're Con and Neve?"

"We are indeed," Con said as we stood.

"You must be Kayla," I said, shaking her outstretched hand.

Kayla settled onto the sofa. "Nice to meet you guys. And thanks for taking me out to lunch. I've never been in here before. It's amazing."

"Our pleasure," Con said. "When we told President Duran—"

"Jeff, please!" She winced and fisted her hands. "I mean, he's Uncle Jeff to me, but please call him Jeff. It still freaks me out a little bit that he's running a country. He needed me to program his TV remote, you know?"

While I laughed at that revelation, Con nodded sympathetically. "Jeff it is," he said. "When we mentioned to Jeff that we were going to be in Cork and he told us his goddaughter was here studying, of course we wanted to meet you."

She rolled her eyes so hard, Con looked worried that she might be passing out. "Okay, you don't have to lie to me," she said. "Uncle Jeff told me you guys saved his life. Is that true?"

"What?" we asked in unison, looking to each other for guidance. Since we had been sworn to secrecy, we hadn't expected Kayla to know anything about what had happened in DC.

She squinted at us. "Wait, you didn't? So, he lied about that?"

I said, "Uh…," while Con said, "Well, not exactly…."

Fortunately, Kayla laughed away our awkwardness. "Okay, so obviously it's true!"

"Well, it's just… it wasn't dramatic like that," I clarified.

"Right," Con explained vaguely. "We stopped the bad guys before anything could happen."

"Exactly," I said, nodding at Con. "President—Jeff was never in any danger."

Kayla shook her head. "You don't have to protect me. I know he's in danger, like, every second of every day. We're all used to it at this point. But I trust the Secret Service. They've kept him safe so far—and you guys did too. Thank you for that."

Con and I were both so unprepared for her gratitude, we didn't know where to look. Thankfully, Kayla spoke again. "He also told me you're here because Con lost a bet to him, so he made you come and check on me."

Evidently, Agent Banai and President Duran had constructed two very different cover stories for us.

Con rubbed a hand across his eyes before replying, "That's not it at all. He got me out of jail last week and asked me to return the favor by dropping in on you."

Her eyes lit up with excitement. "You were in jail? Like, in Ireland? What did you do?"

I had never seen Con speechless before. Smiling, I jumped in. "He didn't do anything. He was framed by a criminal we were trying to catch."

"And eventually did catch," Con added gruffly.

"Awesome!" She reached out to fist-bump Con, and after a moment of awkwardness, he managed to complete the maneuver. "So, what, you guys are FBI or police or something?"

"No. Con is a doctor, and I'm a therapist. Our lives are usually pretty ordinary, believe me. It's just been… an eventful month," I said.

That was the understatement of the year. I still had no idea how we'd managed to land ourselves in so many different types of hot water recently.

"Okay," Kayla said, looking unconvinced. "So, you're doing a favor for Uncle Jeff. That makes more sense. He's terrible at betting."

"We were more than happy to come," Con said, "and would have done so whether or not a favor was owed."

"You guys are nice." She smiled. "I'm glad I didn't make up an excuse not to come."

Kayla's positivity was infectious, and I was amazed at how open she was, talking to two people she'd just met. The fact that Con's arm was in a sling won him some sympathy and served to be a good topic of conversation, perhaps because Kayla seemed to have a morbid fascination with things that had gone terribly wrong. I wondered if it had anything to do with the fact that as president, her godfather was in constant jeopardy.

Over a delicious tapas lunch, we talked about how Kayla was finding Ireland so far, how different it was from her hometown of Boston, and how she liked Cork and the university. She lit up while talking about her studies of folklore, the topic that had brought her here on her study year abroad. Her mother, Fiona, was originally from County Clare and had raised her on stories from Irish folklore. Kayla was grabbing every opportunity she could to visit ancient sacred places, such as stone circles and wells, and was planning to attend a traditional celebration of Samhain, or Halloween, in a few weeks' time.

When Con stepped away to check out the whiskey selection behind the bar, Kayla leaned forward and asked conspiratorially, "Are you guys, like, *together*?"

I couldn't help it. I broke into a wide smile—which apparently said everything, because Kayla bounced on the sofa and said, "I *knew* I was getting a vibe!"

"It's kind of new," I admitted.

"Whatever." She grinned. "You guys are too cute together."

"We are, huh? What about you?" I asked, knowing the typical college student's interests included romance. "Are you seeing anyone?"

"Oh, no." She waved her hand dismissively. "Nope. I mean, there was this one guy, but he kind of made himself scarce after... you know."

Her shrug explained nothing, though. "After... what?"

With a meaningful look, she said, "You know, the visitation thing. The *real* reason Uncle Jeff sent you here."

Now I was genuinely confused. "Okay, yes," I

admitted as Con returned and took his seat, "we have another reason for being here, but I can assure you we haven't heard anything about a... visitation thing, have we, Con?"

He looked as confused as I was. "Uh, no." With a guilty smile, he added, "Are we all sharing our secrets now?"

"Oh, great." Kayla flopped back against the couch cushions and stared at the ceiling. "Uncle Jeff probably doesn't even know yet." She straightened up in her seat. "Why did he send you to check on me, then?"

Since Con once again appeared at a loss for words, I explained, "Con specializes in endocrinology and mental health. Jeff said you'd been having some challenges that might involve both of those areas. He asked Con to give a second opinion—provided you're willing to talk to us about what's going on, of course."

Burying her head in her hands, Kayla moaned.

"I'm sorry," Con said. "We should have told you from the outset—"

"No, it's not your fault. Ugh!" She looked from me to Con and back again. "So, that means Uncle Jeff *does* know about the visitation thing. He just heard it from my *mother*," she said with an accompanying eye roll. "I only went to see an endocrinologist here to make her happy, but I don't need a doctor. I'm fine. If Uncle Jeff had talked to my *dad*, he would know that."

Her scowl told us there was some family drama there, but if we pushed too hard or in the wrong direction, we might lose whatever goodwill we had with her.

"Well," I began, "we're certainly glad to hear you're fine. And no matter what's going on, there's no need for you to feel embarrassed. We're the ones who dropped in on your life under false pretenses, not the other way around."

When her expression softened, Con added, "Neve's right. We're the ones who should feel awkward here. Let me buy you a drink, at least, make it up to you." He raised his hand, and the waitress headed toward us. "What'll you have?"

"I love that eighteen is the drinking age here," she said, smiling. "I like Irish ales."

"Oh? My brother works at a craft brewery in town. I noticed they have a Calfwood ale on tap here. We could try it together if you're interested."

She was, and the temporary change of topic lightened the mood a bit. Not much of a beer drinker, I had a glass of white wine while the two of them enjoyed their craft brews.

Con was pleased that he could give two positive reviews to his brother. Eamonn had offered to give us a tour of the brewery on Kennedy Quay while we were in Cork, so Con invited Kayla to join us. She said she'd love to, provided she was free when we decided to go.

When all our glasses were close to empty, Kayla began fidgeting in her seat. "Look, I feel like I should explain the visitation thing. I mean, it's why you're here."

"It's okay if you don't want to," I said.

"No, it's fine." She smiled. "It's just… it's a little strange."

"No worries," Con said. "If you knew us better, you'd know we have quite a high tolerance for 'strange.'"

"Okay," she said with a shy smile, "you asked for it."

Kayla recounted how a few weeks back, she had been walking home at night with a group of friends. She had fallen behind them a bit when she saw a girl beckoning to her from the river. "The girl looked kind of frantic, so I went over there. Then she waded into the water—it was shallow—and gestured for me to come. She didn't talk, just kept going, so I followed her. Anyway, this is the weird part." Kayla folded her hands in her lap and looked down. "She pointed something out to me in the water, and then she disappeared."

"Was someone in trouble?" Con asked.

"No. I thought that's what it would be too. I was a lifeguard at our pool back home, so I knew how to help. But there was no one. It was just... it was a dead bird."

Before I knew it, the words flew out of my mouth. "A what?"

"A dead blackbird. But that's not even the point," she continued hurriedly. "When I say the girl disappeared, I mean, like, she literally disappeared. Poof. Gone."

She was right; that did sound strange. Disappearing girls were pretty high up there on the "unusual" scale, even for Con and me. However, Kayla didn't seem particularly alarmed about it, so I schooled my features to match her matter-of-fact attitude. "That didn't scare you?"

"Well, I mean, it startled me, of course. It's not what I was expecting on the way home from a volleyball game. But it didn't scare me. When she just vanished like that, I knew what was going on."

As Con's eyebrows slowly rose, Kayla settled back onto the couch and continued. "It was a visitation from the Holy Ghost—I mean, that's my belief about it, anyway. I guess different religions would explain it differently. But I grew up going to my dad's evangelical church. My mom is Catholic, but she only goes to church like twice a year. She never believed it was the Holy Ghost, though, which is why she thinks I need to see a doctor again."

The pieces of information Kayla had shared so far began to fall into place—for me, anyway. Con still looked lost. "So," I said, "this wasn't the first time something like this has happened to you."

"No, it happened twice before. The first time when I was thirteen, and then again when I was sixteen." Shrugging, she added, "Our pastor says it's my spiritual gift. We all have them. I guess I just got a weird one. Not that it's weird to get messages from the Holy Ghost; plenty of people do. But having him appear in a vision like that is unusual. Not unheard of, though. I mean, a lot of religions talk about people seeing unusual things—even Catholicism, but my mom was always skeptical about that stuff. That's why she's convinced I'm hallucinating because of all the concussions I got playing sports."

Now *I* was lost. Thankfully, Con picked up on the

new thread of the conversation. "All the concussions?"

Kayla sighed. "Soccer, mainly. If you play like a beast like I did, it happens."

Nodding respectfully, Con said, "Understood. And she wanted you to see an endocrinologist because...."

"Pituitary failure. I mean, I *did* have that before, but I took hormones for a few years and my levels are fine. It's not an issue now."

Con turned toward me. "Acquired hypopituitarism, secondary to traumatic brain injury. It can lead to a variety of symptoms, including hallucinations." He addressed Kayla again. "As symptoms go, though, that one is quite rare. Still—"

"It's possible. I know. But the thing is, those first two visions couldn't have just been hallucinations, because they turned out to be real."

I felt the connection between Con and me tug as we both resisted the urge to look at each other. Lightly, I cleared my throat. "Real, meaning...?"

"The people I saw were real people who had passed away, who were connected to people in the congregation," Kayla explained. "Like, the first one I saw was our pianist's daughter who had died as a toddler. The second one was an elderly man, the father of one of our Sunday School teachers, who had died of cancer. I had never met either of them, but when I described them, their loved ones recognized them. They showed me photos, and they were of the same people from my visions."

"Wow, that's incredible." While I was listening and responding genuinely, on a parallel track, part of my mind slipped automatically into mental health assessment mode. I noticed that as Kayla told us her story, she remained calm and maintained good eye contact. Although she displayed irritation with her mother, her mood appeared fine, and her speech was normal and consistent in all aspects. Nothing about her presentation or behavior led me to believe she was experiencing any psychotic symptoms. "What was that like for you?"

"The visions were clear, like seeing real people who appeared happy and peaceful. It just seemed normal until they disappeared all of a sudden," she said. "That scared me at first, and when I found out no one else had seen them there, I did think I was losing my mind. That's when my mother took me to the doctor, and I got diagnosed with the pituitary thing. But later, when we figured out that I had seen real people, their loved ones were so happy. I mean, it brought them a lot of comfort because they felt like the Holy Ghost had shown me that their family members were okay and in heaven. It made me feel really good to know I had helped them."

"I'll bet it did," I said.

"It's been four years since the last time, though," she continued, "and I'm an ocean away from our congregation, so it never occurred to me that it would happen here, now."

I stole a glance at Con, who looked deep in thought. The conversational baton remained with me for the moment, then. "Yeah, I can imagine that came as quite a surprise. Do you know who the girl was in your vision at the river?"

"No, but I'm sure she's real," Kayla said confidently. "The Holy Ghost has only shown me people who have passed away. My dad and our pastor checked with our congregation, but no one has been able to identify her yet. I thought it was worth asking, since the other two visions were connected to people in our church."

I nodded. "That's logical."

Con peered at me out from under the dark ridge of his brow as though to say, "*None* of this is logical." But whether I believed the girl Kayla had seen was real or not, *she* believed it, and I couldn't fault her reasoning in light of her past experiences. If my years as a therapist—to say nothing of our recent baffling adventures—had taught me anything, it was not to leap to judgment about someone else's reality based only on the limited parameters of my own understanding.

"Anyway, I'm investigating." Kayla's eyes brightened. "Audrey, one of the girls who shares my apartment, has a friend in the art department who does portraits. He did a sketch of the girl using my description. It's really good, very close. And that dead bird I told you about? It was holding a piece of cloth in its claws. Audrey said it looks like it has the symbol of a sports team on it, so that might be another clue. She's convinced I'm a psychic medium or something, but I don't believe in that stuff."

"Why not?" I asked, curious to know by what thought process Kayla accepted one extraordinary explanation but rejected another.

"Because after people die, they either go to heaven or hell," she said. "They don't come back here to visit. But I mean, that's just my take. No offense if you believe otherwise."

"No offense taken." I gave her a reassuring smile. "And I hope you're not offended by all my questions."

"No." She smiled back. "It's kind of nice, actually, to talk to someone other than Audrey who doesn't think I'm crazy. I mean, you don't, do you?"

"Of course not," I said. "Crazy" wasn't a word I typically used in any event, but I knew what she was asking. "I think you've experienced something that is very much out of the ordinary, and you're doing your best to make sense of it, as any of us would. We're happy to help you in any way we can."

"Thanks." Her shy smile returned. "I really appreciate that. I don't know what you can do, though."

"Well, not to sound like a stuffy old doctor," Con said, "but if you like, I could review your medical records and reassure Jeff if there's no reemergence of that endocrine problem. That might put a few minds at ease."

"If it would get my mom off my back, that would be absolutely great!"

We spent the remainder of our meeting talking about which medical records Con would need and how to get them, as well as how we might assist her in identifying the mystery girl. We discussed reaching out to Banshee, our friend of a friend and resident Irish hacker, for help with research. Kayla used her phone to email us the sketch.

Soon it was time for Kayla to leave for class. When she stood, her energy seemed lighter, as though a weight had been lifted from her. We said our goodbyes, exchanged phone numbers, and agreed to touch base the next day.

After Kayla left, Con leaned forward as though readying himself to get out of his chair. With a hopeful glance in my direction, he asked, "Couch?"

I smiled as warmth whispered through me. "Yes, please!"

We settled in next to each other on the sofa and leaned back. Since I was on his right side, Con was able to lift his good arm, inviting me to tuck in against him. I rested my head on his chest and inhaled deeply. No scent plunged me into instant happiness quite like "Eau de Cornelius."

"So," he murmured, "what's your strategy, then?"

"What strategy?"

"Therapeutically, I mean." When confusion left me tongue-tied, he continued, "The reason you were humoring her, pretending to swallow everything she was feeding you?"

Leaning forward, I twisted around to face him. "I was listening to her, not humoring her."

"I'm not questioning how you handled it. You're

the expert here. I was just curious about your treatment approach."

"Treatment approach? She's not my *patient*, Con! She's the friend of a friend."

"Come back to me." Con pulled me toward him and pressed my head against his chest. "I wouldn't call Duran a friend, exactly. And he does want professional input. That's why we're here."

"That's why *you're* here." I tried to pull away from him again, but Con held me fast. Willing to surrender in the physical sense only, I rested against him as I argued. "You can give President Duran your medical opinion because Kayla has consented to it. But she and I are not in a professional relationship, and it would be unethical for me to behave otherwise."

"True. I hadn't thought of that."

My annoyance softened, and I nestled in a bit closer. "Besides, she was opening up to us about something very private and difficult. I wasn't about to start playing devil's advocate. I can tell you what I think is going on with her, but that's just between us. As far as Kayla and President Duran are concerned, I'm only here to be supportive."

"Understood. You're right, of course." Con placed

a kiss on the top of my head. "So, just between us, then, what *do* you think?"

"Well, whatever it was she saw, I think she was telling us the truth about what she perceived. The conclusions she's reached do follow an internal logic consistent with her religious beliefs. There were no signs of psychiatric problems that I could see, no responding to external stimuli—nothing that would indicate active hallucinations."

"Ha!" Con sounded victorious. "I knew you put on your therapist hat at some point."

I tilted my head back so he could absorb the full power of my frown. "Not the whole hat. Maybe a fascinator or a sparkly headband."

"Hmm. Fair enough." Con inspected my head as though looking for a hidden accessory, then smiled at me like God had placed me on earth just to bring him delight. Once I relaxed again, he continued, "There must be a reason for her hallucinations, though—a real reason, not ghosts, Holy or otherwise."

"Right." The truth was, though, I had no idea what to think. Not until we found out whether the girl in Kayla's vision really existed—and if she did, whether she was alive or dead. Even though, like Con, I had left my childhood religion years ago, we both knew that I remained more open-minded about the spiritual than he did. Nonetheless, he was right; there was most likely a medical or psychiatric cause. "What do *you* think is going on?"

As he inhaled, he stretched his arm out, then brought it back more tightly around me as he exhaled.

"Smooth move there," I said, smiling against his shirt.

"I was going for smooth," he admitted. "Her first two hallucinations could have been caused by hypopituitarism, as could this one. But if her labs are indeed normal as she said, my best guess is that her latest vision was drug-induced."

"You think she was taking drugs?" That hadn't even occurred to me as a possibility. Now that he mentioned it, though, I realized it should have. It was a good thing I *wasn't* Kayla's therapist; my assessment skills were clearly rusty.

"Behold my internal logic," he quipped. "College kid, away from home in a new country—of course she's going to try a few new things. And we know drugs are the most common culprit when young adults suddenly start seeing things."

"Oh, *we* know that, do we?" I teased. "Did you do a study, or is this personal experience talking?"

Con's chest shook as he chuckled. "Going off stories Rosanna's told me from the ER nurses. Either way, we'll find out more when I see Kayla's records. She said her friends took her to the emergency department right after they fished her out of the river. No doubt they did a tox screen there. And those so-called friends of hers should be glad they did one responsible thing that night. It's the only reason I'm not chasing them down right now, one by one, and scaring them straight."

The slight hardening of his tone told me he was perfectly serious about that last part. Kayla had activated Con's protective streak—one of his most endearing qualities, which, when taken to the extreme, could also be one of his most infuriating.

"What if her labs are normal and the tox screen comes back clean?" I asked.

"Then she probably took some new drug they either don't know about yet or can't test for."

"I don't know. I just…." Something about the whole drug theory felt off to me. "I didn't sense that she was hiding anything from us. I really felt like she was being honest, telling us the whole truth—as she saw it, anyway. And she asked for our help, which she wouldn't have done if she had something to hide."

"Well, she may not have taken drugs knowingly." Con's body tensed beneath me. "If that's the case, and

I find out someone dosed her somehow, I will be tracking them down."

"If that's the case, I'll join you." I reached over and stroked his arm. "In your mind, then, the three possibilities are a pituitary gland problem, she took drugs, or she was roofied."

"That's about the size of it."

"For the moment, let's assume you're right." I chewed on the inside of my lip, considering. "With her first two visions, she could have seen pictures of those people who had passed and forgotten about it. Or she and the people in her congregation wanted so much for her visions to be real, they glossed over any inconsistencies between what their loved ones looked like and what Kayla said she had seen."

"Grief can be very powerful. I'm sure they did whatever mental gymnastics were required to convince themselves," Con agreed.

I felt like a deflated balloon—a very warm, well-loved deflated balloon, it was true. But there was a sense of disappointment, imagining how Kayla would feel when we presented her with our counterarguments. Not that our debunking would shake her beliefs; I doubted it would, in fact. But it would create a distance between her and us, and I imagined that

Kayla already felt somewhat alone with her strange experiences.

"Don't worry, we'll get to the bottom of it." Con kissed the top of my head, spilling warmth through me. "But first, I've got to survive a few more hours with Davies."

I snuggled in closer. "Are you sure I can't come to your presentation?"

"You underestimate how distracting you are," he murmured, stroking my hair. Con knew that gesture was my kryptonite and could send me into a nearly catatonic state of relaxation.

I had been a relatively productive person in the first two years we'd known each other as friends. Now that we were together, though, Con had a way of making me feel so content just lying in his arms, I had no idea how I was going to get anything done ever again.

"Look who's talking. Don't forget to text me where we're meeting up tonight."

"You'll really come and save me?"

I melted against him like hot wax. "Just try keeping me away."

CHAPTER 4
CON

FECKING HELL, CON THOUGHT AS HE FLIPPED through his notecards one last time. The morning had been a long one, and the afternoon was already promising a headache. Sitting in the back of the conference room listening to the previous speaker wrap up her question-and-answer session, Con felt the threat of pain pulsing at his temples.

It would help if his shoulder and knee would stop hurting, even for a few moments. The ache in both places was constant, and every time he moved, some tendon, ligament, or muscle caught fire. Not that pain was new to him. They had become old friends in the decade since the tractor he'd been repairing for his father had collapsed onto his leg. But until he had a second injury to contend with, Con hadn't realized that managing his usual pain took so much energy that he didn't have a great deal of excess. And now here he was, running around, giving presentations and meeting goddaughters, when what he really needed was to put his feet up and not move for a while.

Goddamned Banai. Goddamned everyone. Except Neve, of course. She was the one and only thing that was getting him through this "favor" they were doing for Duran. And now their association with Kayla was threatening to stretch beyond the planned two-day window. After lunch, they had all agreed to be in contact the following day, but in the few hours since, Neve and Kayla had already been talking. Neve had texted him that they were trying to find someone who could run facial recognition on the sketch of Ghost Girl.

He couldn't even object, because with the obvious exception that she was seeing people who weren't there and following them into rivers, he had yet to find evidence that anything was medically or psychiatrically wrong with Kayla. Banai must have put a rush on Con's request for her medical records, which had appeared in his inbox almost immediately after he asked for them. He had then spent the first afternoon session of the conference on his laptop, scanning the notes on Kayla's visit to the emergency department and her follow-up with the endocrinologist.

The story Kayla had given at those visits was the same as the one she'd told him and Neve. And just as Neve had noted after their lunch together, there had been no other observed signs or symptoms of psychiatric issues besides the girl's insistence that she'd seen a vision. That was a relief, at least. Whatever this was with Kayla, it seemed relatively contained to this very specific and discrete symptom, which wasn't causing her any distress or problems—yet.

When he saw that all her labs were normal and her tox screen was clean, Con knew the next step should be to interrogate everyone Kayla had contact with the night of the incident. They needed to find out who had drugged the girl, and with what, since it hadn't been detected by the lab. But when he texted Neve about that, she had asked him to wait while she and Kayla pursued another possibility. Neve had made the point that they could theorize about what had happened, but until they found evidence that Kayla's explanation of events was wrong, her belief that she'd seen a vision of something real would likely persist. That made sense, of course, but as far as he was concerned, they had ruled out any endocrine or serious psychiatric issues. Getting much deeper into the weeds with Kayla would be going above and beyond the favor they'd promised to do.

Which was very much like Neve, of course. He loved that she was so compassionate, so caring. Con had always cherished those qualities in her, and now that they were a couple by some incredible stroke of luck, he depended upon them. He just hoped this carry-on with Kayla didn't drag on too long, because more than anything, at this point, he wanted Neve all to himself—preferably alone in a hotel room, with all phones turned off and no one knocking at the door.

So many idle hours of his recovery from that fecking bullet had been spent imagining all the things he would do to Neve once he got her into his bed— exactly how he would bring her to the edge of ecstasy again and again, then push her over repeatedly until she was immobilized by pleasure. He would also ensure she had everything else she might want or need, of course, but his primary plan was to repeat that process for days on end—weeks, if he could get away with it.

And how he would cherish the moments in between, watching her sleep, eating together, lying in bed talking, and generally finding the shape and edges of themselves as a couple. They hadn't really had the luxury of doing that yet. He wanted them to have that chance to get comfortable in their collective skin, to find and savor themselves in each other—preferably before his sister, Una, brought the diamond ring he'd ordered back from Dublin. Then it would be time to take things to the next level.

He would have to wait to propose until they were back in the States, though, since he'd promised Neve that he would ask her father's permission first. He wanted to do it right, choose the perfect time and place. Should he take her on another trip? Con would have to ask Rosanna if there was somewhere Neve had always wanted to go. He knew Neve was in no rush to move things along, but the sooner they got engaged, the better, as far as he was concerned. He would prefer to skip the engagement completely and elope straightaway, but he was determined to make Neve so happy, she would only ever marry once, and he didn't want to deprive her of anything. Con had overheard female coworkers comparing notes on dress fittings, bridal showers, things of that nature. At least Neve had provisionally agreed to say yes, and she was wearing the claddagh ring he'd given her. God willing, the rest would come in good time.

But first, Kayla.

And even before that, his conference presentation.

Davies was up there now, introducing Con as if they were old friends.

He sighed and pressed his eyes closed. This was the annual Global Endocrinology Conference, a major event in their field. He had attended it before, but not since he'd moved to the US. Now that he was back, he needed to give a decent presentation.

Con couldn't step in front of his colleagues feeling resentful about this foist, or hating Duran, Banai, the doctor treating him in Galway, and everything and everyone that stood between him and Neve being naked in bed. If he went out there in that frame of mind, he wouldn't change anyone else's.

And that's what he wanted to do—change minds. His favorite work as a doctor was treating psychiatric patients, but there weren't as many of his colleagues in the specialty as he would like. He wanted to share how deeply satisfying it could be to uncover how the endocrine system was impacting mental health and vice versa, find solutions that would bring relief to suffering, and sometimes even solve complex medical mysteries. Add to that the fact that he had grown attached to the psychiatric patient population with their resilience, humor, and raw, uncompromising honesty. In them, Con saw his own father, who had fought a lifelong battle with cruel depression, and he also saw himself. That could easily have been his struggle as well, but for the grace of God—and more recently, for the grace Neve had brought into his life.

Neve....

And in the second it took to picture her, he was right there again, disrobing her slowly in his mind.

Neve had made it more than clear that the intense desire he felt was mutual. The only thing forcing him to exercise restraint was that a few days remained before he would be cleared to engage in "strenuous physical activity." Not that he had ever let a doctor's orders stop him from doing what he wanted before, God knew. But he also didn't want his first night of passion with Neve marred by blood flowing from a torn-open bullet wound. Not that Con would care, but he was fairly sure it would ruin the mood for Neve, and she deserved better. She deserved perfection.

He blew out a hard breath and forced his train of thought back onto the track of his other passion, psychiatric endocrinology. It was time to go out there and convince his colleagues to take more of an interest in the field. He owed it to his own patients back home, and to their fellows everywhere.

Having given himself his marching orders, Con pushed himself up off the chair and stretched, wincing and cursing under his breath. He tapped his notecards into a neat stack, tucked them into his jacket pocket, and grabbed the handle of his cane.

Whatever unique pleasures the rest of the world held, Ireland rivaled them with the experience of an evening in a local pub. Con had forgotten how much he missed the instant sense of comfort and camaraderie, the feeling of having come home, regardless of where in the country he was.

In fact, Davies had brought him quite a bit farther away from the university than he was expecting for post-conference drinks. They were in the Shandon neighborhood on the north side of the city near Saint Anne's Church. He hadn't been there since he was a boy, climbing the bell tower with his family. They had played the Bells of Shandon and enjoyed the tale of the Four-Faced Liar, the clock tower whose four clocks never displayed exactly the same time, despite the diligent efforts of many an engineer. That story came to mind every time he was treating a patient and something didn't go to plan. It was a humbling reminder that no matter how much he learned or how skilled he became, things would still happen that confounded him.

The pub, called The Close, was tucked away down a side street near the church. Once inside, though, he could have been in a pub anywhere in Ireland. In the forest of polished wood, dark fabrics, and aged but shining brass, a thoroughfare separated the well-stocked bar from the surrounding rabbit warren of nooks and tables. The walls were filled with photos spanning decades, immortalizing local patrons and well-known people who had passed through for a drink, along with a mix of Irish celebrities and historic figures. Strings of white lights winked near the ceiling, possibly hung one year for the festive season and then left up. The tricolor and the flags of various counties and local sports teams added color to the place, as did a few large-screen TVs playing rugby and football games. An unobtrusive soundtrack mixing rock and trad music played in the background.

But the best thing about the pub was the atmosphere, that indefinable quality that was so difficult to replicate elsewhere. He had been to many American establishments that tried, but there was always something missing. As they ordered their drinks, Con tried to put his finger on it. He figured it must come down to the people.

The Close was well populated without being

crowded, and the patrons ranged in age from a few kids running around the place to people well past retirement age. There was that feeling of familiarity and comfort that comes when nearly all those assembled know each other. Con had gone to university with a few people from Shandon, so he knew it was a close-knit community where people were kind and looked after one another. Warmth emanated from the crowd, with everyone rubbing along—no aggression or tension, just a relaxed sense of camaraderie and good cheer.

The feel of the place changed, though, when he followed Davies to the back of the pub and they entered a closed-door private room. Something about the crowd put his back up. There was no music playing, just the sound of low voices. As he stepped in and scanned the room, Con didn't see any familiar faces from the conference. These patrons were all men and all white, unlike the conference attendees. He was also only hearing Irish and American accents, very different from the global crowd of endocrinologists with whom he'd spent the day.

Stepping closer to Davies, he asked, "What's all this, then?"

Davies smiled over his shoulder and replied, "Con, there's someone I want you to meet. Liam, this is Con, the man I told you about. Liam owns The Close, along with some other properties in Cork."

Con nodded at Liam, a tall, stocky man with a shaved head and a tight smile. "Beautiful pub," he said, still wondering what was going on.

"Thanks," Liam replied. "I bought it about twenty years ago, but as you can probably tell, it's been around a lot longer than that."

Con nodded, concealing his surprise that Liam had an American accent. His instincts were telling him to exercise caution around this man. He decided to get straight to the point. "Davies, I don't see anyone here from the conference."

"Well, no. I figured we'd both had enough shoptalk. Much better to enjoy a casual gathering. My friends meet regularly at our favorite watering hole here, and I join them whenever I'm in town." With a crocodile-like smile, he added, "I hope you're not disappointed."

It wasn't lost on Con that Davies took no responsibility for misleading him, or for incorrectly assuming that Con would rather socialize with his friends than spend the evening alone with Neve. To deepen professional connections was the only reason he'd come out in the first place. Now that he was here, though, he supposed he'd make the most of it.

He could take the opportunity to give Neve the authentic Irish pub experience. Christ, he would be glad when she arrived.

"It's grand. I know Neve will be keen to join us." He pulled out his phone to text her. "What's the address here?"

But Davies held his hand up. "What's the rush? Let's sit down and have a drink or two, at least, before we bring women into the picture." He winked in a way that made Con want to flatten him. "There's a free table."

Con wished he and Davies weren't connected to so many of the same people back in DC. He wanted to turn around and get the hell out of there, take Neve somewhere else for the evening. Instead, he was stuck representing his department at Capitol Hill General, at least in part, so he had to be somewhat polite.

He followed Liam and Davies to the table and sat with his back against the wall, not keen to be confronted with any more surprises.

Davies explained that Liam was an importer-exporter based out of DC who lived part-time in Cork. He had made the move to Ireland to establish a commercial foothold with better access to the European Union and the United Kingdom, although Brexit had complicated things a bit. What exactly

Liam imported and exported was never mentioned, although the fact that he was puffing away on a cigar irrespective of the smoking ban suggested the man made his own rules. Listening to Davies talk, Con got the impression that he was a silent partner in Liam's business. In fact, from the snippets of conversation he overheard around them, it seemed other men present were also involved.

It wasn't long before the conversation turned to who they knew in common. Davies suggested that Con and Liam might have a mutual friend.

"Who's that?" Liam asked. Con was curious to know himself.

"Con here is an endocrinologist at Capitol Hill General," Davies said, "but he consults for the psychiatry department."

Liam didn't look surprised in the least, but for some reason, he forced himself to sound that way as he asked, "You know Rodwell, then? Head of psychiatry?"

While nothing had visibly changed, the alarm bells that had issued Con a soft warning when he entered the room began clanging loudly.

Unfortunately, he *did* know Rodwell. That evil snake in the grass was Neve's former boss, and a member of the Brickhaven Foundation, a shady DC think tank whose tentacles reached high up the walls of power. Rodwell had been a central part of the Brickhaven plot to assassinate President Duran. When Neve got in his way, Rodwell had her committed to the psychiatry unit under false pretenses, holding her in an isolation room for hours until Con managed to break her out. The presidential assassination attempt might well have succeeded, too, if not for the interference of Neve, Con's good friend Eric, and himself. Stopping Brickhaven in its tracks had put all three of them in the organization's crosshairs, which was why they all now had Agent Banai's Secret Service phone number in their Contacts lists.

Rodwell was also someone Con would happily beat to a pulp, should the opportunity arise. Certainly, he was someone whose friends Con had no desire to share a pint with.

He worked to remain calm. There were any number of reasons why Liam might know Rodwell. DC circles were small and tended to overlap. There was no reason—yet, at least—to believe these men knew anything about Rodwell's misdeeds.

Con cleared his throat so he could trust his voice. "I do, of course. We've worked together. How do you know him?"

"Old friends," Liam said as he leaned back in his

chair, smiling. "We went to prep school together in DC. Brickhaven Academy."

Con didn't speak, just nodded as the blood in his veins turned to ice. He knew very well that the sinister Brickhaven Foundation was made up exclusively of graduates from the well-heeled boys' school of the same name.

"My brother is also a Brickhaven alum," Davies added. "That's how Liam and I met each other."

"That's right," Liam said. "Davies was too good for us, though. His parents sent him to Wardhall."

"My brother will never let me live that down." Davies smiled broadly as the conversation in the room began to quiet. "Another round?"

Con did a quick scan of the room. The crowd had thinned out. There were about eight men left in addition to Davies and Liam, and they all appeared to be listening in. Unfortunately, they were also all positioned between Con and the door.

In spite of being on high alert, he willed himself to appear unperturbed. After all, Con was in Cork at the request of the president, who wouldn't have sent him if there had been any whiff of a connection between the conference attendees and their recent run-in with Rodwell and the Brickhaven Foundation. Besides, according to the White House, most Brickhaven graduates knew nothing about the foundation's criminal elements or their nefarious activities.

It could just be an unfortunate coincidence, he reminded himself. Though that might have been easier to believe if icy tendrils of unease weren't sliding down Con's back. Whether or not this was an innocent gathering, however, he didn't want Neve anywhere near it. That was priority number one.

Con swallowed the remainder of his pint and placed it on the table. "Why not," he replied. "You were right, Davies. This isn't a night for the ladies. I'll text Neve, tell her to expect me when she sees me."

"Well said." Davies clapped him on the shoulder while Liam raised his fingers at the bartender and drew a circle in the air.

Conscious that both of his drinking companions were watching and could potentially see his screen, Con kept his text message to Neve vague and brief:

> Change of plans. Don't come out tonight. I'll meet you at the hotel. No need to wait up.

He quickly hit Send, then silenced his phone and put it away. "She'll be a bit sore about it, since you *did* invite her."

"Well, I had to, didn't I?" Davies smiled. "Otherwise, you never would have agreed to come. And while it would have made things more interesting, her presence here is not, strictly speaking, necessary."

Not necessary—meaning Davies had brought him here with an agenda. *The jury's still out,* Con reminded himself as he took in the changing scene. The room had grown so quiet, he could hear the sounds of breathing, glasses being placed on tables, and chairs creaking. All eyes had turned to him, and while there were no signs of aggression, he sensed that could change quickly if things didn't go the way Liam and Davies planned.

Keeping the bite out of his tone, Con asked, "Necessary to what, exactly?"

Davies and Liam exchanged satisfied smiles. "Well," Davies began, "we have a business proposition for you. Don't worry, it's a good one—mutually beneficial. It requires a bit of moral flexibility, but we did our research. We know you're not against breaking a few rules for the right cause."

Jesus Christ, Con cursed internally. He never should have allowed Davies to bring him to the pub. In fact, he should have trusted his instincts about the arsehole in the first place. But here he was, and now that he had to assess whether there was a new threat from Brickhaven, the only way out was through.

He picked up his pint and stared down into it. "The right cause?"

"In this case, money," Davies said. "A lot of money, and for very little effort. It's work your Girl Scout of a girlfriend might not approve of, though. No offense, of course. I like Neve, but she's a social worker, right? In my experience, they tend to be do-gooders, and a bit rigid when it comes to ethical matters. So, it would be best to keep this conversation between those of us who appreciate that things are rarely black-and-white, and there are always shades of gray. You understand."

Con still didn't know which "shades of gray" described Davies and Liam. Were they unethical businessmen, murderous conspirators, or something in between? At this point, anything was possible. He *did* plan to keep the conversation confidential, however. No way would he let any of this touch Neve. "I do."

"I told you he would," Davies said, clapping his hands together and smiling broadly.

It seemed to Con that the tension in the room eased ever so slightly—but only for a moment.

"Good man," Liam said before slamming the trap

shut. With a vicious curl to his lip, he added, "By the way, Rodwell sends his regards."

CHAPTER 5
NEVE

> Change of plans. Don't come out tonight. I'll meet you at the hotel. No need to wait up.

"Sorry." I tried not to let Banshee hear how annoyed I felt as I returned to our phone call. "That text was from Con, so I just wanted to check it in case it was something important."

"Was it?"

"No." And it wasn't important to our conversation, or what was happening with Kayla—only to my heart, which now sagged into my shoes. Sitting on the hotel bed, I leaned back on my elbow and asked, "So, any luck with the sketch?"

I had never met Banshee, and indeed only knew her by her hacker name. But Con's good friend Eric, a fellow hacker, had vouched for her as a trusted Irish source when we needed help taking down Mad Max, the cult leader in Galway. She had come through for us in a big way then, so I had contacted her to see if she could help us identify the girl in Kayla's sketch. I was surprised when she called me back after only a few hours.

"Yeah, she's dead, God rest her," Banshee said. "Megan Tóibín, aged nineteen when she was killed a year ago in Cork. Blunt force trauma to the head. Body found in the river. Boyfriend suspected but never found. Apparently, he scarpered, maybe to the UK."

"Oh my God. That's awful." The news felt like a twofold kick to the stomach. The girl Kayla had seen in her vision was not only a real person but a murder victim. "That poor girl. Do they have any idea what happened? Does she have family in Cork? Who was the boyfriend?"

"Stall!" I heard a few clicks on Banshee's end of the line. "I just emailed you the links to the police report and a few news articles."

"So, it was in the news." That made more sense, at least. Kayla must have seen the girl's picture in the paper, and it played into her hallucination somehow.

"Stories like this get a lot of coverage here,"

Banshee said. "These types of crimes don't happen as often as they do in the States."

"Understood." Sadly. "Okay, thanks so much for doing this, especially so quickly and on such short notice."

"It took me less than fifteen minutes."

"Okay, well, send me an invoice anyway. We'll be glad to pay whatever you need."

"No charge. When I saw her name, I was surprised I hadn't recognized her, because I remember hearing about the case. Turns out, no photos of her were ever published. I had to verify the sketch using a picture in the police report."

"Oh." Now I was feeling motion sick from moving so rapidly between understanding and confusion. Where could Kayla have seen her picture, then? "Is it strange that they didn't publish a photo?"

"The police report includes an interview with her parents. They didn't want her picture published because they didn't want their last memories of her to be her picture plastered next to headlines about her death. The press respected their wishes."

"Oh, wow." I tried hard but couldn't imagine a circumstance under which the US press would show the same restraint.

"Anything else I can help with? Need me to bug Con's phone or something?"

"What?"

"I could tell whatever he texted you earlier got up your nose. If you think he's cheating or something, I'd be happy to pair—"

"No, no, thank you!" I shook my head. "Everything's good, just a scheduling mishap. There's nothing else. We both really appreciate this."

"No bother. You know where I am if you need me. Cheers!"

I smiled to myself as she clicked off. Con, cheating? Or me, for that matter? *Not in a million years.* Whatever differences we might have—and there were a few—we were both faithful, some might even say loyal to a fault. And I wouldn't have it any other way.

My heart warmed as I looked down at the claddagh ring Con had given me back in Galway. I admired it, turning it around on my finger. A pre-engagement ring, he had called it—the symbol of a promise. The joy I felt when I thought about what that meant....

Flopping backward on the bed, I tossed my phone to one side, grabbed a pillow, and screamed into it. Sometimes the idea of what was happening between Con and me was so exciting, I couldn't contain myself. It was hard to believe that after two years of friendship, crushing on him the whole time but never imagining anything would ever happen, here we were. And here I was in his home country, having met his parents, wearing his promise ring on my finger.

The light moment evaporated, though, when I remembered the text Con had sent.

I picked up my phone and read over it again. *Don't come out tonight. Don't wait up.* Banshee was right; it *had* pissed me off. What kind of text was that, anyway? Dismissive, cold, and with no explanation or apology for cutting me out of his plans?

It also worried me, though. That was so unlike Con, I could only conclude that something unexpected must have happened.

I hope everything is okay....

Stop it, I ordered my brain before it started down a panic attack rabbit hole. I couldn't afford to let irrational thoughts get the better of me; there was too much to do. Con would explain everything later, I was certain of it.

When has he ever let you down?

The answer was "never."

Holding on to that thought, I forced myself to shelve my annoyance and anxiety. We would sort it out later, together.

For now, there was poor Megan to read about, and Kayla to call. Instantly sober, I picked up my phone again and opened Banshee's email.

I spotted Kayla in the back of the coffee shop, which was still bustling in the early evening. She explained that the Brooklyn Bean, opened by an American expat, catered to students and insomniacs. The interior was cheerful and bright, with the walls covered in flyers and eclectic art and worn leather armchairs surrounding tables, nearly every one of which was currently home to a laptop. There was also a smattering of paraphernalia from Brooklyn, like New York subway signs and photographs of the skyline.

I ordered a latte and sat with Kayla. "This is where she wanted to meet?"

"I know, right? Not what I expected."

We had about half an hour to talk before we would be joined by Rose, a local psychic medium and friend of Audrey, Kayla's roommate. While Kayla was clear that she didn't believe in psychics, she had agreed to indulge Audrey by showing the sketch of the girl she'd seen to Rose, who Audrey thought might provide useful insights.

Kayla was relieved to hear that Con agreed with the other endocrinologist that her labs looked normal and there was no resurgence of her pituitary issues.

"I can't wait to tell my mom," she crowed. "You know, it was only later that she decided my visions were caused by my concussions. The first time I had one, she actually tried to get me to see an exorcist!"

"What?" I froze, cup midair, glad I hadn't yet taken a sip when she dropped that bomb.

"Yeah," Kayla said with an eye roll. "In her defense, I was also acting really weird at the time. I was forgetting things, I had a terrible temper, my mood was all over the place. She didn't know what was going on, and neither did the doctors for a while. So, she tried to get me an appointment with the exorcist for the Boston Archdiocese. Fortunately, his secretary said he was booked out for six months, and I had my pituitary diagnosis by then."

I blinked. Then blinked again. "Hang on, the Boston Archdiocese has an exorcist?"

"Yup."

"With a six-month waiting list?"

"Yeah, so, you know, good luck if you have an

emergency demonic possession—as opposed to the other kind!"

To avoid laughing at the absurdity of it all, I bit my lip so hard, I tasted blood. "I'm sorry, I just... I don't even know what to say about that."

"Well, what *is* there to say when the combat of evil spirits gets bogged down by bureaucracy?" Smiling, she asked, "You said you had two pieces of news?"

"I did." I hesitated, reluctant to take the conversation from absurd to chilling. I cleared my throat and began, "My friend was able to identify the girl in your sketch."

"Oh, wow, really?" All levity disappeared as Kayla leaned forward, her forehead crisscrossed with worry lines, and whispered, "She's dead, isn't she?"

I nodded, and it felt as though a heavy black curtain had fallen over our table. I told Kayla the story of Megan's tragedy, careful to share only the basics. There was no need to traumatize her with the details I'd read in the police report, like how Megan had been hit in the back of the head with a blunt wooden object that left splinters under her skin before she was tossed into the river. Or how she had been found by children on their way to school, half of her body visible above the water where she had washed up on a shallow bank. It was already dreadful enough, telling Kayla about the murder of a girl with whose spirit she believed she'd interacted.

As I spoke, she leaned back in her chair with her eyes closed, listening carefully and nodding. After I finished, I asked if she was okay.

"I don't know." Kayla shook her head. "That's horrific, what happened to her. And it's really scary to think the guy who did it is still out there somewhere." She shuddered. "If I knew she was happy and at peace, I would feel better, you know? But in my vision, she was in obvious distress." She blew out a hard breath and looked off at a point in the distance. "I just wish I knew why she was shown to me. Maybe I should talk to her family? I think that's what I was meant to do with the last two."

"I don't know," I said, trying to work out how to phrase my opinion on that plan delicately. "I think if you put yourself in their shoes, it might be less than helpful for them to hear what you saw, possibly even traumatizing."

With a sigh, Kayla admitted, "Yeah, I guess you're right. I wouldn't want to hear that somebody I loved who passed away might still be upset." Her eyes lit up a bit. "Hey, maybe the Holy Ghost wants me to find her boyfriend, bring him to justice."

The last thing any of us needed was Kayla getting mixed up with a murderer. I had to get her to change course, and fast. "Now that you know who she was, do you remember ever seeing her picture anywhere?" From the information Banshee had given me, the only pictures of Megan were in the police report: one from her family for identification, and multiple grisly photos from the crime scene and postmortem medical examination.

Kayla gave me a tired look. "No, I never saw her picture, and I'm not imagining things. I saw what I saw, Neve. I mean, I do get why you and everyone else question it, but I was the one it happened to, and I'm telling you, it was real."

"Right. Okay." I gave her a conciliatory smile. "Look, I'm just worried about your safety. Maybe you can tell the gardaí what you saw, but you don't want to put yourself on the radar of a person who could do what Megan's attacker did to her. And I'd be willing to bet the Holy Ghost doesn't want you to be in harm's way either."

She thought for a moment. "Fair enough, you're probably right about that."

"Kayla?" a warm voice called from behind me.

"Oh, hi!" Kayla smiled. "Are you Rose?"

The woman sat in the empty chair we'd saved at

our table. Far from the psychic wrapped in scarves and jingling gold jewelry I had imagined, Rose blended in easily with the students in her leggings, sneakers, and oversized hoodie. She appeared to be about my age, and her expression was warm and welcoming.

We all greeted one another and exchanged brief introductions—who we were, where we were from, how we were connected to Audrey.

At a natural lull in the conversation, Rose adopted a professional, no-nonsense demeanor. "Kayla, Audrey said you'd like me to look at a sketch?"

Kayla nodded and pulled the sketch of Megan up on her phone. "So, this girl—"

"Wait," Rose said gently, holding up her hand. "I'd rather you not tell me anything yet. I said the same to Audrey. I prefer to hear what Spirit has to say first. Is that all right?"

"Of course." Kayla and I exchanged surprised looks as she handed Rose the phone and sat back. Leaning toward me, Kayla whispered, "That's true. Audrey said she didn't tell Rose anything either."

I had never met a medium before, or really given them much thought beyond advertisements I'd seen on the internet and late-night TV for psychic hotlines charging exorbitant rates. Those ads didn't exactly inspire confidence, nor did the stories I'd heard of spiritual scammers who had convinced my therapy clients they were under a curse, and the only cure was to pay them large amounts of money.

As I sat watching Rose examine the sketch, I realized I had a lot of preexisting assumptions about how she worked. I'd expected her to ask Kayla questions, then share insights drawn from the answers and informed by empathy and sensitivity to subconscious cues, perhaps with a bit of archetypal psychology thrown in. Her request that Kayla not give her any information about the sketch in advance came as a surprise.

It wasn't the first time recently that I would be prying my mind open a bit further. Back in DC, our patient Amos had claimed it was an angel who helped him lead us to the evidence we needed to stop the assassination attempt on President Duran. Even the drama with Mad Max had taught me new things about the mysterious impacts of traumatic events, including those that occur when we're in an unconscious state.

Working in a hospital, we all lived and breathed the Western medical model—which was only appropriate. That's why patients came to us, after all, not in search of spiritual support. Lately, though, forced confrontations with the mysteries of the universe had made me realize I had developed tunnel vision, and that science wasn't the only place to look for answers or deep truths.

Rose pushed her long brown ponytail back off her shoulder, folded Kayla's phone between her hands, and closed her eyes. "Okay," she began, "an older gentleman is coming through. I'm getting that he's on your maternal side, and he had a problem with the lungs—he died from fluid in the lungs. He's wearing a tweed flatcap, and he has a dog with him—black-and-white, about knee-high." Opening her eyes, she turned to Kayla. "Can you confirm this?"

Kayla leaned forward, her expression hesitant but hopeful. "Well, that could be my grandfather, my mom's dad. He had a border collie, and he always wore a tweed cap. But he died from heart failure, not a lung problem."

"I see. Well, heart failure can cause a buildup of fluid in the lungs. You can check on that, but for now, I'll take that as confirmation that he's here for you."

I had liked Rose immediately, so I had hoped she wouldn't confirm my skepticism. But so far, she hadn't said anything that would undo my existing assumptions. Lots of people Kayla's age had a grandfather who had died, lung problems were a frequent cause of death, lots of grandfathers wore caps, and plenty of dogs were black-and-white. I sat back, folded my arms, and began to strategize how to help Kayla manage her inevitable disappointment.

"All right. He's bringing through another spirit, the girl in your sketch. She has passed. Not long ago, maybe within a year. There was violence in her passing." She set the phone down and lifted a hand to the back of her head. "Someone hit her just here. She's showing me water…. I think she was found in water, but she didn't die by drowning."

Wait… what? My whole body stilled. Everything Rose had just said was 100 percent accurate. Even the part about Megan being dead before she entered the river. The medical examiner's report had concluded the same, since she didn't have any water in her lungs. That detail had not appeared in the articles about Megan, so it wasn't something Audrey, Kayla, or Rose could have known.

Excitedly, Kayla tried to jump in, but again, Rose held up her hand, saying, "Just one second, I'm getting more details." She turned to Kayla, eyes wide. "She's saying she came to see you. I mean, after she passed. Did you see her?"

Still frozen, I could only watch as Kayla nodded in slow motion.

"Got it." Rose nodded as though listening to

someone. "She came to you because she wants you to find a man, someone who was there when she died. I'm getting the letter *D* and the word 'pearl.' Now she's showing me the word 'blackbird.' Something like 'you'll find him near the blackbird'? Okay, now she's pulling her energy back. Your grandfather has come forward again. He says he's proud of you and wants you to know he's keeping an eye out for you. Now he's pulling his energy back as well."

As Kayla and I sat there, slack-jawed and staring, Rose slid the phone across the table to Kayla and leaned back in her chair, eyes closed. "Hang on, there's someone else coming through."

We exchanged wide-eyed looks. Rose nodded periodically, as though listening to someone speak. After several minutes, she opened her eyes and surprised us by saying, "Sorry, nothing else to add right now. That's all I've got for you, Kayla. Did any of it make sense?"

"Wow," Kayla murmured, looking as stunned as I felt. "I mean, wow."

Rose smiled gently, as though she was well accustomed to having this effect on people. "I take it that's a yes?"

"Yes, that's a yes!" Awestruck, Kayla reached out

and grasped Rose's hand. "You really talked to her, and to my grandfather!"

"Well, the conversation was a bit one-sided," Rose said, smiling. "They tend to be, though. I need a coffee now, after that. Anyone else need a refill?"

In that moment, as our beliefs and assumptions were being rearranged in a profound sense, I was grateful for Rose's well-timed use of humor. We smiled back as Rose gestured to our empty coffee cups.

"I'm okay," I said. "Kayla, how about you?"

"Yeah, I could use an Americano. I'll come with you."

But the looks on our faces must have told Rose that Kayla and I needed a few minutes to recover. "No," she said, waving her hand. "You two relax. I'll be right back."

Once she was gone, Kayla looked at me, mouth open wide. "Oh my God, Neve, she's for real!"

My instinct when confronted with something paradigm-shifting was to proceed with caution, never to jump to conclusions. But Rose had genuinely blown me away. "She's left me speechless, to be honest."

"Oh, wow." Kayla flopped back against her chair. "What *was* that? I mean, my grandfather! I wasn't sure about that part, but then she told us Megan came to see me, and how she died. And the blackbird…. That's too crazy, Neve. She *knew* things. I didn't understand some of the stuff, though, like the letter *D*? And what's the significance of the word 'pearl'?"

"Yeah." I rubbed my eyes, which were dry from prolonged staring. "I can't say for sure, but the *D* might refer to Declan. That was the name of the boyfriend."

"No way!"

I nodded. "And I did look up the name Megan online earlier. I was just curious to know if it was Irish. Turns out, it was originally a Welsh form of Margaret, and the meaning of the name is 'pearl.'"

"Whoa!" Kayla slid down in her chair, her head lolling back.

Honestly, I felt like doing the same, but I figured one of us should try to remain as sharp and analytical as possible.

Rose returned with two fresh coffees in hand. "Here we are!" Her mood was bright as she sat down again. "So, do you have any questions for me about your reading?"

Kayla popped back up in her chair. "Thanks so much, Rose—for the reading and for the coffee. That was truly incredible." She reached for her bag. "How much do I owe you?"

"Oh, no." Rose waved her hand dismissively. "No worries. I'm happy to help any friend of Audrey's. Was there anything more you wanted to know?"

"Well, I guess we figured out the letter *D* and the 'pearl' thing." Kayla looked to me for confirmation.

I nodded. "*D* could be Declan, her boyfriend, and the name Megan means 'pearl.'"

Rose blinked in surprise. "Oh, that's interesting! I don't always have a sense of what the information means that I'm getting, especially those kinds of details. Often that's for you, for validation. There was one strange thing, though."

Before I could stop myself, I laughed, a bit incredulously. "Just one?"

Fortunately, Kayla and Rose laughed along with me.

"What was it?" Kayla asked.

"It was the blackbird. Usually, when Spirit shows me a word, I see it like it was typed on an old-fashioned typewriter, black letters on a white background, like paper. But this time, when I saw the word 'blackbird,' it was different—all capital letters, for one thing, and they were red on a yellow background. The word appeared in a rectangle with a black outline.

Also, it looked like the letters were raised off the surface." Rose shook her head. "Sorry, I have no idea what that means."

Kayla and I shrugged at each other. "Me either," Kayla said. "When Megan appeared to me, though, she led me to a dead blackbird."

"Huh." Rose shook her head. "Well, often the meanings behind these things become clear in the days or weeks after the reading. I'd love it if you would let me know when you figure out what it means."

"Of course, I'd be happy to!" Kayla's smile faded slightly. "You know, I've had these sorts of visions before, but I was told they were from the Holy Ghost."

"And I'm not here to tell you otherwise," Rose said. "My job is just to share with you the information I received." With a knowing smile, she looked at me. "I'm not trying to change anyone's beliefs."

"Ha!" I grinned. "Epic fail, then."

Rose's genuine laughter rose above the sounds of the coffee shop, drawing a few curious looks. The conversation became easy and comfortable as she explained to Kayla how she communicated with Spirit, how she'd learned that she had a gift, and what she'd done to develop it.

Kayla shared more about her grandfather and how meaningful it was to receive his message. She spoke about how, because of her own faith, she had always believed in heaven and an afterlife, but it never occurred to her that her loved ones who had passed on would stay so connected to her here on earth.

I didn't say much at all. Rose had given us as much information as she could about Kayla's visit from Megan, and I didn't want to interrupt as the two women compared notes about their similar gifts. Instead, I sat back and thought about what Rose had shown us, not just about Megan but about concepts of the spiritual.

Eventually, we all stood up to leave. Kayla couldn't wait to tell Audrey about her reading, and Rose had dogs at home waiting for their dinner. She and Kayla hugged and exchanged information.

Kayla headed out first, and as I began to follow her, Rose put her hand on my arm. "Neve, someone came through for you as well, but I don't think this is the best time or place for me to give you their message." She pulled a business card out of her pocket and pressed it into my palm. "It's about your recent medical news. Call me when you're ready."

"Oh." Her words felt like a blow to the solar plexus. I couldn't inhale. "Um...."

"When you're ready."

She was giving me a reprieve, and I took it. I tucked her business card into my phone case as I rushed ahead of her and out of the coffee shop. Outside the door, I sucked in a deep breath.

After what I had just seen, I strongly suspected Rose did have a real, genuine message for me. That was extraordinary, and such a generous gift. But I really didn't want to hear what my grandparents, for example, might think about my infertility, especially since I didn't even know what *I* thought about it yet. Besides, they might be devastated, or even feel sorry for me. I didn't think I could handle being pitied by someone who was dead.

We said our final goodbyes, and Kayla and I climbed into a taxi. After we gave the driver our destinations, she turned to me. "I can't thank you enough for all your help. I know you're a lot younger than my mom, but hanging out with you reminds me of having her around. Even though she's a skeptic, she has always been supportive. If she were here, she'd be doing all of this with me." Reaching over for a quick hug, she added, "You'd be a great mom, Neve."

I knew I should thank her for her compliment, but every word I could think of to say stuck in my throat.

Instead, I smiled, nodded, and tried very, very hard not to cry.

It was all too much. I knew what I needed, though.

Con. I just want to be with Con.

With everything that had happened, maybe it was just as well that I wouldn't be joining him at the pub. In my current state, I might not be much good at saving him from Davies, or anyone else for that matter. I would just go back to the hotel, slip into one of the white fuzzy robes they gave us, distract myself with room service and trash TV, and wait.

CHAPTER 6
CON

Rodwell sends his regards.

Con froze, pint glass halfway to his lips.

That meant Rodwell knew they might be meeting. Liam must have spoken to Rodwell in the month since Con and Neve thwarted Brickhaven's presidential assassination attempt. How much Rodwell had told them, he couldn't be sure, however.

The White House had assured Neve, Eric, and Con that Rodwell no longer posed a threat to them. But all he knew for certain was that Rodwell had disappeared from view, with the official story that he was on indefinite personal leave from work. If Liam and Davies had been in touch with Rodwell, however, they might know all about Rodwell's crimes. And if they did know the whole story but remained friends with the man, that meant they, too, felt at home in Brickhaven's sick swamp of corruption.

"Does he now?" Slowly, Con put his pint back down on the table and glared at the two men. "What do you want, boys?"

"Straight to the point." Davies nodded. "We were told to expect as much. Well, then, I'll do you the courtesy of being straightforward as well."

Con leaned forward slightly. "Please."

"It's simple, really," Davies began, spreading his hands out on the table. Con was glad to see the smiles had disappeared from both men's faces along with any pretense of camaraderie. "We do some off-the-books surgical work for people who need it. Nothing frivolous or cosmetic; this is lifesaving stuff. But we help patients who wish to 'jump the queue,' as they say over here, and whose goodwill is valuable to us."

Christ almighty. Con knew this sort of thing went on, of course, but he'd never actually spoken to anyone involved. "Jump the queue? You mean skip the waiting lists."

"That's right."

"For…?"

"Organ transplants, mainly."

Con kept his expression as neutral as possible, acutely conscious now that he was sitting in a room full of serious criminals. "And the donor organs come from where?"

"We're connected with people who have access to large numbers of highly motivated potential donors."

"Motivated by…?" Con wasn't going to let them get away with any vagueness. He had to know just how dangerous this crowd was.

"Money, mainly." Davies threw the word out casually, as though its meaning in this context wasn't sinister in the least.

"I see." Con nodded. "And these patients whose goodwill is valuable to you, who might they be?"

"They might be anyone." Liam's tone was sharp. "That's not your concern."

Davies shot Liam a stern look, as though urging calm. "We're saving lives. As the surgeons, that's all we need to know. Decisions about donors and recipients are made at another level of the organization."

Con kicked himself once again, unable to believe he had allowed Davies to draw him into this festering morass. "You've performed these surgeries, then."

"Yes, of course. In fact, I'm in town for that very reason." Davies's smile was tight and professional. "Early on, we set up Cork as one of our hubs of operation. As US citizens, we can come and go, and with the long coastline and the proximity to France and the

UK, we can bring others in under the radar. Since it's a popular tourist destination, my regular vacations here don't raise any eyebrows, and this Global Endocrinology Conference provides me with another legitimate reason to visit annually. We had already been working out how to recruit you. When your name appeared as a last-minute addition to the conference schedule, it just presented us with the perfect opportunity."

Recruit him? Con wanted nothing more than to stand up, overturn the table, and make a hasty exit, flattening as many of the goons in the room as he could on his way out. But Davies was being suspiciously free in sharing information about their operation. He wouldn't be telling Con all of this unless something else was going on. The wiser part of his mind advised that before getting into a brawl, he needed to know what that was. At the very least, Con could get as much information out of them as possible, something concrete to share with the authorities when he finally got away. With the hostile looks he was getting, he only hoped that when that time came, he'd be leaving in a taxi, not an ambulance. "And who is 'we,' exactly?"

"You'll just be working with Liam and me, with our team." Davies lifted a few fingers to keep Liam from jumping in. "It's a good deal, Con. Better than you're ever going to get from a hospital. A lot of us do this kind of work. You just don't hear about it when you're coloring inside the lines, so to speak. Trust me, it'll be a good move for your future, and for Neve's future."

Hearing Neve's name on Davies's lips sent tension shooting through Con's body like an electric shock. "Neve's future?"

"As I said, the compensation is generous," Davies continued. "Neve will be able to buy whatever she likes, and she can accompany you on your trips. As an Irish citizen, of course, you have the freedom to come here anytime and stay as long as you like without raising any eyebrows. But when you need to travel elsewhere, we'll set you up with cover stories. Beth comes along on most of my trips, and she loves it. She doesn't know about my off-the-books work, of course, but she'll take any excuse to take a break from DC."

Davies brings his wife? Con remembered meeting her at some fancy dinner event. So that's what Davies envisioned for him: being married to Neve while performing black market organ transplant operations on the side.

Con couldn't stand a fecking gobshite like Davies

thinking about Neve at all. If he said her name again, in fact, Con wasn't sure he could be responsible for his actions. He had to get her out of their heads and, most importantly, disconnect her from him in their minds. "I appreciate the thought, but Neve and I aren't serious."

"Ah, that's too bad," Davies said, and Con could practically see the adulterous wheels turning in the man's head. "I thought you made an attractive couple."

"Sorry to disappoint," Con said dryly. "I'm a confirmed bachelor, I'm afraid. Helps me focus on my work." He didn't add that if he *were* involved in some kind of illegal activity, unlike Davies, he'd keep himself and his shady dealings well away from anyone he cared about.

"Good man." Davies nodded. "In that case, you might want to go ahead and cut her loose—to help you focus, that is, because your first surgery is tomorrow night."

"What are you on about?" Con shifted his focus from Davies to Liam, who wore a smug expression. "I haven't agreed to anything."

"Oh, but you will." Liam leaned forward, ignoring Davies's gestured objections. "It's the least you can do for Brickhaven after the mess you made."

Brickhaven. Fecking hell. His worst suspicions were officially confirmed. At the very least, Davies and Liam knew he had made trouble for Brickhaven somehow, and they had brought him here to extract payback. And Con had followed Davies right into the belly of the beast.

Davies sighed heavily, but Con rubbed a hand across his mouth as he kept an eye on Liam.

"Yeah, that's right," Liam continued with a punchable smirk. "You didn't really think you could kick the hornet's nest without getting stung, did you?"

"Ah, no." Con shook his head. "I don't run around kicking hornet's nests. I'd never heard of Brickhaven before that unfortunate business. I was trying to save a man's life—the same thing you're asking me to do here, by the way—and it just so happened that you feckers turned out to be on the wrong side of it." Shrugging, he added, "Nothing personal, and I don't owe you a damned thing."

Liam blew a huge puff of cigar smoke in Con's direction. "Oh, okay, then! You were just trying to be a good guy and save the president, is that it? He's not *your* president, though, so why did you even give a shit?"

Con had been careful not to mention President Duran, so Liam's words revealed that he, Davies, and the other men in the room knew all about Rodwell's planned assassination attempt. That meant Con was in the room with a bunch of murderers, and in as much danger as he had ever been.

Focus, he ordered himself as he tried to stop his thoughts from spinning. He had to make it clear from the outset that whatever they had in mind for him, he wasn't going to be a pushover. "You got me," Con said, looking Liam in the eye. "He's not my president, and it *was* personal. I was just trying to get on your wick."

Liam pushed his chair out sharply and began to stand, but Davies laid a hand on his arm. "Everyone relax, okay? We're all going to be working together, after all." He waited to continue until Liam was sitting back down in his chair, arms crossed. "Con, look," Davies said, "I know what you're thinking, but Dr. Rodwell and the rest of us at Brickhaven, we're not psychopaths. We realize that when plans are carried out in secret, there's always a risk of interference from people who might not know or appreciate who they're dealing with. You were simply ignorant before, and you can't be blamed for that, which is why no harm has come to you. Now, though, you know who we are."

"Yeah, now you fuckin' know!" Liam declared.

Con sublimated the violent urges the two men were inspiring in him by imagining how he would pummel them both at some future date. "Brave words spoken on foreign soil," he pointed out. "It's my understanding that back home, they have you boys *well* neutered."

Con knew he'd hit a nerve when Liam appeared ready to froth at the mouth. "You know nothing!"

"Gentlemen, please!" Davies paused for a few moments, pinching the bridge of his nose while he waited for Liam to settle down. "Dr. Rodwell pointed out—wisely, I think we can all agree—that another doctor would be a valuable addition to our team. That's especially true now that his freedom of movement is somewhat limited—something else for which you're responsible, Con. Like I said, we're not out for retribution. But we do expect debts to be repaid. You took one of our doctors off the board. Now you'll replace him. Fair's fair, wouldn't you say?"

Every pair of eyes in the place bored into Con. He picked up his pint and took a sip to emphasize that his next question was merely curious. "And if I don't agree?"

"Con, come on now," Davies pleaded, turning his hands palms up.

"The organization decided," Liam said, "that *if*

you're willing to work for us, killing you would be a waste—if and only if, though." He and the other men in the room looked as though they were already fantasizing about how to dispose of Con's body.

Davies gave Liam a long-suffering look, but he didn't deny the threat. Instead, he shook his head at Con as though the two of them were friendly comrades who had to tolerate the others. "Try to see the opportunity here. As I mentioned, I came to Cork to harvest a kidney. But given all the inconvenience you've caused, Brickhaven has decided you should do it instead—with me assisting, of course," he added with a glance at Con's sling. "We have a donor currently en route and a recipient waiting overseas. The surgery is tomorrow night."

It had been taking a great deal of effort for Con to appear invested in what Davies was saying while simultaneously imagining ways to thwart Brickhaven's whole seedy operation. If they wanted him to perform a surgery, though, there was a chance he could nail down the details of when and where it would be happening and inform the authorities. Then they could catch these arseholes red-handed, snapping up Davies and crew and saving the poor bastard who was going on the chopping block.

That's presuming the authorities believed him, of

course. Right now, it was all pub talk and hearsay, and outrageous sounding at that.

"Think of this as an audition," Davies said. "If all goes well, you're hired. We want you to be part of our team."

"The surgery will be filmed for collateral," Liam added.

"Collateral I'm sure we'll never need," Davies said, the picture of insincerity. "I'm confident that when you see the details of the compensation package, you'll choose to join us. Another part of the deal is protection, of course, and a guarantee of your safety. As long as everything goes well with the surgery and you agree to work for us, no harm will come to you—or to Neve, for that matter."

Hearing Davies speak Neve's name again, this time with a threat attached, set Con's blood boiling. "What about Neve?"

"Well," Davies explained, "she also meddled with Dr. Rodwell's plans for the president, so like you, she owes Brickhaven a debt now. And while you say you and Neve are not an item, Dr. Rodwell assures us you're close friends. That being the case, as a goodwill gesture, we thought we'd offer to let you work off her debt along with your own. You can say no, of course, in which case—" He waved his hand through the air. "—Brickhaven will find another way to collect from her."

The other men in the room chuckled and exchanged lecherous glances. Through sheer strength of will, Con managed to contain his burgeoning rage.

He had failed to protect Neve from dangerous situations in the past. He would never forgive himself for that, and he certainly wasn't going to fail her again. Not this time. Not with Brickhaven. Whatever else, he had to get her out of harm's way. If that meant temporarily convincing these bastards he was on board, that's what he would do.

Meanwhile, the look on Davies's face showed he knew perfectly well what Con's answer would be. Before he gave them the satisfaction, however, Con had to find out whether his friend Eric was also considered "in debt" to them. "Anyone else I need to worry about?"

"Ah, you mean your hacker buddy?" Liam smiled and shook his head. "No need to worry about Eric. He already had some credit built up with us."

Credit built up? What the hell is he talking about? "Meaning?"

"We consider Eric a valuable asset. He's done good work for us in the past," Davies said, "although he didn't know it. The kind of work he does, sometimes it's unclear who's paying your fee. He'll work for us again in the future, too, without ever realizing it." With a low chuckle, he added, "He is a handful, though, that one."

Oh, hell. Eric wasn't going to like hearing *that*—if it was, in fact, true. Thankfully, Eric and his wife, Katie, were off the grid camping in Colorado for another week. He didn't have to worry about Eric's safety, then—at least not immediately.

"Right, so. I agree to work for you, and you'll leave Neve alone?"

Davies nodded. "That's the deal—along with generous compensation, protection, free travel, and other attractive benefits we can get into later."

"Done." He stretched his hand out. Looking pleased but not surprised, Davies shook it, then winced as Con squeezed hard. Infusing his voice with the promise of violence, Con said, "You'd better hold up your end, though."

Davies had the audacity to look offended. "One thing you can count on with Brickhaven: we always keep our promises."

Con released his hold, and Davies snatched his hand back.

"Let's drink to it," Liam said, calling for yet another round.

Con's mind raced. Now that he knew for certain that Neve had a Brickhaven-shaped target on her back, his first job had to be getting her out of Cork and somewhere safe. For that, he could ask for help from Banai and the Secret Service. Once Neve was out of harm's way, he could try to put a stop to the surgery while gathering as much information as he could about this criminal network. He would have to be certain she was safe first, though, since blowing up Brickhaven's operation would invalidate the deal he'd just made for her safety.

How the hell he was going to convince Neve to agree to leave town, though, he had no idea. Knowing her like he did, Con was well aware that if he told her the real reason he needed her to go, she'd insist on staying and helping him take Brickhaven down—again. On the other hand, if he didn't give her a good reason to get on a plane home, she would definitely refuse to do so.

Feck. He'd have to figure that out later.

For now, he sat back, fixing his eyes on the new round of drinks being delivered. Brickhaven might know a lot, but their information was patchy. For example, they didn't appear to know the real reason for his visit to Cork. If they had known he was doing President Duran a favor, no doubt they would have crowed about it to show off how clever they were and leveraged it to issue more threats. At least he didn't have to worry about Kayla, then.

To get the details of the surgery to pass on to the authorities, he'd first have to convince these thugs he really would go along with their plan. Con picked up his fresh pint. "What exactly am I meant to do tomorrow?"

With a self-satisfied smile, Davies visibly relaxed at the shift in topic. "We won't have a laparoscope on hand, so it'll be an open nephrectomy. It's a simpler procedure anyway. Then we'll store the kidney for transport. The transplant will be done on the recipient's end."

"And you'll be there, assisting me?" Con pointed at his slinged arm. "Not only am I one-handed at the moment, but I'm also neither a surgeon nor a urologist."

"Yes, I'll be there. I've done this many times" came Davies's sick boast. "Don't worry, it's relatively straightforward. You'll have the day tomorrow to study up. I printed out some materials for you."

This is some unbelievable bollox, he thought as one of the goons brought a thick file folder to Davies, who then handed it over to Con. "And if I make an error and something happens to the donor? If this is an 'audition,' as you put it, I need to know what defines success or failure."

"We're not worried about the donor," Liam sneered, "just his kidney."

Observing Con's stormy expression, Davies clarified, "The donor doesn't have much to look forward to right now. If he survives the surgery, though, he'll be doing very well for himself—and I'm confident he will be fine. There's always a risk when we have to operate in unsuitable conditions, but that's not an issue in Ireland. Our setup here is to a high standard."

Con felt the hair on the back of his neck prickle. How many of the worst-case scenarios he'd imagined were going to be proven true tonight? "What do you mean, not much to look forward to?"

"It means we'll be improving *two* lives tomorrow," Davies said, his expression smug. "Most of our donors are currently indentured servants from places where that sort of thing still happens. But by selling his kidney, our donor will pay off his debt and have money left over to start a new life for himself and his family."

"In Ireland?"

Davies squinted at Con. "I don't know where he wants to go—"

"Not what I meant." Con wiped some condensation off his pint glass, trying to appear unbothered. "The donor is from another country, but we'll be performing the surgery in Ireland. I'm assuming the donor's not known to the state. If he were, he'd be classed as what? An asylum seeker? A refugee?"

"No," Davies replied dryly, "he is not 'known to the state,' as you put it, nor will he ever be. The donors only stay in the country as long as needed for us to perform the surgery."

"Ah. So that's what you meant by bringing people in under the radar." Con paused to sip his pint, trying hard to appear neutral as the full horror of the situation sank in. "That's good Guinness, by the way."

Appearing annoyed by the compliment, Liam said abruptly, "Of course it is."

Con made a show of enjoying his lager as he took a few moments to rein in his anger. "So, you sell organs," he observed coolly, "and you traffic people to do it."

"Good God, of course not!" Davies shook his head in disgust. "We're not human traffickers—what an ugly concept. We simply work with people who are in the business of connecting motivated individuals with opportunities to improve their situations."

Con shook his head, marveling. Either Davies actually bought his own bullshit, or he thought Con might. Either way, it was a display of extraordinary self-deception.

"Where the people in charge find these individuals," Davies continued, "how they gain access to them, that varies. It's also not our concern. As I said, those decisions are made on a different level of the organization. All we have to worry about is the kidney. Don't make it more complicated than it needs to be."

"That's right," Liam added. "We didn't start the fire; we're just warming our hands by it. And don't try to act high-and-mighty around us. We know about your criminal record."

If Davies and Liam knew about his history of assault, that meant they'd done quite a bit of digging on him in preparation for this meeting. Con castigated himself. Brickhaven had seen him coming, laid their trap—and he had walked right into it.

It was true that in secondary school, Con had broken the nose of a boy who had tried to assault his sister, Una. The boys were in the same class, but Con had turned eighteen while the gobshite he'd hit was seventeen, making the charges against him more serious. It was a part of his past he'd had to explain whenever a background check was required—for example, when he applied for his green card, his medical license, and his job at Capitol Hill General. And although Neve had reassured him that it didn't worry her, Con feared his history might become a problem again should they decide to adopt or foster. While that remained the worst possible consequence his old conviction might have, Con certainly wasn't happy that Brickhaven was using it to argue that they all had things in common.

With a smug grin, Liam added, "Besides, you're one of us now, Mr. Good Guy."

Seldom had Con ever met someone begging for a beating quite as desperately as Liam. "Just trying to calculate how many international laws I'll be breaking."

"Just enough to keep you honest," Davies said smoothly, earning a chuckle from Liam.

"I see." Breathing the same air as these gobshites was beginning to suffocate Con, to say nothing of the cigar smoke. He needed to speed things along, get his information, and get out. "All right, gentlemen, if there's nothing else, can we wrap this up? I'll need a decent night's sleep if I'm going to spend tomorrow studying. I'll also need a couple of hours to get Neve to the airport."

"She's leaving?" Davies looked much too disappointed for his own good.

"I'll see to it," Con said gruffly. "Like you said, it will be easier for me to concentrate on what we need to do if she's out of the way."

"Well, I can certainly understand that." The salacious smile Davies tossed at the other men in the room put the final nail in the man's coffin. Con couldn't wait for the moment he would find that arsehole's jaw with his fist. Finally, Davies stopped digging his own grave and said, "I'd say we're done here for tonight, then. Before you go, though, we'll just need your phone and laptop."

One of the goons who had been sitting at the bar appeared behind Liam, holding his hand out.

Christ, these feckers.... "For what?"

"We'll install a tracker on the phone," Liam said. "Can't have you getting on that plane with Neve, now can we?"

"That's not necessary," Con said as he fished his phone out of his pocket and handed it to the goon, along with his laptop bag. "You'll find that I, too, keep my promises."

"Of course," Davies replied, "but it's also for your protection."

"I'm sure." Con was born on a Sunday, but it wasn't *last* Sunday.

"If you ever get into trouble," Davies continued,

"we'll know where to find you. Needless to say, you'll want to make sure you keep your phone with you at all times. We'll be listening in as well, and monitoring your usage—just until the team can be sure of you, of course."

"We'll also have other eyes on you while you're in Cork," Liam added, gesturing to the men seated behind him. "If you were having any more Mr. Good Guy fantasies, like thinking about calling the gardaí, I would kill those ideas right now. Besides, you should know we have friends everywhere—and I do mean *everywhere*, in uniform and out."

So, they had some guards in their pockets—or at least Liam wanted him to think they did. Not that he didn't believe it was possible. Con had a very high opinion of the gardaí, but he also knew the extent of Brickhaven's surveillance and other capabilities in the US. They seemed to have tentacles everywhere and certainly weren't beyond blackmail and other threats —threats which were far from empty, since Brickhaven members had founded their very own private military contractor. With Liam on the ground in Cork, they could well have extended their influence into Ireland.

If Brickhaven was going to be monitoring Con's phone and tailing him through Cork, getting help from someone he could trust would be more complicated than he thought. And if he couldn't arrange backup, the grim possibility existed that he might just have to do this surgery. The thought was so abhorrent, it made his stomach lurch.

If his hand was forced and he had to operate, maybe he could at least secretly record the surgery somehow and gather real, ironclad evidence. After all, it sounded like once the surgery was done, Brickhaven expected him to return to his life in the States. Once Neve was in some sort of protective custody, he could go straight to Banai with his recording and take them down. At least he knew Banai and President Duran weren't in Brickhaven's pocket. Con would be implicated by the recording, of course, since he would have committed a crime himself. But there were bigger issues at play.

Grimly, it occurred to Con that if he had to perform the surgery, there would be another silver lining: he could make sure it was done properly and the donor would be all right. He had no such confidence in Davies.

"I'm sure Con's not that foolish," Davies said with a crocodile smile. "Liam's bedside manner notwithstanding, you'll find we're a good outfit to work for."

Davies actually sounded like he believed that, which strained Con's credulity. He'd get the details now and worry about how to get help later. "Time and place for tomorrow?"

"Don't worry about that yet," Davies said. "We'll contact you tomorrow afternoon and arrange to pick you up. The fewer people who know where we're going and when, the better. Operational security, you understand."

Con tamped down his disappointment. He should have known it wouldn't be that easy. "Of course."

"Excellent!" Davies stood as the goon handed Con's phone back to him.

"And my laptop?"

"We'll return it to you after the surgery," Liam sneered.

"Well, don't waste your time trying to break into it," Con said. "Eric installed the security."

"We have no interest in the contents of your laptop," Davies reassured. "We just can't have you losing focus, can we?"

"Don't try to be sneaky and get any messages out on the hotel's phones or computers either," Liam added. "We've got really good hackers, as you know."

The hotel? If they knew where he and Neve were

staying, all the more reason to get her out of the country and under Banai's protection as soon as physically possible.

Davies shook his head at Liam. "The man said he keeps his promises, so he's going to stick to the program, aren't you, Con? A car is waiting out front to take you to the Hotel Gairdín—presuming that's where you're going."

Con got to his feet, forcing himself not to wince as his leg, shoulder, and several other body parts groaned in complaint. His adrenaline must have kicked in earlier, because it was dropping now and making things worse. He needed to get the hell out of the lion's den. "Good night, gentlemen."

"Good night, Con," Davies called after him as he made his way out of the room. "Glad to have you on board!"

It was all Con could do not to turn around and bash the man with his one good arm.

As quickly as he could, he pushed through the crowded pub and burst out onto the street, sucking in a breath of cool air. Just as Davies had promised, a car was waiting by the curb, engine running.

One short ride and he'd be with Neve. Con still had no idea how he was going to convince her to leave. All he knew was that he had to find a way.

CHAPTER 7
CON

It was late when Con returned to Hotel Gairdín. He went into the lobby and around the corner to the lifts, then waited a few moments before looking back at the front entrance. At one end of the circular drive, a dark car pulled up, parked at the curb, and turned off its headlights. He saw two men in the front seat, neither of whom appeared to be making a move to leave the vehicle. Liam hadn't been exaggerating when he said they'd "have other eyes" on him while he was in Cork. He spit out a few silent curses, not wanting to be overheard by whoever was using his fecking phone to "listen in," and then headed up to the room.

Outside the door was an empty tray with the remains of dinner waiting to be picked up by housekeeping. At least Neve had eaten, then. At this hour, though, she was likely asleep, so after he slid the key card into the handle, Con took care opening the door. A dim glow of light came from both bedrooms, but there was no sound. As quietly as he could, he shuffled down the hallway into the main bedroom.

No Neve. However, there were signs of her, and they weren't comforting. Tiny, drained bottles from the minibar cluttered the table, along with several nearly empty glasses of varying sizes and shapes.

Con had never known Neve to be much of a drinker. Worry coursed through him as he made his way into the smaller bedroom, tempered by relief when he found her sprawled out on the bed, snoring lightly.

In spite of his concern about her uncharacteristic intake of alcohol, he couldn't help smiling. Neve had that effect on him. It didn't matter what the circumstances were or how she appeared; whenever he laid eyes on her, emotion rose up inside him, making his heart swell.

She looked like a furry white starfish, lying on her stomach with the hotel robe cinched around her waist, arms and legs stretched out. Her dark, wavy hair was fanned out across the duvet. Not even the thick robe could disguise her divine curves, the luscious delicacy of her skin, and all the places he couldn't wait to devour. As a buffer against the unpleasantness soon to come, he allowed himself to indulge in a few moments of mental fantasy.

Con was greedy. He knew it, and he wasn't in the least bit sorry. It wasn't enough to have Neve's love, as miraculous as that was. It wouldn't even be enough to marry her. No, he was determined that once he joined her back in DC, he would bring her such intense pleasure and make her so hungry for his touch that even a lifetime together would never quite satisfy her. While his career would remain important to him, of course, making Neve permanently languid with ecstasy would become his new reason for living.

But reality struck again all too soon. Con remembered the empties in the other room. Had she brought a guest over, perhaps? That would make the volume of alcohol consumed less worrying.

Slowly, he lowered himself to sit on the mattress, leaned his head toward hers, and inhaled—then had to pull back suddenly to keep from waking her by coughing loudly. The scent of alcohol seemed to ooze from her very pores. He'd better take a closer look and see what he was dealing with.

Con went back into the main room and evaluated. He was right; she had cleaned the minibar out of vodka. Several other glasses were nearly empty. He drank the remaining drops of liquid, tasting the contents. Thankfully, he discovered that in addition to cocktails, she'd had some water as well.

Regret clutched at his chest. To drink like this, Neve must have been feeling lonely and bored. She was also probably upset with him for canceling, as she had every right to be. His first impulse was to think about how he would make it up to her. But then he remembered what he had to do the next day: convince her to go home. Maybe it would help his case if she was angry with him and having a disappointing time.

Con took his mobile into the bathroom, placed it on the counter, and turned the water in the shower and sinks on high. At least that would give Brickhaven something to listen to. Then he yanked the cable for the hotel phone out of the wall, destroying the connector so Neve couldn't use it and inadvertently be overheard by those thugs.

He had an impulsive thought: if he could get online undetected, he might be able to find help somehow.

Con spotted Neve's laptop on a chair and tried to open it, but it required both a PIN and a fingerprint scan. *Smart girl*. It had been a poor idea anyway, considering he didn't have any actionable information to share yet. Nor did he know which authorities could be trusted, and he certainly didn't want anyone connected to Brickhaven flagging Neve's IP address.

Con searched around until he found Neve's phone. He took it out onto the balcony and quietly closed the door behind him. Neve had told him the password for that device before—it was his birthday. He had asked her if she did that so she wouldn't forget the date. Making him fall in love with her even more, she had replied that she already had his birthday memorized, but she enjoyed having an excuse to think about him every time she opened her phone.

Con looked up Banai's number—or what he assumed was Banai's number. Neve had it saved under "Secret Agent Man." He hoped she only knew one.

"Miss Keane?" It was a woman's voice.

"I'm using her phone. This is Dr. Cornelius O'Brien. I'm looking for Agent Banai."

"He is off duty at the moment. This is the White House answering service. How can I help you?"

It was a hell of a time for Banai to take a sick day. At least he'd dialed the correct number. Con cleared his throat. "I need to leave him a message. It's urgent."

There was a pause on the other end. He heard the soft clicking of a keyboard. "Urgent, got it. I will contact him right away. What is the message?"

Feck. Con hated leaving messages, especially when it was something important, but he didn't know when he'd get another chance to make a private call without arousing Brickhaven's suspicion. Rather than trying to explain everything, he would have to boil down what he needed to say to its most basic parts. "We're in Ireland. Agent Banai must get Neve on a plane home under his protection tomorrow before...." Con paused to calculate. The surgery was tomorrow night. It shouldn't be asking the impossible to get her on a flight by 5:00 p.m. "Before noon eastern standard time. And when she gets home, he'll need to keep her in some kind of protective custody until I give him the all clear."

More clicking. "Is Miss Keane in danger?"

"Not right now, no," Con said, relieved that the woman on the other end of the line was taking him seriously. "But she will be if he doesn't get her out of here. Please ask him not to tell her that, though. I don't want her panicking."

"I'll tell him. Is there anything else?"

There was so much—far too much to leave in a message. And Con didn't want to risk dividing Banai's attention by mentioning Brickhaven. Above all else, he needed Neve out of here, quickly and quietly. Once she was in the clear, he'd worry about the rest of it.

"One more thing, please," he said. "Once Neve is in the air, ask him to leave a message for me with our hotel's front desk. He knows where we're staying." Because Brickhaven might intercept the call, Con quickly invented a coded message he could pass off as having come from Neve. "Tell him to say it's from 'Herself,' with the message 'Home safe.'"

"And the alternative message?"

"What alternative message?"

"What message should he leave if things don't go to plan?"

Con felt the urge to reach through the line and grab this innocent person by the throat. "That's not an option!" Hearing his voice rise, he forced himself to sound calm. The woman was just trying to be helpful. "I suppose, still say it's from 'Herself,' but make the message 'Missing you.'"

"Got it. Can he reach Miss Keane on this number to make arrangements?"

He pictured Neve passed out on the bed. "Not

tonight, but in the morning, yes. And he should call this number only, not my mobile number. It's not secure." Con swallowed hard. "I can't stress the importance of this message enough."

"Understood." A few final clicks, and the woman added, "Don't worry, Dr. O'Brien, we'll take care of it."

Don't worry. What futile instructions. "Thank you."

His next call was to Banshee. Fortune was smiling on him, as she answered, so he didn't have to leave another message. God bless her, Banshee didn't ask any questions when he said he needed to figure out how to record something surreptitiously. She thought for a moment, then said she had a techie friend named John who traded suitable devices under the cover of a cigarette stand in the English Market. She said she would place a call and the goods would be ready by midmorning.

If Liam and Davies had been telling the truth and he couldn't trust the gardaí, Con would have to get help elsewhere. But where? After his tractor accident, he hadn't had the time or energy to maintain close friendships. And living in the States for the past five years, he had lost touch with even his casual friends in Ireland, though he never would have imposed upon them with something this serious.

He played around with the idea of calling Sergeant O'Leary from the garda station in Rosaveel. The man had assisted them in taking down Mad Max, and Con believed he was trustworthy. But he had nothing solid to share yet, and he knew the sergeant did not enjoy having his time wasted. Besides, Rosaveel was near Galway, so Sergeant O'Leary would no doubt have to contact someone local for assistance, and Con couldn't be sure at this stage who else they could trust.

For a fleeting moment, it occurred to him to call his brother. He knew Eamonn would help, no questions asked, but it was bad enough having Neve on Brickhaven's hit list. The last thing he wanted was to get his family tangled up in this mess as well.

Any thoughts of seeking help were premature anyway. Con wanted to stop the surgery from happening tomorrow night and hopefully destroy yet another ring of Brickhaven hell while he was at it. But he couldn't even think about doing those things until he was certain Neve was safe.

Back inside, Con plugged her phone into the charger on her bedside table. She was still asleep in the same position, beautiful, perfect—and so vulnerable. He hoped to God Banai would follow through and protect her.

Feckin' Rodwell, and feckin' Davies. It was bad enough that those maggots had decided to spit on the Hippocratic oath, but to try to get Con involved…. He had no doubt this whole thing was really Rodwell's idea of revenge. Con had never liked the head of psychiatry, and ever since he'd played a role in thwarting Rodwell's presidential assassination plot, the bad blood flowed both ways. This whole thing stank of Rodwell's twisted mind, trying to taint everything that meant something to Con by forcing him to use his medical skills to help the same organization that threatened Neve.

He had just wanted a week away with her, undisturbed. Now he wondered how far away from DC they'd have to go to get it. Bali, perhaps? Fiji?

Neve moaned lightly in her sleep. Con debated whether to wake her and say good night, given how unhappy she'd been when he failed to wish her a good morning. But that would be cruel. She looked too peaceful, too unconcerned.

And Con was determined to keep her that way.

CHAPTER 8
CON

As Con gazed at her there on the bed, Neve shifted onto her side. Her hair fell across her face, and she began sucking it into her mouth when she inhaled, then trying to spit it out. He again lowered and sat on the bed next to her, reaching over and smoothing the hair away. Neve's tantalizing pink tongue darted in and out of her mouth, searching for the last few strands, but Con had brushed them all aside. Slowly, her eyes fluttered open.

"Con?"

He traced her cheek with his fingertips. "I'm here."

"Hi." Her eyes closed again as she smiled and curled around him. "That man's on the balcony again."

Instantly, Con tensed, tossing a protective arm across her body. "What? Who?"

"Oh," she murmured, sliding her arms around his waist. "Oh-rion. You remember him?"

"Jaysus," he whispered, "you put the heart crossways in me." She meant the constellation Orion. He took a deep breath, trying to slow his heartbeat back down. "Orion's still out there, is he? A bit of a stalker, that one."

"Mm-hmm." She shifted upward and rested her head on his lap.

With Neve lying on top of him, all the tension in Con's body slowly melted. In its place, an intense heat grew, his heart pumping warmth through every artery, vessel, and capillary. "You two had some drinks together."

"I wanted to have them with you, but…." Neve's eyes opened, this time fully. "Why did you tell me not to come out tonight?"

As he quickly thought up a lie, Con leaned down and kissed her forehead. "I'm sorry about that. By the time I got to the pub, Davies was already langered, and when he drinks, he gets handsy. I didn't want you anywhere near that, besides which I had to focus on keeping him away from our female colleagues, lest he create an international incident."

"Oh." Neve's mesmerizing sea-glass-green eyes stared up into his. With a bluntness aided by inebriation, she declared, "I don't like him."

Never had Con felt a common sentiment more deeply. "Neither do I, love. Neither do I."

Her eyelids fluttered, and he smiled as she fought to keep them open. She shifted into a sitting position and readjusted her robe, which had fallen askew in ways that sent his imagination to scandalous places.

"Did I leave a mess in the other room?" A blush pinked Neve's cheeks as her eyes darted toward the doorway. "I'm sorry. I don't know what happened. I just thought, since I wasn't having drinks with you, I'd have some by myself. So I ordered a screwdriver with dinner, and then another one, and then it just seemed silly to bother room service again, so I looked in the minibar, and there was more vodka, so I started in on that, and then… well, the more I drank, the more it seemed like a good idea to keep going, you know?"

"I do." Con smiled as he rubbed circles on her back. He had fallen victim to the very same alcohol-induced logic on more than one occasion. "Can I get you some water?"

Neve's brows knit together as she thought much

harder than would normally be necessary. "Um, yes, okay, thanks. That would be good."

"Don't move." When Con pushed up off the bed this time, he felt every ache and pain in his body object. He got Neve a drink from the tap still running in the bathroom. Let Brickhaven think he was taking the longest shower known to man. He just wanted a few private moments alone with Neve before he had to start thinking about tomorrow.

Neve sipped the water, which seemed to give her a bit of new life. "Oh, I saw Kayla, and you're not going to believe…. You know how Amos made me believe in angels?"

She'd never stated her belief in such definitive terms, but when they were back in DC, Con knew Neve had found their mutual patient's report of interactions with the supernatural to be compelling. "I recall you saying something like that, yes."

Smiling brightly, she reported, "Well, now I believe in psychic mediums too."

Her guileless excitement about it made him fall just that much more deeply in love with her. "You don't say?"

Con listened as Neve recounted a remarkable story about a meeting in a coffee shop between herself, Kayla, and a woman who claimed to talk to the dead. He wasn't a believer in that sort of thing himself, but given what Neve told him, he could certainly understand why she was convinced. In the end, she felt they had obtained some potentially helpful information on Kayla's Ghost Girl. He hoped that was true. "Sounds like the meeting was very useful."

"Wait a minute." Neve leaned back, wobbling slightly, and folded her arms. "You're not going to play devil's advocate?"

"Not tonight." Con reached out to steady her. "It wouldn't be fair."

"Why not?"

"You've been drinking."

Neve sighed and leaned against him. "There was another reason for that too."

"Oh?" Con heard a note of melancholy in her tone. "Let's get comfortable so we can talk."

Trying not to show her how much pain he was in, he piled some pillows up behind him, then reclined against them. He patted his chest, and Neve arranged herself next to him, resting her head on his shirt and draping her arm across his waist.

"What drove you to drink, then?"

Neve blew out a hard breath. "Estrogen, mainly."

That answer was so unexpected, Con had to stop

himself from laughing. But she sounded serious, so he refrained from making any light remarks. "What about it, exactly?"

"It's just so stupid," she began. "Dr. Mohinder told me I'm probably still going to get my period—not every month, maybe, but sometimes—for the next twenty years or so. And for what?"

His heart dropped as Con realized what was on her mind. This was about her recent medical tests. He had been with her the previous week when she got the results. Then, a few days ago, she'd had a follow-up video appointment with the surgeon who was coordinating her care. Afterward, Neve had told Con that with the usual caveats about how nothing was ever certain and there were other tests they could perform, Dr. Mohinder had confirmed there was less than a 0.1 percent chance she would ever be able to conceive, even with medical intervention. In other words, as Neve had put it, "it's not happening."

Although it was what she'd been expecting to hear, the news had still hit her hard. Neve had confided that she'd never had an active desire to have children, but Con knew that just having the option taken away could be devastating, whether or not she'd ever planned to avail of it. Plus, it was adverse health news, and that would be a blow to anyone. He also knew there was a lot more to it—things that he, as a man, would never be able to fully understand.

From his own experience giving patients serious news, he expected that Neve's reactions would be complex and unfold over time. Last week, she had asked him to sit with her as she called her parents to give them the news. Con knew her mother and father were fine people, and she was very close to them. One of the hardest parts of the infertility diagnosis for Neve had been her feelings of guilt that her condition might cause them disappointment. But if her parents had felt that way, they hadn't let on. Rather, they had reassured her, comforting her and expressing relief that she was otherwise healthy. He'd noticed that the conversation had taken a lot out of Neve, but her parents' reaction had helped release some of the emotional weight she'd been carrying.

Con knew Neve had a tendency to process things internally, only talking them out when she needed support, so he had been watching her closely, knowing she would bring things up when she was ready. He pushed his physical pain to the back of his consciousness so he could focus on her completely.

"My cycle has no purpose now," Neve continued, the mixture of anger and grief in her voice raking at him. "It's just needless aggravation."

And a regular reminder of her diagnosis, he read between the lines.

This was uncharted territory for him. Con wasn't sure what to do or say, and the last thing he wanted was to make things harder for her somehow. "What do you need, love?" he asked softly. "Just to talk?"

"No!" She made a fist and pounded it on the mattress. "I need information! I need my doctor boyfriend to tell me what the point is of all these useless hormones coursing through my body."

"Ah." Con felt some measure of relief. That, he could help with. "Well, then, you've come to the right place."

She relaxed her fist and settled back against him. This time, though, when she spoke, her voice sounded small, defeated. "Go on, then, explain."

Neve was deeply emotional, but Con knew from experience that the cerebral was her comfort zone when she felt overwhelmed. If she needed her mind engaged as a way of soothing her emotions, he would oblige. He began stroking her hair, a gesture he knew gave her comfort. "For starters, those hormones of yours are important all throughout the body. Most people don't know this," he murmured conspiratorially, "but there are estrogen receptors in the brain, the liver, and the kidneys."

"Hmm." He felt her body begin to soften. "I like it when you 'talk doctor' to me. Continue."

Con made a mental note of *that* comment. "Well, for its part, progesterone is important to the GI and nervous systems. Your lovely hormones keep your cholesterol down, regulate your blood sugar, improve bone mass, and protect your heart. Also—" He tapped softly on the top of her head. "—they help you focus."

"Really?" Con felt her cheek press against his chest as she smiled. "They do all that?"

"They do." He leaned down and kissed the hairline just above her temple. "Was there anything in particular that put your mind on this?"

Her sigh was so heavy, Con just wanted to lift her up, wrap her in his arms, and take her away—preferably to a beach somewhere warm and sunny, with the soothing sound of waves and no one else around.

Neve closed her eyes and pressed her fingertip between her eyebrows. "Kayla told me I'd be a good mother."

Con's heart fell on Neve's behalf—down through the mattress, into the ground, and deep into the cold earth. "Ah, I see."

"Yeah." She nestled against him, turning her face

toward his chest. "I still don't know how I feel about... you know. All of it."

Con set about stroking her hair in a steady rhythm, hoping she would talk on and say everything that was weighing on her until it lightened enough for her to feel at peace.

"I told you I've never been someone who always wanted to be a mother," she began. "And with Stephan being so... well, *unsuitable*..."

"Fecking abusive gobshite" was the term Con would have chosen for Neve's ex-boyfriend, but he kept his counsel on the matter.

"I had already accepted it probably wasn't going to happen," Neve continued. "Being a therapist, caring for my clients—that's always been enough for me. I don't even know if being a mother would fit in with that. I mean, I know other therapists who are parents, and they balance everything beautifully. But for me, I just... I don't know." She rolled onto her back and looked up at him. "It's embarrassing to admit, but I'm starting to realize there are limits to how many things I can handle. Most of the time, I feel like I'm already at full capacity."

Con had seen firsthand how Neve put her whole self into her work. It was one of the things he admired most about her, but it was also why he worried about her being a therapist. Neve always took her work home with her. After hours, she would still be thinking through cases, researching mental health issues, looking for resources, troubleshooting. He was happy to help and honored to be her sounding board. God knew he did the same with his own work, so he could hardly criticize. But his work wasn't as emotional or intimate as Neve's. He treated physical ailments; she dealt with hearts, souls, and minds. Con worried that one day, the gravity of all she carried might prove to be too much.

He also understood her feeling of being "at capacity." Since the tractor accident banjaxed his leg nearly twenty years prior, a great deal of his physical and emotional energy had been expended first on his recovery, then on living with chronic pain and diminished mobility. Con did his best to hide his struggles. The last thing he wanted was to be pitied, or to have people worrying about him. But putting a brave face on required even more effort, and he worried that he wouldn't have enough left in him to raise a child, too, and do it well.

Still, they had talked about alternative routes to becoming parents. If that was what Neve wanted, he would go all in and do his very best, and he had told her as much. After all, he would do anything for her.

And while the idea of parenting remained daunting in the abstract, Con knew from experience that he and Neve made a formidable team. Besides, everything they did together was infinitely more enjoyable than anything else in his life. He couldn't imagine that ever changing.

Neve dipped her chin down to her chest and murmured, "But when I start to make peace with the situation—when I think about how it fills my whole heart just being with you, just the two of us—then I feel ashamed for being selfish and so self-centered."

Her words stole Con's breath. God knew being with Neve was all and everything he wanted from life. Hearing that she might feel even a small bit similar illuminated something exquisite in a hidden corner of his heart. But her self-reproach took him aback. The last words he would ever use to describe Neve were "selfish" or "self-centered," and she certainly shouldn't feel ashamed for considering her own needs and limits. Con didn't want to interrupt her, though, so he remained silent as Neve squirmed a little, settling into his arms. She fit so perfectly there.

More than ever, his determination hardened to get her out of Dodge the next day, far away from any risk of harm. She'd had to deal with so much already.

Her voice softening, Neve added, "Anyway, thank

you for being honest and telling me you never wanted kids. And for still being willing to try to be a parent with me if I want to. That's just so loving, so generous. There are no words. It means everything, knowing you're with me either way. And don't you *dare—*"

Neve's hand flew up for emphasis, but with her alcohol-impaired proprioception, she nearly smacked Con in the face. He ducked away just in time.

Blissfully unaware, she continued, "—say anything more about your assault conviction making you a 'liability' to me! You are the best person I have ever met or could ever even imagine, and I'll tell any fostering or adoption agencies the same thing. Besides, you were protecting your sister from a sexual predator. That should be considered a plus, not a minus."

Con smiled as she slowed down dramatically to be sure she made her argument without slurring her words too much. "I won't say another word about it, and please don't thank me. You never have to thank me for anything." But he wanted her to keep talking, so he didn't press the point any further.

"Good. And I know." Her smile held a heartbreaking mixture of love and sadness. "But it really does help, knowing you support me no matter what."

She shifted back up into a half-sitting position. "And it does take some of the sting out of this whole thing to know my hormones aren't *totally* useless."

Con felt her energy shift. Neve was done with her emotional deep dive on the issue and was ready to return to her cerebral comfort zone. "Definitely not useless." He moved his arm to support her. "In fact, they're quite miraculous."

Neve ran her fingertip around and around his belt buckle like it was a singing bowl. "I thought you didn't believe in miracles."

"I didn't." He lifted her hand, brought it to his lips, and placed a tender kiss on her palm. "But then you said you loved me. Now I'm a true believer."

She smiled, stretching like a cat and flopping onto her back again. "What time is it?"

He checked her phone. "Just after midnight."

Neve moaned. "I have to be up at eight." She rolled onto her side and closed her eyes. "I think my alarm is set."

He checked her phone again. "It is."

She didn't reply this time, though. Her eyes were closed, and her breathing began to even out and slow.

Guilt pricked at him. Neve was lying there, so relaxed and trusting, with no notion that he was going to send her home the next day. Should he lance the boil—tell her now and give her time to adjust? But he would be presenting it as a fait accompli, not giving her an option. He knew that would trigger conflict, and he couldn't bear to start an argument tonight, not with all she had weighing on her mind. Plus, he knew from experience that it was hard enough to win an argument with Sober Neve. He didn't rate his chances of victory against Drunk Neve.

Con wondered if she had fallen back to sleep. He waited a few minutes, then carefully began to shift out from under her.

Just as he succeeded in laying her on the bed, she awoke again. Narrowing her eyes at him, she asked, "What's wrong?"

"Nothing. You just fell asleep again. Sorry for waking you."

"No." She leaned up on her elbow. "I mean, what's wrong? I can tell something's wrong. What is it?"

Ah, Jaysus. Not too drunk to be empathetic, then.

Con fought the sharp, sudden urge to tell her everything about Davies, Rodwell, the whole mess. He didn't want any space between Neve and him, especially not the type of gulf that could be created by secrets. Not to mention, she was adept at creative problem-solving. If anyone could help him figure out a way to deal with those Brickhaven thugs....

But the mere act of telling her the truth about what was going on would get her involved, and he couldn't let that happen. Her intuitive senses were alert now, though, so he had to come up with an answer that had some element of truth, or else he feared she'd know he was lying.

He settled on something that was true but unusual for him to admit. "I'll be honest with you," he said with a sigh, letting his shoulders fall. "Everything hurts."

"Oh, Con!" As quickly as she could with the vodka still in her system, Neve got up onto her knees and wrapped her arms around him, careful to avoid his shoulder. "I'm so sorry! Here I am, complaining to you...."

"Don't apologize," he called after her as she slid off the bed and went into the other bedroom. She returned with the bottle of opiates his Galway doctor had prescribed.

"I know you hate these," she pleaded, "but you're about to go to bed. Does it matter if your head's cloudy? You need at least one good night's sleep, and you know you won't get it if you're in pain."

"All right, all right." God, he loved this woman.

He had no intention of either taking the meds or sleeping—he had too much to think about—but he would try to appease her. "I'll take one, all right? But only if you go back to bed right now. You need sleep more than I do, thanks to the minibar."

"Whatever," she said, but in a sign of how tired she must be, she didn't argue with him. "Good night kiss?"

He leaned down and kissed the top of her head again. "That's all you're getting until you sober up. Into the bed with you."

Neve climbed beneath the blankets. As Con helped her pull the duvet up to her chin, remorse stung him. He had promised Neve that after Kayla was sorted, they'd spend the week in bed together. Now, who knew how long it would be before he'd get a chance to fulfill that promise?

"What?" she asked, squinting at him again.

"Nothing." When she appeared unconvinced, he added, "I love looking at you. I'm storing this moment in my head for later."

She rolled her eyes and flashed him a cheesy grin. "Smooth talker."

"Good night, love."

Con's heart nearly burst with the sheer galactic size of the love he had for her. But when he reached over and clicked off her light switch, the feeling transformed into a blade, stabbing him with a pain so acute, it nearly knocked the wind out of him. He was sending her away tomorrow, and even with the weight of Banai's authority backing him up, Con couldn't predict how smoothly that would go. If he knew anything for sure, it was that Neve was a bit of a wild card.

When he reached the doorway, he heard her reply softly, "Good night." With a catch in his throat, he watched her roll onto her side and curl up around a pillow.

Con turned off the water in the bathroom and retrieved his phone so the thugs from Brickhaven wouldn't think he'd drowned in the tub and send someone looking for him. Then he took a micro bottle of whiskey from the minibar, sat down at the table, and tried to think.

CHAPTER 9
NEVE

Bang, bang, bang!

I rolled over, taking my pillow with me and scrunching it over my head. What kind of hotel allowed construction to be done in the middle of the night?

"Room service!" The voice calling from outside the door pierced my consciousness like the screech of a Valkyrie.

Good God. They must have got the time wrong. I had ordered breakfast for 9:00 a.m. That couldn't be for hours yet.

I reached over and felt around on the bedside table until my fingers made contact with my phone. I yanked it from the charger, pulled it in under the pillow with me, and clicked it on.

Nine o'clock on the dot. My alarm had gone off at eight, but I must have turned it off and gone right back to sleep.

"Oh no." As I moaned the words, my head throbbed with the vibration. Memories of the night before began to trickle in. I remembered ordering a drink. It was delicious, so I ordered another. Then I remembered checking out the minibar. Things got a little fuzzy after that, but I did remember Con coming in. I had curled up with him, my face against his chest. I remembered his scent….

Where is Con now?

Slowly, I eased into a sitting position. My head throbbed on the way up, but the pain ebbed once I had been vertical for about a minute. I stood up and took a moment to steady myself. *Not too bad,* I observed, then shuffled into the larger bedroom. No Con, but there was a piece of paper on the table folded over with my name written on the front—along with some cocktail glasses and nearly a full chess set of empty minibar bottles.

So many bottles.

"You are not a drinker," I whispered to myself, since apparently I needed the reminder. "You are a lightweight."

Another set of bangs came at the door. I stumbled

down the hallway, not yet accustomed to the length of my own feet.

"Morning!" A man who was aggressively awake wheeled a cart into the room. Glancing at the table, he asked, "Will I clear this for you?"

Embarrassment pinged my brain, asking if it was time to come out yet, but I was too hungover to care. "Um, I'll take care of it. Unless you need to…." I ran out of words.

"No worries! I'll leave the cart here. Just wheel it outside when you're ready. There's a whole pot of coffee on here, per the request of your gentleman friend. Cheers!" He gave me a kind smile and closed the door very softly behind him.

My gentleman friend. A whole pot of coffee—very thoughtful. No surprise that Con knew I would be hungover, given the evidence I'd left lying around. I sat back down at the table and unfolded his note.

> SORRY I HAD TO GO. CONFERENCE FOLLOW-UP. EXPECT A CALL FROM BANAI THIS MORNING. I CAN'T TAKE CALLS RIGHT NOW, BUT I'LL TEXT YOU LATER WHEN/WHERE TO MEET ME FOR LUNCH. DRINK PLENTY OF WATER AND ENJOY YOUR BREAKFAST. DOCTOR'S ORDERS.

Con

Not the most romantic note, but the "doctor's orders" part made me smile, and at least he had apologized for not being here. I didn't remember him waking me to say goodbye, but he might well have.

I did remember, though, that we had talked the night before. Snippets of conversation came back to me like objects that were underwater floating slowly to the surface and bobbing into view. There was something about… estrogen?

Moaning, I cradled my head in my hands. Now the memories came rushing back. Kayla telling me I'd make a good mother had triggered a whole avalanche of thoughts and feelings about my infertility diagnosis, and I'd unloaded on Con. Although he hadn't made me feel like I was burdening him, of course; Con was always there when I needed him. Over the last couple of years, he'd shown me that time and again as my friend. But since we'd started dating, we had encountered one crisis after another, and his steadfastness had never wavered. It was one of the reasons I wanted to spend my life with him, and I had told him as much. I knew he planned to propose at some point, but not before we got back to the States and he could ask my father for my hand. It was old-fashioned, I knew, but Con had a great relationship with my parents, and they would appreciate the gesture.

For what must have been the millionth time, I admired the claddagh ring he'd bought for me in Galway as I twisted it around my finger. The hands represented friendship; the crown, loyalty; and the heart, love. *That sums us up all right.* I smiled as the thought sent a tiny shiver of pleasure through my body.

I reviewed the details of our conversation as I picked at my breakfast. He had been so wonderful, listening to me ramble and indulging my demand to know if my hormones were of any use to me now. Thinking back on our exchange was bittersweet, given the soup of emotions I was feeling about my infertility and what it might mean for me.

The night before, I was feeling betrayed by my body, leading me to the "anger" stage of grief—although it wasn't a stage as such, as I had learned from being a therapist. Rather than moving through grief in a linear way and finding resolution at the end, people usually jumped around between the various stages, sometimes indefinitely. Grief could creep up on us at the most unexpected times and in the strangest ways, sometimes years or decades after the loss that had carved it into our hearts. But regardless of whatever internal struggles I was having, I knew in the deepest part of me that Con would be there, supporting me, holding me. That gave me confidence that I could handle whatever the future held, including grief and its stealth attacks.

A gentle warmth surged through me as I reflected on what a miracle Con was in my life, just as he'd said I was in his. Maybe the constellation Orion had truly heard and answered my prayers.

I managed to eat and keep down fried eggs, toast, and a little bit of yogurt, sipping water the whole time. A long, hot shower and a few ibuprofen pills later, I felt like a new woman, or at least a "gently used" one.

A text came in from Kayla. She asked if we could meet in an hour's time to talk about Megan and offered to come to the hotel. Given the delicate state of my head, I didn't fight her. I figured I could order whatever she wanted from room service; no doubt the Secret Service wouldn't mind footing the bill for President Duran's goddaughter. We decided to contact Banshee as well to see if she had learned anything new. The previous evening, before hitting the vodka, I had emailed Banshee the details of our meeting with

Rose. I texted her and asked if she could meet with us via video chat and compare notes.

I was flipping channels on the hotel TV when my phone rang. "Secret Agent Man" popped up on-screen. I had forgotten that Con had said Agent Banai would be calling. Most likely he wanted to check in about Kayla.

I swiped up to answer. "Hello?"

"Good morning, Miss Keane. Agent Banai here."

"Good morning! How are you?"

"I'm fine, just calling to give you your flight information for later today."

Agent Banai was changing our flights? That came as a surprise, though not an unwelcome one. Maybe it was a perk for doing President Duran a favor, and we'd get to fly on a private jet or something. But he'd gotten the date wrong, obviously.

"I didn't realize you were arranging our travel. That's very kind of you. But you mean for next week, right?"

There was a brief pause. I heard some papers shuffling on his end. "This flight is just for you, and yes, it's for today at 1600 hours. That's 4:00 p.m., departing from Cork Airport."

"I'm sorry, there must be some misunderstanding. Con and I are flying out together next week."

This time, the pause was longer. "Apologies, Miss Keane. Did Dr. O'Brien not speak with you?"

A cold, heavy sensation began to swirl in my stomach. "He told me to expect a call from you, if that's what you mean, but he didn't say what it was about. Why?"

"Oh. Well…."

Never had I heard Agent Banai hesitate before. I recognized the feeling in my belly as uncomfortably close to dread.

"Dr. O'Brien called me last night," he continued, "and he called from your phone, so I assumed you were with him or at least knew what was happening. He left a message requesting that we put you on a flight to DC today before noon eastern standard time, 5:00 p.m. your time. He stressed that it was important."

I only realized I'd stood up suddenly when I heard the thump of the chair falling over onto the floor behind me. "What?" Conscious that no sound had come out, I cleared my throat. "Wait… *what*?"

Agent Banai returned to his usual calm, in-control demeanor. "I take it Dr. O'Brien is not there with you at the moment."

"No, he isn't." My mind cast about, grasping. "What time did he call you?"

"6:12 p.m., eastern time. That would be—"

"11:12 p.m. Irish time." I remembered it was after midnight when Con and I finished our conversation. So, he had called Agent Banai before he spoke to me but hadn't said anything about it? "There has to be some mistake."

"The phone call was recorded. I listened to it myself several times."

That made zero sense. "Are you *sure* that's what he said? Was he okay? Is something wrong? Wait, is everyone all right?"

"I am sure of what he said. He was fine. Who do you mean by everyone?"

Now was not the time to be obtuse. "My family, his family. Our friends."

"Yes, as far as I know, everyone is fine."

My brain was like a dog in a room into which a hundred tennis balls had been thrown at once—jumping around with no idea where to go next. "Well, then, did he say why he wants me to fly home? Because we talked for nearly an hour after he called you, and he didn't say a word about this to me."

"He did not provide a great deal of detail. However, he did leave specific instructions for me not to call his phone, only yours, so I have not attempted to contact him for clarification."

I began pacing the room. "Okay, yeah, he left me a note this morning saying he couldn't receive calls."

"Perhaps his phone isn't working."

"Right, I guess not. I'm sorry, I'm just really confused right now. He called and left you a message telling you to fly me home for no reason, so you're just… doing it? I don't understand. There's got to be something more to this."

"I'm afraid I'm not at liberty to say."

My heart skittered. *What the hell is that supposed to mean?*

Agent Banai was normally adept at concealing his emotions, but I thought I detected a note of annoyance in his voice when he asked, "Did Dr. O'Brien tell you anything else?"

I willed myself to squeeze any relevant memories of the previous night's conversation from my brain. Con hadn't said anything to me about this, had he? No, not a chance. If he had, I certainly wouldn't have forgotten about it… right? But I couldn't be sure—not absolutely, anyway. Nor did I have any desire to explain my minibar exploits to Agent Banai. "Just that he'll text me later where to meet him for lunch."

"No doubt he'll explain then."

The tang of blood on my tongue alerted me that I

was chewing on my lip. "You're *sure* everyone's okay?"

"Yes, rest assured. I will send the flight information and e-ticket to you via email. You will be flying into Reagan National. Either I or another Secret Service agent will meet you when you get here."

I blurted out a nervous laugh. "That's not worrisome or anything."

"You will be fine, Miss Keane," he reassured, as if that was my main worry. "You have a seat booked on a private flight, so no need to go through security, but I would advise you to arrive at the airport at least thirty minutes in advance. Would you like me to arrange a car to pick you up?"

Anxiety bubbles began to rise in my chest. In an attempt to squelch them before they transformed into abject panic, I inhaled deeply through my nose and blew the breath out slowly through my mouth.

"Miss Keane? Are you all right?"

"I'm okay. And no, please don't arrange anything else. I want to talk to Con first."

"Understood. After you speak with him, if you need a car, just call. I look forward to seeing you in DC."

That's what you *think.* I knew he was just trying to do his job as best he could with the information he had. That information must be wrong, and I had no intention of getting on a plane without Con, but we could clear that up after I talked to my "gentleman friend."

"Right. Thanks, I guess? For calling, I mean."

"Of course. See you soon."

Immediately after hanging up, I dialed Con's number. No answer, and his voicemail wasn't accepting messages. Maybe Agent Banai was right and there was something wrong with his phone. Surely he could get access to one, though, since he'd said in his note that he would text me.

Or maybe his Wi-Fi was working and only the cell network was down? To test that theory, I tried to type him a lengthy text a few times. But my thoughts were so discombobulated, my fingers wouldn't cooperate. Eventually, I was able to send him a brief message:

> I got the call. Are you okay? Is everyone else okay?

I poured myself a cup of coffee and sat staring at the phone, waiting for his reply. A bubble with an ellipsis showed up and then disappeared a few times. So he could text, at least, and he was thinking about what to say, then deleting his responses. Finally, his reply came:

> I'm fine. Everyone is fine. I'll explain everything at lunch. Meet me at noon at Un-Corked on the Grand Parade. I'll send you a link to the location. Can't converse right now.

Although his message was somewhat reassuring, it explained nothing. My already-tender head now felt like it was at high risk of exploding.

I tried to comfort myself by focusing on the positives. Everyone was fine, according to two reliable sources, and I was meeting Con for lunch in two short hours. At least he hadn't texted anything ominous like **Pack your bags.** This *had* to be some horrible mistake, and being overly cautious—as was his job—Agent Banai had jumped the gun. After all, the two men hadn't actually spoken, so something might easily have been lost in translation.

As I calmed down a bit, my rational mind kicked in, and it finally occurred to me that the whole thing might be work related. We worked at a hospital, after all; crises did arise. I could check in with Rosanna.

My phone pinged when Con sent another text with a location link. Since he didn't want to chat, evidently, I replied:

> Okay. See you there.

More ellipsis bubbles appeared and disappeared. Finally, he sent me a thumbs-up emoji, confirming that I wasn't going to get anything more out of him before lunch.

I nearly jumped when another text came through right away. It wasn't from Con this time, though. It was Banshee, letting me know she was free and could join the video chat with Kayla and me. I thanked her and forwarded the meeting link we had set up.

While I waited for Kayla to arrive, I called Rosanna to ask if there were any work emergencies Con had for some reason neglected to tell me about the night before. There was no answer—not surprising, given that it was still early morning in Washington. I also checked my work emails, but there was nothing that would indicate they needed *me* back in DC, anyway. Honestly, I would have been shocked if they had. I was a therapist—not exactly indispensable. Other team members could cover for me, and Rosanna had practically ordered me not to even think about work while I was away.

Con, on the other hand.... His friend and trusted colleague, Dr. Kamali, was covering for him on the endocrinology unit. But if Dr. Kamali had an emergency and wasn't able to come to work, the hospital might conceivably ask Con if he could come home early. Upon reflection, that seemed the most likely scenario. Agent Banai must have gotten his wires crossed, thinking I needed to go back instead of Con. And Con might have asked for one ticket only, thinking I'd want to stay in Ireland without him—not an unreasonable assumption, but an incorrect one. I'd set him straight over lunch. Meanwhile, I'd wait to hear from Rosanna. If Con had been called back to Washington, she likely would have heard about it from HR.

For now, though, I had to try to push Con and Agent Banai to the back of my mind so I could focus on my upcoming conversation with Kayla and Banshee. At least a bit of research on the Ghost Girl case would keep me from going stir-crazy before lunchtime.

CHAPTER 10
NEVE

Once Kayla arrived, we started the video chat with Banshee. It hadn't occurred to me that being a secret identity type, she wouldn't want to reveal her face. Her on-screen image was an elaborate painting of a mythical banshee, naked and perched on an ocean cliff with red eyes, long, pointed nails and teeth, and wild hair caught in a chaotic wind. I turned away from the screen to hide my smile at the stark contrast between that terrifying creature and Banshee's friendly, cheerful voice.

Banshee started off the meeting with a bang, announcing that she'd found out what the "blackbird" meant. She pasted a link in the meeting chat. It took us to the website of a pub in Cork called the Blackbird. The image on the home page showed the front door of the pub. Hanging over it was a rectangular wooden sign with a yellow background outlined in black and the word "blackbird" in raised red capital letters. Recalling our conversation with Rose, Kayla and I turned toward each other, mouths falling open.

"It appears your psychic was right," Banshee said. "The pub's on the river, about two kilometers upstream from where Megan's body was found."

"Oh my God," Kayla gasped. "Maybe that's where her boyfriend Declan killed her!"

"I don't know about that," Banshee said. "She's not the only one who got a knock on the head that night. Have a look at the CCTV from in front of the pub. The pawnbroker across the intersection there has a hidden camera. The image quality is shite, though, and it looks like it was pissing down rain, which doesn't help."

Banshee's screen began playing a grainy black-and-white video with poor contrast. Still, we could make out what appeared to be a young man in a branded tracksuit and a young woman in a miniskirt stumbling out the front door of the Blackbird. They were followed immediately by four burly-looking men, two of whom wielded wooden sticks about three feet long that were broad and flat at one end.

My hand flew up to cover my mouth.

"That's Megan," Kayla whispered as she gripped my arm, her nails digging into my skin.

Although there was no sound, we could see that the two young people were shouting at the four men and struggling against them. But they were no match for the group of men, who forcibly pushed them toward the alley next to the pub. The young man shoved his way between the group and the woman, spreading his arms out as if to shield her. But the thugs grabbed him and pulled him to the side, then grabbed her arms as well, dragging both of them into the alley.

Due to the angle, now we could only see the backs of two of the thugs. Nausea threatened to overtake me as one of them raised his stick above his head and brought it down quickly and with great force—not once but three times. His motions reminded me of a scene from a movie I'd seen once where a man wielding a machete had killed a poisonous snake.

"What are we watching?" Kayla asked, horrified, as the video sped up.

"I'll fast-forward through this bit," Banshee said.

We saw the thugs moving in fast, jerky movements, gathering under the pub roof's overhang, pulling their collars up against the rain and talking. While the others smoked cigarettes, one of the men went in the front door of the pub, then returned to the alley carrying what looked like a large tarpaulin. Banshee slowed the video back down to regular speed as all four men disappeared into the alley.

Shortly afterward, one of the men stuck his head out, looking in every direction. He disappeared again, and a different man came out carrying something long and heavy folded over his shoulder, wrapped in the tarp. He walked across the street and off camera.

"He's heading in the direction of the river," Banshee said.

Kayla stood up abruptly and ran into the bathroom. I heard the sound of retching.

"Should I stop?" Banshee asked.

While I wanted to run to Kayla and see if she was okay, I felt like being sick myself. Instead of helping her, I might make things worse. Besides, one of us had to get all the way through this video, and I didn't want to subject Kayla to any more of it. "No, keep going."

The video played on. A few minutes later, the man returned with the empty tarp. After another pause, the same scene repeated itself.

"Bodies," I heard myself say aloud as the bathroom sink turned on.

"Maybe, although we can't be sure," Banshee

pointed out. "And while I'm working on improving the quality of the video, we can't prove yet that it was Megan and Declan who came out of the pub, although it's certainly possible given their descriptions."

Kayla walked out of the bathroom holding a wet towel to her forehead. "It's definitely Megan," she said. "She's wearing the same thing I saw her wearing in my vision."

"That may be," Banshee said, "but visions don't tend to hold up in court."

"Right. Well, we're not there yet," I said. "We're still just trying to piece together what happened."

As Kayla sat down beside me, I put my arm around her shoulders and squeezed. We watched as the man returned once again with the empty tarp, folding it over his arm. The other three men emerged from the alley and shuffled back toward the entrance of the pub, two of them still carrying their sticks.

Banshee paused the video and hovered her cursor over one of the sticks. "They're called hurleys," she explained. "They're used in hurling and camogie, Irish sports. And check out the big fella, second from the left."

They were all pretty big guys, by my reckoning, but I looked at the man she had indicated. He was lifting a lighter to the cigarette dangling from his lips.

It appeared he had tattoos on the backs of his hands. They were very similar to one another, thick black lines from knuckle to wrist, but with other lines crossing them like irregular hash marks.

I squinted at them. "What are those?"

"Ogham," Banshee said. "It's an ancient Irish system of writing. I can't see the tattoos clearly enough to make out what they say. They're unusual, though. Might help ID him." She hit Play again, and we watched the four men go back inside. Then the screen went black, the video replaced by her banshee illustration.

I poured a glass of cold water for Kayla and nibbled on a scone in an attempt to calm my stomach.

"Maybe your man Declan didn't kill her after all," Banshee declared. "From the description in the police report, he was pretty lean and not nearly as tall as those other feckers. That could have been him trying to defend her."

"Yeah," Kayla said softly. "If that was him protecting her, maybe…." She turned toward me, eyes wide and glistening with tears. "Maybe that's what the vision was trying to tell me, that he's innocent."

Maybe she was right. In fact, I didn't doubt it, and that shook me to my core.

Con's words after our first meeting with Kayla

rang through my head. He had said it appeared I was swallowing everything she was feeding me. Not that I believed she was "feeding" me at all, at least not in the sense of lying or trying to mislead anyone. I could tell Kayla was 100 percent genuine. But whether she was *right*... well, that was another matter entirely.

All of my education and training had taught me to remain skeptical, keep my critical thinking cap on, and not get sucked in to bizarre narratives. Part of my role as a therapist was to help my clients engage in reality testing, examining their perceptions and helping them to see what was real and what wasn't. But my experiences over the last several weeks had taught me that my own perceptions also needed careful examination. A patient who claimed to have an angelic guide; a woman whose body reacted to trauma she didn't even remember; and now, a college student having visions and a psychic medium who knew things she couldn't possibly know.

There was a part of me that couldn't help but believe in these phenomena; I had seen and experienced too much to deny them any longer. But a decade ago, after becoming disillusioned with the religion of my youth, I had found a new home in the solid certainty offered by logic, reason, and the scientific method. They had brought me so much comfort, and a part of me was loath to release my grip on those foundations, even with just one hand.

Then there was the small voice inside me whispering that Con wouldn't believe any of this and might lose respect for me because I was considering it. I swallowed hard as I rooted around in my head for rebuttals to that deeply disturbing possibility.

Thankfully, Banshee interrupted my thought spiral. "Neve's notes said the psychic told you that you'd find him near the Blackbird, right?"

Kayla sniffed and rubbed her eyes. "Yeah, she did."

"Maybe those men dropped them both in the river," Banshee continued, "but Megan's floated further downstream."

"Right," Kayla said, nodding. "The report from the gardaí said it appeared Megan had been killed elsewhere and her body had been carried some distance by the river. But since Declan's body hasn't been found…."

"It could still be closer to where they dumped it," Banshee said, finishing the thought.

They were both moving too fast, charging headlong toward conclusions while I hung back, trying to engage my brain through the hangover fog. I suggested it would be good to pause the conversation and take some time to process the information. Banshee said she was still working on refining a few images taken from the CCTV footage to see if what appeared to be a sports team crest on the young man's tracksuit matched the cloth Kayla found in the blackbird's claws. She agreed to contact me with any updates.

We thanked Banshee and ended the video call. Kayla popped up and started pacing the room. The color had returned to her face, and she buzzed with nervous excitement. "We know where they killed her," she declared, "and that they killed Declan, and who they are—or where they hang out, at least. There might be more footage from somewhere else that's better quality. We could use it to identify them—"

"Oh, no, no, no." I stood and held both hands up. "Hold it right there."

Kayla paused, looking confused. "What?"

"There is no 'we.'" I had seen too many people I cared about, too many vulnerable people, put in danger recently, and there was no way I was going to let that happen again.

"What are you talking about?"

"Come." I sat back down at the table and patted her chair. "Sit."

Squinting at me, she obeyed.

"Look," I continued. "You have done enough, Kayla. You have done what whoever sent you the vision wanted you to do—the Holy Ghost, Megan… whoever it was, you've fulfilled your mission."

Kayla shook her head vigorously. "But we've just found out who killed her! We're just at the beginning of investigating—"

"No," I declared loudly and firmly enough that she stopped midsentence. "*I'm* just at the beginning of investigating, and I'll make sure the gardaí also investigate. We will find Declan, and we will find their killers. They will be brought to justice. But none of that is your job." I tapped the table in front of her for emphasis. "Your job right now is to be a college student. And not to pull rank or anything, but I'm 100 percent certain your parents and your godfather would agree with me on that."

She delivered the expected eye roll, but I could sense relief behind it too. "I can help, though!"

"You can't." I laid my hand atop hers. "In fact, if you stay involved, it'll muddy the waters. You've done the part that only you can do," I reassured as she opened her mouth to speak, then closed it again. "You followed Megan, found the blackbird, and shared what you saw. No one else could do that. But the rest of it? That's for law enforcement. That's their area of expertise, not yours, and not mine. I'll find a way to give them the information we've found so it will be useful to them."

"But how?"

I had no idea, but I was going to keep her away from the case entirely, no matter what. There was no way I was going to allow Kayla to put herself in the crosshairs of murderers. "Con and I have contacts in the gardaí," I half bluffed. "We'll figure something out."

"Are you sure?" Now that her initial excitement at solving part of Megan's murder had melted along with the adrenaline rush, anxiety was etched across Kayla's face.

"I'm absolutely positive."

We talked for a while longer, getting our facts straight and figuring out what loose ends I still needed to tie up, including contacting Rose to let her know what we'd found out. I also promised to keep Kayla updated once significant progress had been made.

I could sense a weight coming off her shoulders as she opened the hotel room door to leave. I knew she would have continued chasing justice for Megan if I had let her. But now it was time for her to hand the case off to someone else and return to normal student life.

Kayla pulled me into a tight hug. "So, you guys will call me about the brewery tour?"

"Yes, as soon as we know when it's happening." I smiled and lifted her fallen backpack strap onto her shoulder. "You take care of yourself in the meantime, okay?"

"I will. See ya!"

Once she disappeared down the hallway, I shut the door and leaned back against it, closing my eyes against the world and trying to ground myself before returning to the table and checking my phone. No new texts, and about forty-five minutes to get ready before lunch.

Thank God I'm going to see Con. More than anything, I just needed to be with him, to feel his presence and talk through the morning's events, even if he didn't believe the psychic parts. Or maybe *because* he wouldn't believe the psychic parts. I wasn't sure what to believe myself anymore—or I was, but I needed confirmation from someone I trusted to be sufficiently skeptical.

"*After* we get this flight home nonsense sorted out," I muttered to myself. With everything Banshee had shown us, I'd almost forgotten about the whole Agent Banai mess.

I checked my messages. There was a voicemail from Rosanna.

"Hey, Neve! I hope you're having a good trip! In answer to your question, no, I don't know of any emergencies related to Con's patients, or any reason why someone might be trying to call him back to work. Not to mention, if they did try, they'd have to go through me first, because I'm not letting anyone ruin your vacation! If something's going on that you need me to know about, call me back. If not, don't you dare call me back, just go out and enjoy yourself!"

With that, my best guess about what had been going on with Con and Agent Banai evaporated. Now I was completely at a loss.

I threw back another cup of coffee and tried to brace myself for whatever would come next.

CHAPTER 11
CON

Un-Corked was an upscale restaurant packed with people, and Con had chosen a table just inside one of the large front windows. Hopefully, that would keep Neve from giving out to him too loudly when he delivered the bad news.

He spotted the two men who had been tailing him all morning. They'd been in the back room of The Close the night before. Now they sat across the square at an outdoor café.

Con had called Davies earlier and told him that he needed privacy during his lunch with Neve. He had argued that he couldn't think on his feet properly if he knew people were listening in on their conversation, in which case Neve would sense something was wrong and refuse to leave. Davies had agreed to let him turn off his phone so they couldn't hear what was being said but told him to keep the phone with him so they could still track him. That seemed unnecessary since they clearly had eyes on him, but apparently Brickhaven wasn't taking any chances.

He had taken advantage of Davies's permission to turn off his phone and done so just as he reached the Grand Parade. He arrived at the restaurant early, then pretended he had forgotten something and walked over to the English Market. Once inside, he headed to Foley's Flints, the cigarette stand run by Banshee's techie friend. John Foley introduced himself and sold Con a pack of cigarettes and a lighter, which he described as "the special one you requested." John said it was a voice-activated recorder, and it was turned on by lighting it up. As he left, Con checked on the goons tailing him. Thankfully, they looked as bored as ever and didn't appear to suspect that anything unusual had occurred.

Once Con was seated in the restaurant, he saw Neve before she saw him. A taxi dropped her off at the curb. Con glanced at the goons again, but they didn't see her; their attention was on him. His gaze returned to Neve, drinking in the sight of her as she looked around, spotted the sign for Un-Corked, and began to walk toward him.

He discovered that watching Neve when she didn't know she was being watched was a singular pleasure. Usually, there was a small element of self-consciousness about her, but not now, not in this moment. She was fully herself, fully Neve. Seeing her like that made Con feel like he was discovering yet another hidden layer of the woman he loved. He knew he could spend his whole life learning her without ever growing tired of it.

But first, he had to get through this lunch.

He stood as she approached the restaurant door, waving her over as she walked in. The way her face brightened when she spotted him made his heart swell —and then break, knowing he was about to ruin her day. She accepted the offer of his outstretched arm, though, and they shared a quick embrace.

Stepping away, she looked him over like she was expecting to see new gunshot wounds. "So, you're really okay? And everyone else too?"

"Yes." Con cursed himself. It hadn't occurred to him that Banai's call would make her think of worst-case scenarios, but it should have. "As I said, everyone's fine. Don't worry."

She searched his face. "What's going on, then? Agent Banai—well, there's been some mistake."

"Has there?" Con had known this conversation

would be difficult, but regret was already grating at his heart. He leaned around the table and pulled out her chair.

Neve shrugged off her jacket and sat down with a heavy sigh. "Yes! He said he got me a ticket to fly home. Today. Alone." She shrugged, wide-eyed. "Obviously, he's confused. What's going on? What did you tell him?"

The genuine concern on her face made him feel like a monster. Neve always assumed the best of him, and of everyone, so of course she thought this was all an innocent mix-up. Now, it was his job to crush that illusion. Her natural optimism, her lack of guile and artifice—these were some of the things he loved most about her. They were also some of the reasons he had to get her on that plane.

Con looked down at the table and cleared his throat. It was time to lower the boom. It took all his courage to look her in the eyes again as he said, "I told him he needed to fly you home today. I have to stay here for a few more days, at least."

"What?" Neve blinked. "Is something wrong at the hospital? I called Rosanna, but she said she wasn't aware of anything."

Her question caught him off guard. "No, nothing's wrong at the hospital. Why would you think that?"

"I don't know. I just…." She threw her hands up. "That's the only thing I could think of, Con! Why do you want me to go, then? And why do you have to stay? Is it to do with the conference?" Neve dropped her head into her hands and rubbed her face vigorously. "What is it you're saying here?"

Good grief. This was harder than he thought. At least Neve had given him an idea for an explanation that was partially true and better than anything he'd come up with on his own. "It's something confidential related to the conference. That's why I have to stay. But I need you to go home. Agent Banai is not confused, and there has been no mistake," Con said, speaking slowly and deliberately in the hopes that his words would sink in. "I called him last night and asked him to put you on a flight to DC today. I'm sorry, Neve. I know this is confusing and comes as a shock."

Different emotions swirled around her expression like watercolors mixing on paper. She blinked again, her face blank with confusion. "But why?"

"I'm afraid I can't tell you that right now. All I can tell you is that it's important. I wouldn't be doing this otherwise." He reached his hand across the table and was relieved when she took it. "I should have known Banai's call would cause you to worry about your family and friends. I apologize for that, truly. Everyone is fine."

Neve squeezed her eyes shut and pinched the bridge of her nose for several seconds. Con waited while she processed the information.

"Let me get this straight." When she opened her eyes this time, they focused on him with a new sharpness. "You're telling me that I need to fly home today, but you can't tell me why. And you need to stay here to do something related to the conference, but you can't tell me what."

When she put it to him like that, Con realized how unreasonable it must sound to her ears. "Yes, that's about the size of it."

Neve slid her hand away from his. She crossed her arms over her chest, and Con watched with grim fascination as her walls went up. "Okay, well, first of all, no."

Con waited for her to continue, but she did not. "No, what?"

"No, I'm not flying home today, and I'm not going home without you." Her lips pursed like she had sucked on a lemon. "Second, why didn't you talk to me about this last night instead of having Agent Banai spring it on me over the phone and then ambushing me at lunch? In a restaurant, for God's sake!" She swept her arms out, barely missing the vase of flowers at the center of the table.

Con closed his eyes and thought carefully about what to say next. Neve was starting to get upset. He needed her compliance, not a repeat of previous arguments where she'd had a panic attack, run away from him, or both.

He reached across the table again. "Give me your hand, Neve." When she didn't, he repeated his request softly but with insistence. "Please."

Exhaling audibly, she gave him her hand. He held on firmly, drawing her eyes to his. "I know this is confusing and upsetting and doesn't make any sense right now. But it will, I promise. Once you're back home, I'll be able to tell you more. In the meantime, I need you to trust me. I wouldn't be asking you to do this if it weren't important. I didn't bring it up last night because—and there's no judgment here—you were in no state to discuss it."

He was relieved to see the change on her face as her anger and frustration appeared to abate. They were morphing into worry and a small bit of embarrassment, but those were easier for him to deal with.

"Welcome to Un-Corked!" They pulled their hands apart as a cheerful young man approached, laying two menus on the table before pulling a small pad and pen from his shirt pocket. "I'm Michael, and I'll be your server today. Can I take your drinks order?"

It took Neve a moment to pull her focus away from Con before politely ordering a diet soda. Con called for the same. He really wanted a shot of whiskey, but given that Neve was likely still hungover, he didn't want to remind her of the night before.

Once the waiter departed, Con asked, "How's your head?"

She just glared at him for a moment. "Look," Neve began, "I get the part about you having to do something work related here. It's not what we planned, but hey, things come up." Her half smile gave Con hope that the risk of a panic attack had passed, at least. "The part I don't get is why I need to go home. If you have things to do, that's fine. I can entertain myself. I'll go sightseeing, maybe take a bus tour, hang out with Kayla. I've been wanting to explore Cork anyway. Don't worry about me. I'd rather be spending time with you, of course, but I'll be fine on my own. When you're done, we can go home together, or maybe even explore Ireland a bit more. I mean, we have the time off work. Why not use it?"

It was an entirely reasonable proposal, which made it that much more painful for him to refuse her. "I wish I could agree to that plan, believe me, but I can't."

She leaned back in her chair, sputtering. "Why not?"

"I can't tell you that either," Con said as remorse threatened to swallow him whole. "I've told you all I can for now. I know this sounds crazy, Neve. I promise, though, when I get back to DC, I will explain everything in detail. Then you'll understand why all of this had to happen the way it did."

"I'll understand?" Neve closed her eyes again and massaged her temples. "I bet I won't agree, though."

Sensing he needed to tread carefully, Con asked, "Agree with what?"

When she looked up this time, her annoyance was clear. "You can explain it to me, but I doubt I'll agree that sending me home with no explanation—via the Secret Service, no less—was the best course of action, or the only one. You know I trust you. I trust you with my life," she said, "but that goes both ways. I need you to trust me too. Haven't I earned that?"

Neve's voice cracked slightly, and Con nearly gave in. He thought of all they'd been through together over the past several weeks and all the ways in which Neve had been there for him, whether he'd wanted her to or not. In fact, if it hadn't been for her stubborn insistence to stick by him, he could easily be dead now. It broke his heart that she might interpret his request for her to leave as a lack of confidence on his part. "Of course I trust you. I'd trust you with my life, too, in a heartbeat. That's not what this is about."

Neve was about to launch into a rebuttal when the waiter brought their drinks. Their emotional conversation had left them parched, and they both paused to take a sip, releasing some of the tension that had built up in the space between them.

"Okay, then *what*?" Neve continued. "Don't we come up with better ideas when we put our heads together? Why send me away instead of bringing me in?"

Con rubbed his hand across his face. She wasn't wrong. Her help had always been invaluable to him. But this time was different. If he told her what was going on, he knew her well enough to state with certainty that she would refuse to leave. And if he betrayed Brickhaven, that would put her in immediate danger. In his mind, that was the *real* worst-case scenario. Neve's anger, he could deal with. But if she got hurt—well, he refused to go down that road.

"And don't tell me it's because of confidentiality,"

she warned. "We both know how to talk about the general shape of a situation without disclosing the details."

Con was reminded once again why he avoided arguing with Neve. There would be no winning here, so there was no point in engaging further. "No one is more aggrieved than I am that we have to cut our holiday short. I'm confident that I impressed upon you how much I was looking forward to this week." He gave her a look that he hoped was laced with enough heat to underline the truth of that statement. "Believe me, if there were any other possible way of handling the situation, I would do it. But there isn't, and as I've said, I can't explain why right now."

Her mouth fell open. "Did you just completely dodge my question?"

"Neve." He bowed his head. "I just need you to *give* me this one."

A thousand thoughts played out across her face as she considered his request. It was a big ask, but he was hopeful that her faith in him would overcome her need to understand the "why" behind everything. It was an admirable trait of hers, and one of the things that made her such a gifted therapist, but it could be a stumbling block here.

Finally, she said, "This is a big one."

She was thinking about it. *Thank God.* "No argument here."

"You really mean it," she murmured, incredulous. "You're seriously asking me to just get on a plane, go home, and wait."

Pushing against everything inside him, especially the instinct that wanted to keep her with him at all times, he said, "Unfortunately, I am, yes."

Con hated witnessing the moment that she decided to do as he asked. Sadness crept into her expression, and her shoulders slumped in defeat. Neve sipped her drink as though trying to soothe herself. "You'll owe me a freebie, then, at least?" she asked, her voice soft and low. "At some point in the future, you'll do something for me without asking any questions?"

"Without asking…?" But Con stopped himself when he saw her eyebrows begin to lift. Right now, getting her agreement was far more important than pointing out the double standard in what she was proposing. "Yes, I'll owe you a freebie. And not just one. As many as you like, love."

Neve placed her glass back on the table. She lifted her hand, cool and wet with icy condensation, and patted it across her forehead. Then, as though she couldn't quite believe she was saying the words, she gave her head a vigorous shake. "I'll hold you to that. Okay, then."

"Really?" Con leaned back in his chair as relief poured over him. The first and most crucial task of the day was going to plan. Still, it felt like something of a Pyrrhic victory. "Thank you, Neve. Thank you. I mean it. Now, let's order. I don't want you getting on the plane hungry."

They ordered and ate in agonizing silence. Con was afraid to say anything that might change her mind. He wasn't at all happy that Neve had grown sullen. She had agreed to go, though, so he focused on that. There was a good chance that when he finally did explain things to her, she'd be furious. It might take a lot for her to forgive him, in fact. But at least she'd be alive to argue with him. He would gladly accept that outcome.

Con was dimly aware that the food was excellent, but the mood being what it was, it turned to ashes in his mouth. Judging from the look on Neve's face, she was having the same experience. By the time the waiter brought the check, Con was impatient to get moving. Thankfully, when he offered to go back to the hotel with Neve so she could pack her things and then take her to the airport, she agreed. Until her plane was wheels-up, he wouldn't be able to concentrate on anything else.

Each step they took toward her departure felt like a walk to the gallows—even more so whenever he caught a glimpse of the men tailing them. Not wishing to give Brickhaven's goons any excuse to get closer to Neve, Con turned his phone back on when they reached the airport.

It took some looking, but they found the private flight check-in desk, the point where he'd have to leave her. As Neve produced her documents, it felt like a weight was lifting off him, but it was also the most painful moment of his life thus far.

Con had tried to sound confident when he'd told her they would sort everything out between them when he got back to DC. But when she arrived, she'd be taken into protective custody, something that would no doubt cause her anxiety to spike. Her fear would only be made worse when she learned they were under threat from Brickhaven again. But Con couldn't afford to worry about that yet. He'd made sure she had anxiety meds in her carry-on bag, but that was all he could do for now.

"You're all set, ma'am!" The employee at the check-in desk handed Neve back her documents.

She tucked them into her purse, and just as they

were about to say their goodbyes, his mobile vibrated. It was a text from Davies:

> It's time. Meet your ride in front of the airport in five minutes.

Possibly the worst timing ever. Then again, what did he expect from Davies?

"What is it?" Neve asked, tension spiking in her voice.

"It's nothing." He put the mobile in his pocket and embraced her with his good arm. "I just have to be somewhere. I think I'd have to leave you here anyway, though."

"Yeah," she said, looking so dejected that Con wanted to whisk her off to some hidden corner of the airport and kiss her deeply until they both forgot all their worries. She pointed at a sign on the wall. "Super-fancy private jet customers only beyond this point." For the first time since lunch, Neve's lips turned slightly upward in a half smile.

The sight gave Con's heart the uplift it needed to keep him going. "Be safe and enjoy the flight. I promise we'll sort everything out. I'll be home soon."

She leaned in, wrapping her arms around his waist. "You be safe too."

"Always," he said, and then they both laughed

lightly at the wild lie that was. They'd been a lot of things over the last several weeks, but "always safe" was definitely not one of them. "From now on," he clarified. "I promise."

Neve sighed audibly. "You *really* want me to go?"

The heartbreak in her voice nearly did him in. He reached down and took her hand in his. She was doing what he'd asked; the least he could do was give her something to hold on to, some semblance of a reason. "I don't want you to go. God, no, I don't want that. But I *need* you to go." He fell in love with her just a bit more when her brow wrinkled, her mind struggling to understand. "Do you remember at our breakfast in the stone circle, when the sun came through and temporarily blinded you?"

Neve nodded.

"Well, you're a bit like the Irish sun for me. You shine so brightly, it's blinding sometimes. Don't get me wrong; I love that about you." He lifted the back of her hand to his lips, kissing it softly. "But for the next few days, I need to be able to see straight. I'm sorry," he said when she started to look even more confused. "It's a tortured metaphor. I should just say thank you again. Thank you for giving me this—what did you call it? This freebie."

"It's okay," she replied, eyes flashing. "I guess it's

not too bad a deal for me either, since I'm getting as many freebies as I like in return."

Con smiled. Of course she remembered that part.

The employee at the desk called out, "You can go through now, ma'am. They're getting ready to board."

"Thanks." Turning back to Con, Neve said, "That's me, I guess." She pushed up onto her toes and gave him a quick peck, whispering, "I hate this."

He cupped her cheek and locked his eyes on hers, desperate to drink them in for one more second. "I hate it too."

As though she could no longer stand the intensity of the emotion, she turned her head. "Bye."

"See you soon," he called as she flitted away from him.

Con watched as Neve followed the employee's directions as to where to go next. She looked back and gave him a quick wave before stepping behind the desk and disappearing around a corner.

The moment he lost sight of her, Con felt like he'd been hit in the chest by a flying cement block. Even though Brickhaven had promised to let Neve go, he knew anything could happen—her flight could get canceled or delayed, for example. That was why he'd wanted to wait at the airport until her plane departed, but Davies had to screw that up too. From this moment until he received a message at the hotel confirming Neve was in the air, Con would have to trust Banai to handle things.

The five minutes Davies had given him were up. It was time.

Steeling himself for what was to come, Con made his way to the front of the airport where a car, as promised, was waiting to take him to hell.

CHAPTER 12
NEVE

As impossibly hard as it was for me to "just give this one" to Con, I fully intended to get on that plane. I'd resigned myself to acquiescing, even though my instincts were screaming and it went against everything in me. It was obviously important to Con, though, and I trusted that he had his reasons. I also knew he was a man of his word, so if he said he would help me understand everything later, I believed him. It might be the last time I'd ever do something so bizarre with no explanation, but I was willing to give it a try, just once, as an experiment.

Which was not to say my brain hadn't gone rogue, trying to think up a plan to make Con think I'd gotten on the plane without actually doing so. Knowing he intended to hang around the airport until my flight left, I'd been concocting a scheme for getting off the plane right before departure. Never having flown on a private jet before, I wasn't sure exactly how it worked. But I thought maybe I could board the plane, then tell the crew that it was my boyfriend's birthday tomorrow and I was surprising him by staying in Ireland, even though he thought I was going home. I wouldn't request a refund, just ask that they let me off the plane and refrain from updating my boarding status until the last possible minute. Then I could hide out somewhere and leave the airport once the plane took off and the coast was clear.

When Con got that text and said he had to be somewhere, my potential escape became tantalizingly simple. I just had to head toward the plane but refrain from boarding, give it ten minutes or so to be sure he was gone, and then walk right back out of the airport.

I wasn't going to do that, though. I had given him my word that I would fly home, and I fully intended to.

But as I made my way toward the final door that would lead me out to the plane, Con's "Irish sun" speech kept playing over and over in my mind. What did he mean when he said I blinded him, and for the next few days, he had to be able to see straight? If whatever he had to take care of was related to the conference, what was it about my presence in Cork that would bother him so much? It didn't make any sense. We worked together, for goodness' sake. We *helped* each other to focus.

Maybe it would be enough for him to believe I'd left. If Con thought I was gone, he wouldn't be distracted. He could focus on what he needed to do, and when he was finished, I could surprise him and show up at the hotel. He might be angry at first, but the possibility that our first time sleeping together could be mind-blowing makeup sex had definite appeal.

But no. I would stick to my word, end of story. I would start off this relationship as I intended to continue—keeping my promises, not breaking them. Besides, Agent Banai was waiting for me in DC. No doubt if I failed to show up, he'd contact Con and my whole plan would backfire.

There were still a few minutes left before I had to board, though. I found a cushy seat near an outlet and plugged in my phone to charge. There were notifications for two unread texts. The first one had been sent to both Kayla and me from Banshee:

> Finished refining the crest image from the tracksuit on maybe-Declan. Mayfield Raiders AFC (Amateur Football Club—that's soccer to you). Also, reviewed more footage, and it looks like our boyos might be nightly regulars at the B-bird. Can't say for sure since I still can't make out faces. But there are four guys who hang out together with gaits and builds similar to the ones from our footage on the night.

Attached was a close-up of the crest on the tracksuit of the young man in the CCTV footage from outside the Blackbird. The image was rough but well-defined enough to see it was the same crest as the one Kayla had taken from the bird's claws in the river: white embroidery on a red background, with the letter *M* and a tall ship sailing between two towers.

While that didn't prove the man in the video was Declan, given the other context clues, it certainly increased the probability. Kayla would definitely be convinced. And if our four thugs went to the Blackbird frequently, they would be easier to apprehend.

I texted Banshee back to thank her, then read the next message, which was from Kayla:

> Hi! I know I said I was done, but I'm thinking, no harm in going to have a pint at the Blackbird tonight. Maybe do some recon. If you're not busy, care to join?

"No, no no no no no," I muttered, drawing curious glances as I dialed Kayla. I stood up and walked to a quiet corner of the gate.

"Hi, Neve," she said brightly. "Did you get my text?"

"Yes," I hissed softly. "That's why I'm calling!"

"Why are you whispering?"

"I'm… in a public place and don't want to be overheard. You cannot go to the Blackbird tonight!"

"Look, I know you and Con have a romantic week planned. I'm not trying to interfere; I just thought on the off chance you were free—"

"That's not the issue!" My voice was rising. I willed myself to calm down. "Kayla, we talked about this. You can't involve yourself in this any further, okay? It's not safe, and it's not your job. Not to mention, your godfather would definitely not approve!"

"Oh my God," she said, and I could almost hear her eyes rolling. "Okay, yeah, all of that. But listen, I called the gardaí—"

"You did *what*?"

"I just wanted to tell them about the CCTV footage and see if they'd follow up. I described it to them, but they said it sounded like there was no evidence of a crime on there. Which I guess is true, technically, since you can't actually see the murders happening, or see the bodies, since they're wrapped up. I tried to explain why it was significant, but then they started asking me why I had the footage, where I got it, why I was so sure a crime had been committed…. Obviously, I couldn't answer those questions, so after a while, they just hung up. I think they thought it was a prank call or something."

I tried not to think about how livid Agent Banai would be if he found out about Kayla's extracurricular activities, to say nothing of President Duran. "Please tell me you didn't give them your name."

"No, of course not. I'm not stupid. And I called from a burner phone, which I bought in cash. Banshee told me where to get one."

I breathed a sigh of relief. She had at least sought advice from Banshee first. Maybe Kayla had more common sense than I was giving her credit for.

That hope proved to be short-lived, however.

"But Neve, seriously, think about it," she continued. "Just because these guys have been going to the

Blackbird lately doesn't mean they'll keep going there forever. If I go tonight, I can just have a pint, act casual, and if I see those guys, I'll take pictures of them on my phone when they're not looking."

Oh Lord, she's going to get killed. I tried to massage the tension from my forehead. "Kayla, you're not a secret agent! They'll catch you. Besides, we don't even know what kind of pub this is."

"What do you mean? It has a website."

I reminded myself that I was just as naive as Kayla before I began working as a therapist. "That doesn't mean anything. We don't know what kind of people hang out there, what they do there. And we're definitely not locals, so it would be that much harder for us to pick up any cues people might give us that we weren't welcome or were in the wrong place."

Thankfully, that gave her pause. "But we have to do something!"

"No. *We* are not doing anything. *You* are going to go right back to being a regular college student, just as we agreed, or I swear to God, I will call the Secret Service."

There was an exasperated sigh on the other end of the line. "But somebody has to follow up on this. The more I think about it, the more I'm convinced I had this vision because the Holy Ghost wants someone to find Declan's body, to put him to rest and clear his name. I swear, Neve, I won't have any peace until everything that can possibly be done for Megan and Declan has been done. We can't let this opportunity pass us by."

"Again, no 'we,'" I exclaimed.

"Fine! Could you take Con, then, maybe? He's a local, sort of. And he's, like, intimidating. I mean, nobody's going to mess with him, even in a sling."

Somehow, I just knew—maybe because "like knows like," and I'd made plenty of unwise, impulsive decisions when intense emotions were involved. But I knew in my bones that if I didn't agree to check out the Blackbird, Kayla would do it herself—if not that night, then some night soon.

But here I was, sitting in the airport, having promised to board a plane. Were that not the case, I would have offered right away to visit the pub myself. I wasn't worried about my own safety. I had enough common sense and situational awareness—or "cop-on," as Con would call it—to keep myself from getting into trouble. Kayla, on the other hand….

"What is it? Do you think he wouldn't go?"

"It's not that." *Dammit.* There was no way I was getting out of the airport without disappointing somebody. If I didn't fly and disappointed Con, he would be angry, yes, and we'd have to work that out. But if I flew and disappointed Kayla, it could lead to her getting hurt, or worse.

That settled that.

"Sorry, I was just thinking. You're right, it's an opportunity we shouldn't allow to slip by. We might find some useful information at the Blackbird, something to put with the CCTV footage that would force an investigation by the authorities. And by 'we,' I mean Con and me. I don't want you anywhere near this, Kayla. You have to promise me."

"Oh, thank you," she gushed. "This means the world to me. And I promise, I totally promise. You'll tell me what happens, though, right?"

"After I've done everything that can be done, I'll fill you in," I said. "I don't want you waiting around to hear from me about every detail, though. You have classes and other things to concentrate on. Okay?"

"Deal." I could hear the smile in her voice. "Thank you so much again, Neve!"

"No problem," I lied. "Talk to you soon!"

I held my head in my hands and tried to think. So, I was staying in Cork. I needed to get a room in a different hotel from Con, so he wouldn't know I was around and I wouldn't distract him. But first, I needed to call Agent Banai so he could cancel my ticket. I dialed his number.

"Hello, Miss Keane," he said, startling me by picking up on the first ring. "I can see you've checked in. Are you ready to board?"

"Well, I was." It was slightly creepy that he knew so much about my movements, but I didn't dwell on it. "There has been a change of plans, though. I'm staying here. You can cancel the ticket. I'll be happy to pay any resulting fees," I added, praying to God there wouldn't be any. I didn't know how much a ticket on a private jet cost, but I was pretty sure it would clear out what little I had in my savings account.

Several beats of silence passed before he replied. "Does Dr. O'Brien know about this?"

Somehow, I stopped myself from asking why in the hell that mattered. Instead, I said, "No he does not, and I would request that you refrain from telling him. I will give him the news myself."

There was some muttering, and I thought I heard him say, "Not a couples counselor." Agent Banai cleared his throat. "Miss Keane, Dr. O'Brien communicated to us in the strongest possible terms how important it was to get you Stateside as soon as possible."

These two, I swear. "I spoke to him over lunch, and I know more about the situation now." That last part was an extreme exaggeration, though not an outright lie. "I was prepared to fly, but new information has come to light, and now I'm going to stay. I am a United States citizen with permission to be in Ireland, and although he likes to pretend otherwise, Dr. O'Brien is not in charge of where I travel and when." *Nor are you,* I thought, but since I wasn't sure what powers the Secret Service actually had, I decided not to poke that bear. "Thank you very much for arranging the ticket, but I won't be using it after all."

"All right, Miss Keane. If that's what you've decided, I'll take care of it. And don't worry, there won't be any fees."

He was being quite kind to me under the circumstances. "I really appreciate that, Agent Banai, thank you. I'm sorry you went to all this trouble."

"No trouble. I heard from Dr. O'Brien yesterday that you both met with Kayla and she's in good health. We appreciate your help, there."

Grateful for the change of subject, I said, "It was our pleasure, really. Kayla's a sweetheart."

"Please call me if you change your mind about

flying home, or if you need anything at all. We're here to help."

"I will. Thanks again."

I returned to the check-in desk and let the employee there know I wouldn't be getting on the flight after all. Relieved to have that taken care of, I used my phone to book a hotel online.

Knowing I had made the best choice possible under the circumstances did nothing to ease the feelings of guilt and defeat I wore like a weighted vest. I absolutely hated deceiving Con. It went against everything in me, chafing my conscience. Besides, how many times had I lost it with him for lying to me? And now here I was, doing the exact same thing I loathed. As the reality of that hit, my stomach churned.

Unfortunately, for the life of me, I couldn't imagine how else to resolve the situation. Officially out of options, I carried my bags outside, stood at the taxi rank, and waited.

CHAPTER 13
NEVE

Although I had been in Ireland for just a little over two weeks, I found myself unpacking my suitcase for the sixth time—and this time, alone. Not what I'd had in mind, that was certain.

I tried to cheer myself up by admiring the art deco hotel. It wasn't as sumptuous as the Hotel Gairdín, but it was majestic in its own way, with high ceilings, black and bronze styling, and, most importantly, a comfortable bed. I had managed to get a good "last-minute" deal—fortunately, since I was paying for this one myself.

I was lying down, trying to let the stress of the day wash out of me, when a new text came in from Banshee, asking if we could talk. She had new information but said it was too much to put in a text. I sat up and grabbed my laptop to take notes before calling her.

"Hey, Neve!"

"Hi, Banshee. What's up?"

"Thought I should call you instead of Kayla on this one," Banshee said. "Not a criticism, she just seems a bit… eager."

"Right." After my earlier conversation with Kayla, I certainly couldn't fault Banshee's judgment. "What did you find?"

"These feckers," she began. "I found another gardaí file with Megan's name in it, separate from the murder investigation. She called in a few times to report suspected prostitution in the house just next door to where she lived. She was worried about the women in the house, said they looked thin and scared and were covered in bruises. She reckoned they were Eastern European for the most part, judging from the languages she heard spoken. Megan was keeping tabs, said the gals stayed for a few weeks at a time, then got replaced. Sketchy guys hung around outside, and some scary-looking boss lady kept everyone in line."

"Oh my God, those poor women." I knew too well how vulnerable sex workers could be, having treated several patients on the psychiatry unit back home who were involved. "What happened?"

"That's the kicker. The last report she gave them, she called in the day before that scene we saw at the Blackbird."

My stomach dropped. "You mean the day before she was killed?"

"That's the one. In that report, Megan told the guards she'd been caught spying on the house by the boss lady. They had a confrontation, and Megan said she was scared for her safety. That must have been enough to trigger some action, because the gardaí went to the house the next day. It had been abandoned —in a hurry, by the look of things."

"Wow." This provided a chilling replacement for the now-disproven "murdered by her boyfriend" narrative. "And no one connected this with her murder?"

"Two separate files, two separate garda stations," Banshee pointed out. "And she never called from her own number or gave her surname when she made the reports. She must have been scared, and rightly so. Plus, there were a fair few people calling in about what was going on in that house; it wasn't just her. I only stumbled on the report and figured out who she was because I did a first-name search and looked at the similarities in postal addresses. If I hadn't been fishing for information, I wouldn't have found the connection either. There's no way of proving it was her, of course, since she covered her tracks."

I brought my hand up to apply pressure to my chest, trying to hold in my pounding heart. "What if the guys at the Blackbird were connected to the prostitution ring? Maybe they figured out Megan was calling in the reports, got angry…."

"And took revenge," Banshee finished my sentence. "Megan gave the gardaí descriptions of the fellas hanging around the house, and four of them sound like the same langers from the CCTV footage. She even said one of them had distinctive hand tattoos."

"Let me guess." I shuddered. "Ogham tattoos?"

"Yes. Not that they're uncommon in Ireland, but hand tattoos are rare enough, and to have multiple ogham designs on both hands? I've not seen that before."

That information confirmed who I'd be looking for at the Blackbird that night—or more specifically, who I'd be trying to avoid. "Look, Banshee, I'm just going to tell you this because I can't tell Con, and I feel like someone should know. I'm going to the Blackbird tonight, just to observe. I might not even go inside. I just want to see if these thugs show up, maybe take some pictures that are clearer than the images from the CCTV."

I heard Banshee make a clucking sound, and it gave me the distinct impression that she was judging me. "Can't tell Con. Well, as I told you back in Galway, I don't get involved in domestics. I'll grab the CCTV from tonight just in case you need something to back up whatever observations you make. I will say, I hope these bastards don't show up. If they're bringing in women from abroad and forcing them into prostitution, those are some serious feckers you're dealing with."

I thought back to when we first arrived in Ireland and I was waiting in line at the airport, going through Customs. There had been signs explaining what to do if you were a victim of human trafficking. Intellectually, I'd known it was a global problem, but it had still been a shock to see those signs interspersed with tourism posters featuring the beauty of the Irish landscape. Now, Banshee's news made the whole issue horrifyingly real. "You sound like you know something about it."

"My work sometimes takes me to places online even darker than the dark web," she said matter-of-factly. "You rub elbows with some real scum there. I'm just saying, watch your back even more than usual, and call me if you need any help that's in my wheelhouse. If you can find something that'll take those bastards down, grand, but don't put yourself in harm's way doing it. And if you want my advice, don't go alone. If you can't take Con, take somebody else, at least. Preferably a man, given the lads you're dealing with."

A nervous laugh bubbled up from my throat. "Not Kayla, then."

Banshee didn't laugh, however. "No, not Kayla. I like her a lot, but she's young and seems to have limited experience of the world. In a tough spot, she'd be about as much use as a chocolate kettle."

"Right. Okay, well, thanks for offering to help. I'll be careful, I promise. And thanks for everything, Banshee. I mean it."

"No worries. Glad to help."

Banshee had done an excellent job scaring me to death about visiting the Blackbird, especially alone. But aside from Con—and his family, who would definitely rat on me if I contacted them—I knew no one in Ireland. Well, I sort of knew the gardaí who had helped us nail Mad Max in Galway. But they were hardly going to drive to Cork to join me on a stakeout for fun—which was all it was, at this point. I didn't have enough information yet to justify an actual investigation. That's why I needed to go to the Blackbird in the first place.

First, I had to figure out my transportation. I could have the hotel call me a taxi, but getting home was a different issue. The concierge from Hotel Gairdín had told me about a phone app for ordering local taxis… but as I searched for the app, I remembered I *did* know someone else in Ireland: Thomas the Taxi Driver! He had been so kind to me on my first day in Cork, showing me the sights before dropping me off at the university—and he had given me his business card.

Of course, there was every chance that he wouldn't be available to spend the night ferrying me around town, but it was worth a shot. I fished his number out of my purse and gave him a call, keeping my fingers crossed.

"Good of you to bring me along, gal." Thomas winked at me.

We were parked along the curb next to the pawnbroker shop whose CCTV Banshee had hacked, our eyes on the Blackbird. It was around 7:00 p.m. and already dark. I was delighted that Thomas had agreed to go with me, although he could only stay with me until eight, when he was due home to relieve his daughter. They were looking after his wife, post–knee replacement, in shifts. But his son-in-law worked nights, so his daughter had to get home to her kids by a certain time. Secretly, I was relieved to have a time limit on how long we'd be in the orbit of Megan's murderers. I had explained the situation to Thomas in general terms, who thankfully had understood without needing too many of the bone-chilling details.

We had been sitting there for an hour at that stage, sharing the front seat and chatting occasionally to break the tension. Tense on my end, anyway; nothing seemed to ruffle Thomas. At the same time, I could tell that his senses were tuned-in, and that beneath his relaxed exterior, he was poised and ready for anything.

"Are you being sarcastic?" It wasn't exactly an exciting night out, and I had trouble reading his tone and speech inflections at times.

Thomas chuckled. "Not at all. Sitting here talking to you is far preferable to battling traffic, which is what I would be doing otherwise. I'm also glad you didn't come on your own, given what you're up to. And while this isn't the worst part of town, I wouldn't like to think of you being out here without a local guide."

"I really appreciate it." While we hadn't yet seen the Gang of Four—Thomas's new nickname for the thugs I was hoping to spot—several shady-looking characters had gone in and out of the Blackbird. The darker the night became, the more grateful I was to have Thomas with me.

Another twenty minutes passed before we saw a group of four burly men walking up the hill toward the pub, illuminated by streetlights. The closer they came, the more I thought they resembled Megan and Declan's killers. Sitting still and trying not to stare, I whispered, "I think that's them!"

"Those are some likely lads, all right. You wanted pictures?"

I chewed on my lip as they got closer. "Yeah, but I don't want to go in there now."

"Step out," Thomas said. "I want some pictures of myself with my taxi."

Trusting Thomas, I pulled out my phone and got out of the car. He walked around to my side of the taxi, looked back at me, and put his hand on the hood. As he leaned in, he created a frame in which I could take a picture of him and also capture the front of the Blackbird.

"Perfect!" I began positioning the camera just as the four goons reached the pub. As though following my unspoken instructions, they stopped in front of the building to have a smoke.

Thomas began goofing around a bit, changing up his poses. When I spotted the ogham tattoos on one of the man's hands, nerves hit me so hard that I almost dropped the phone. But Thomas distracted me, even getting me to laugh as I went about my work snapping one picture after another, pretending to take a lot of time to set up each shot. Eventually, the men entered the pub.

"Got it!" I declared, and Thomas and I climbed back into the taxi. "You're a genius," I told him, breathless. "Are you sure you haven't done this before?"

"Just using a bit of creativity there." Thomas pointed at the phone. "Going to show us what you got?"

We flipped through the photos. Sure enough, I had clear pictures of all four of the men's faces. I had even captured a good shot of the hand tattoos.

"You're a good photographer," he joked. "I look ten years younger in these."

Thomas had an easy time making me smile. "Want me to send them to you?"

"Ah, stop." He waved the idea away. "Is there anything else you need? Want me to go in there and chat 'em up, get their names, dates of birth, and so on?"

The idea of getting more information was appealing, but the thought of either of us going into the pub after a group of known murderers felt too terrifying to contemplate. "Thanks for the offer, but no, I'd say...."

I trailed off as the four men came back out of the pub. One of them cast us a fleeting glance, but we quickly looked away. Thankfully, it seemed we had succeeded in not drawing their attention. They conferred for several moments before heading back down the hill the way they'd come.

"What do you want to do, girleen?"

I realized I had stopped breathing at the sight of them. "I'm not sure what you mean."

"Well, I've got more than half an hour left before I need to get home. Want to see where they go next?"

"You mean follow them?" It hadn't even occurred to me, but when Thomas suggested it, it seemed like the obvious choice. "Can we do that? Without getting caught, I mean?"

"Sure, no bother." Thomas started the engine. "I've been at this a while, you know. Many a night

I've had someone in my cab, trying to find out if their other half was cheating on them. You learn stealth in this business."

"I guess so." Evidently, he was much more adept at stakeouts than I was. "If you have the time, sure, it might be helpful to see where they go next. Maybe we'll find out where they live."

"Here we go, then!" Thomas pulled away from the curb and eased the car into the street.

True to his word, he managed to keep from raising the thugs' suspicions. It took a lot of work on his part, since they were on foot at first, but he managed to stay out of sight. Then they turned and walked down a driveway. I took note of the location, and we decided to wait a few minutes to see if anything else happened.

Soon, a boxy white van pulled out of the driveway with three of the men visible sitting in the cab. The van sported a round logo on the side with a picture of a fish jumping out of water and the words "Rocky Creek Seafood." Thomas said it was a Transit van, a commercial vehicle typically used for transporting cargo. We followed it all the way down the hill and along the river. After crossing a bridge, we entered an industrial area where it looked like most of the buildings were warehouses. According to Thomas, we had reached Kennedy Quay, part of the commercial port of Cork. Recalling what Con had said about the place Eamonn worked, I asked Thomas if Calfwood Brewery was nearby. He said it wasn't far away and pointed down the river.

We parked on the main road while the cargo van turned right down a narrow side street. They passed two warehouses but appeared to drive into the third.

"Not sure I want to know what they're doing in there," Thomas said, echoing my thoughts. He tapped the clock on his dashboard. "All right, I'm afraid it's time for me to be getting home. Drop you back to your hotel, I'm guessing?"

The practical, self-protective part of me that very much enjoyed being alive wanted desperately to say, "Yes, please." But the image of the women Banshee had described haunted me. If there was something I could do to help them, or possibly impede the human trafficking ring, I had to do it, even if there was some risk involved. By walking down there and taking some photos, there was a chance I could get evidence not only of the identity of those men but of something else—maybe an actual crime being committed. That would definitely give the authorities something concrete, something to act on.

"No, you can just drop me off here." I smiled at Thomas in a way I hoped was reassuring.

"Jaysus, girl," he muttered, pressing his palms together as though in prayer and holding them up to his forehead. "Whoever your man is, he's got his hands full. You're sure I can't talk you out of it?"

I reached over and squeezed his arm. "I promise I'll be safe. I won't do anything stupid. And I'll remember all the stealth moves you taught me."

"Take this, at least." He reached over and retrieved a small flashlight from the glove compartment. "Here, hand me your phone. I'm giving you the number for a friend of mine who works the late shift for when you're ready to come home. I'll tell him to expect your call."

"Thanks, I really appreciate that."

He input the number with the name "Finn Taxi." "Sure you don't want to go back now?"

I wasn't sure at all. I was the furthest thing from sure, in fact. But what I felt compelled to do was a whole other matter.

"I'm good. I'll be fine, I promise."

We took care of payment, and despite his objections, I added on a hefty tip this time, insisting it was payment for the flashlight. "Take care, Thomas. Thanks again!"

"Mind yourself!" he called as I climbed out. "Slán!"

As he drove away, I swallowed hard. The sudden absence of his companionship made my isolation quite stark.

For the hundredth time since he'd dropped me off at the airport, I wished with all my being that I could call Con. But no. He had wanted me gone for some important reason, so as far as he knew, I was going to stay gone. I would give him the time and mental space to do whatever it was he needed to do. Meanwhile, I had to stay focused on my own task if I was going to keep my word to Thomas and stay safe.

Streetlights provided sporadic illumination of the warehouses and the pathways between them. With the flashlight in my pocket, I stepped down the road the van had taken. I walked along the far side, opposite the warehouse they had pulled into, and tried to stay in the shadows.

CHAPTER 14
NEVE

As I approached the warehouse the Blackbird thugs had pulled into, my heart began to pound out an uneven beat, like a heavy metal drum solo. It occurred to me that this would be a really horrible time and place to have a heart attack, or a panic attack for that matter. I tucked myself against a long row of storage units across the road. Hiding in the shadows, I willed myself to breathe as a curtain of dread closed around me.

Ever since I'd been stabbed by my patient, anxiety issues had dogged me. They were improving, but not nearly fast enough in my estimation—which was ridiculous, I knew. I would never tell a patient they needed to hurry up and heal. But the symptoms could be extremely uncomfortable, not to mention inconvenient. They tended to crop up at the worst possible moments—like this one, for example. I had taken my antianxiety meds before leaving the hotel, hoping they would keep my nerves under control. I knew myself well enough at this stage to know that as long as I could keep taking slow, deep breaths, I could stave off a full-blown panic attack. I closed my eyes and focused.

Inhale, hold. Exhale, hold.

To ground myself, I imagined tree roots growing from my feet down through the pavement and deep into the earth, holding me in place. I called up a few affirmations I'd taught myself to talk down my heightened emotions: *You are alive. You are safe. You are unharmed. You are not in danger. Nothing bad is going to happen.* I forced myself to repeat those thoughts like a mantra, even though a tenacious part of my brain countered that in fact, at that very moment, I was courting danger, and something bad very well might happen.

Slowly, slowly, the affirmations had their desired effect, and my heart rate returned to normal. The sweat felt cool as it began to dry on my skin, and my hands began to feel less clammy.

Thank God.

I opened my eyes to discover they were better

adjusted to the dark. One large garage door was open on the warehouse the men from the Blackbird had driven into. The interior was fully lit, and their van was parked just inside the entrance. There appeared to be a lot of movement happening on the other side of the van, but I couldn't quite see what was going on. I would have to get closer.

As I crept across the road and dove into a shadowy area at the corner of the warehouse, I made up a story in my head: what to say if I got caught. I decided to try "lost American tourist" first, and if that didn't work, switch to "union organizer researching working conditions for dockers in Ireland." If that failed as well, I'd say I was an investigative reporter writing an exposé on—well, I didn't know what, but something as far from human trafficking as I could think of. Maybe lead paint or water quality.

On second thought, better not to get caught at all.

I fumbled with my phone, trying to pull up the camera while keeping the light from the screen hidden. Scooting up to the edge of the garage door opening, I set the camera app to video mode, hit the Record button, and extended my arm with the camera pointing into the warehouse. From that angle, I could see the screen, and the camera could show me what was inside.

At first all I saw was the van. Moving the phone left and right, I captured more of the interior. There were at least a dozen men walking around who resembled the men from the Blackbird. Everyone was wearing darkish clothing, and rock music I'd never heard before blared from somewhere. There were two other vehicles with the Rocky Creek Seafood logo parked inside. The far end of the space seemed to be sectioned off by fencing of some kind, and there were groups of people on the other side. Unlike the men in the foreground, those people appeared to be stationary.

In order to see more, I needed to get a different angle on the inside. I slipped back across the road and hugged the front wall of the storage units, avoiding illuminated spots as I made my way to the far end of the warehouse. There were two more large garage doors, both closed, and a regular-sized door at the very end. If I could open that door even a crack, I could slide my phone in and take another video. At least I hadn't drawn any attention to myself yet. I slipped across the road again and headed for the small door.

Carefully, I pressed down on the metal lever handle. When the latch clicked, my heart leapt into my throat. The door was open, but my nervous system couldn't decide whether that was good news or bad. Biting down hard on my lip, I pushed the door in just enough to slide my arm through, holding the phone. I looked through the crack at the screen as it recorded the scene.

The fenced-in area I'd seen from the far side of the warehouse was only about ten feet away from where I stood. The fence enclosed the area entirely, and there was a single entry door with a heavy padlock and chain around it. People were crowded inside, some sitting but most standing. In the dim light, I could make out that the majority were women, with some men as well, and a few who might have been teenagers. They were so thin, their clothes hung off their frames. Cowering with shoulders slumped, all looked fearful—and all had their hands cuffed in front of them.

It's like a horror movie. I swallowed to force down the bile rising in my throat.

Holding the camera on them for a few moments longer, I rotated the phone to capture as much of the warehouse interior as I could. Then I pulled my arm back through the door and allowed it to close quietly.

I rounded the corner of the building and fell back against the cool steel wall. My legs lost their strength, so I slid down until I was sitting on the pavement.

There was no indication that I'd been seen, and the spot where I was sitting was in shadow, so I allowed myself a moment to regroup. The still-functioning part of my brain prompted me to back up the videos and photos I'd taken. The best way I could think of to do that was to send them to Banshee. I emailed them to her and dropped my phone back into my pocket.

What on God's earth had I stumbled into? The fact that all those imprisoned people were at the port might indicate that they had come in or were preparing to go out by sea. The Rocky Creek Seafood vans might also be used to transport them over land. In any case, it appeared to be a much larger operation than would be required to supply a local prostitution ring. Banshee had been right—these were *not* people I wanted to confront.

I slapped myself lightly on the cheeks to get the blood flowing to my head. It was time to get out of here.

Using the wall for support, I pushed myself to my feet and tested out my legs. They were still shaky but functional. Rather than risk going past the open garage door again, I decided to go behind the warehouse, walk a block beyond it, and then turn back toward the main road, calling Finn along the way.

The tension began to drain from my body as I

crossed the road behind the warehouse and stepped out of sight, walking along the far side of a similar building. It also appeared to be lit up inside, though not quite as bustling. It could have been a legitimate business, but for all I knew, there might be more than one criminal enterprise operating on the quay. Just to be safe, I made my way quietly, staying as much as I could in the dark.

Having walked past the second warehouse without getting caught, a feeling of light hysteria took hold. One more turn, one more three-block sprint, and I would be safe back on the main street. Quickly, I rounded the corner to the left, heading for freedom.

Bam!

I slammed into something and felt myself falling backward. But two hands gripped my upper arms, stopping me in midair. I looked up to find that I had run directly into a wall of a man who was now lifting me into a standing position.

"Who's that?" a deep voice called from behind him.

The wall-like man kept one hand on my arm but took a step back. Now they both peered at me.

"Oh, I'm sorry!" I forced a smile. "I didn't mean to run into you. Thanks for… you know—" I gestured toward his hand, which still gripped my arm. "—catching me. I didn't hurt you, did I?"

My question, meant to be ridiculous enough to elicit a smile, did not have the desired effect. Their startled curiosity transformed into something sharper.

"What are you doing here?" The second man was a head taller than me and a head shorter than his partner.

"I'm so sorry," I apologized again, thinking fast. "I'm lost. Maybe you gentlemen can help me. I got separated from my tour group. Can you tell me how to get to the main road from here?"

"Your tour group?" The men exchanged skeptical glances.

It had not escaped my attention that the wall-like man had not loosened his grip on my arm. When formulating my alibi, I'd forgotten what a woeful liar I was. With a light laugh, I tried, "It was my fault. I slipped away from them around dinnertime. I wanted to go on an authentic Irish pub crawl, and the rest of them just wanted to get to bed early. As you can see, though"—I swept my free arm around me—"I got a bit off course."

"A bit?" the second man asked. "What do you say, Keto? Does 'a bit' describe it?"

"More than a bit, I'd say, Ace."

They weren't using each other's real names. I took that as a bad sign.

In desperation, I tried batting my eyelashes. "Exactly! Any help you can give me, I would really appreciate."

"Would you now?" Ace sidled up close to me, taking me by the other arm. "How appreciative would you be?"

"Yeah," Keto chimed in. "No pubs here, but *we* could pour you a drink."

"That's right, plenty of drinks inside." Ace smiled at me then, but he also licked his lips.

I tried to step back, putting tension on their grips. "Thanks, but no, I'm afraid not. The tour group is waiting for me. They'll call the police if I don't show up in the next few minutes. That's why I need to get back to the main road."

"I don't know about that now." Ace brought his face uncomfortably close to mine and squinted. "You see, this is private property, and not only are you trespassing, I think there's a strong possibility you're lying."

Good grief. Something was betraying me—either my horrible poker face or my nerves. I thought about pulling out my "union rep" or "reporter" identities, but it felt like changing my story at that stage would only further damage my credibility. "I'm telling you the truth, I swear! I just need some help—"

"All right, calm yourself," Ace said, stepping back again. "Maybe you are telling us the truth."

"I don't think so, Ace," Keto added, once again the picture of helpfulness.

"Come now," Ace replied, "she might be. But I think we should take her back to the office, check into her story. Don't you agree, Keto? Just to be safe."

My growing fear must have shown on my face, because Keto grinned like a shark that smelled blood in the water. "Yeah, I agree. Just to be safe."

"That's totally unnecessary," I said, voice rising, as they began to walk along the back of the warehouse, dragging me between them. "I didn't realize this was private property, honestly! I'm a tourist; I'm not from here!" I was slowing their progress, trying to keep my feet planted, so they tightened their grips on my arms and lifted me off the ground.

Damn, they're strong, I thought as my feet swung through empty air.

My instincts yelled at me to kick and scream. With these two, though, I doubted attacking them physically would end well for me. And since I hadn't seen another soul around, if I drew attention to myself, it could easily come from the Blackbird thugs and their colleagues. Getting involved with that crowd could take me from whatever frying pan I was currently in and throw me directly into the fire.

Unable to think of any other options, I just kept arguing. "Call the police," I pleaded, purposefully using the wrong word for the gardaí to underline my "tourist" status. "Have them come down here and charge me with trespassing if you like. At least then I'll be out of your hair. I really need to get in touch with the tour group. I just want to go back to the hotel. I'm so sorry about all of this!"

"If you're lying to us," Ace snapped, "you'll be even sorrier soon!"

By now, we had crossed the street and were approaching a small door that led into yet another warehouse. The well-known kidnapping survival advice ran through my head: "Never let them take you to a second location." My heart sank as Keto jerked the door open and they thrust me inside.

CHAPTER 15
CON

THIS FECKING CHAIR. GROANING, CON SHIFTED AGAIN, trying to find a slightly less painful position on the too-small, too-hard metal chair Davies and Company had given him. It didn't work, though. He would just have to endure it.

Con's ability to focus was going, but still he tried to read up on the surgery. At least he'd already reviewed the materials a few times and felt confident he could perform a nephrectomy without killing the patient. He also had some idea what to expect, having assisted with a similar surgery while in medical school.

Not that he had any intention of operating. But if his hand was forced somehow, since Davies was so proud of his vast experience doing these illegal chop-shop procedures, Con hoped he would prove useful, if not do most of the work.

He had no idea where he was. The driver who'd picked him up at the airport made him put on a blindfold before leaving, and it felt like he'd taken Con the long way to wherever they were now. He had tried to keep track of the turns and distances, but the driver had gone in circles, either to confuse him or kill time, Con didn't know which. Once inside what appeared to be a warehouse, they had removed his blindfold. Davies had greeted him before stashing him in the office so Con could "study." Meanwhile, the Brickhaven crew had begun setting up while they awaited the donor's arrival.

Since the office was up a staircase and had windows, from where he was, Con had a good view of the warehouse interior. There appeared to be a dozen security guards and four other people setting up a makeshift surgical suite. He had been observing the security guards' movements, figuring out their blind spots and getting familiar with the exits.

A plan was forming in his mind. The surgical suite was close to the staircase leading up to the office. Its four walls were large metal frames hung with blue curtains. The sink was located along an outer wall of the warehouse, just under the staircase.

They had brought Con in through an exterior door just next to the sink. Once the surgical suite's walls were assembled, the security guards had all but abandoned that corner of the warehouse. Maybe they assumed that the folks preparing for the surgery were keeping an eye on things. Con had been observing that crew, who appeared to be medical professionals of one stripe or another rather than hard men. Most likely, then, if he showed up ready to operate, they wouldn't view him with automatic suspicion if he stepped away to scrub up.

Once he got to the sink, he would start the water running to cover the sound of the exterior door opening and closing behind him as he slipped outside. Scrubbing properly took time, so he would be able to get some distance away before his absence was discovered, or at least get his bearings and find a hiding place.

That was the plan, at least.

Con had a couple of things working in his favor. While he hadn't let on to anyone, the arm he kept in the sling had improved to the point where he almost had full use of it. He estimated that if needed, he could get a good few punches in before the shoulder gave out on him. Also, he knew Davies was arrogant as hell and way too sure of himself. If Con played along until Davies was convinced he would operate, he was fairly certain his colleague wouldn't even consider the possibility that he'd been deceived. Liam was another matter, of course, but thankfully, Con hadn't spotted that shitehawk yet.

There was only one more thing he needed, and that was to check his messages at the hotel. If he was going to pull off this escape, he first needed to be certain that Neve was safe and sound.

He heard someone climbing the stairs, opening the door. It was Davies again, and he looked quite pleased with himself.

What now? Con rubbed his tired eyes.

"All going well?" Davies asked, sounding positively chipper.

"A bit more to do, but yes."

"Not too much, I hope. I just got a call. The donor will be here shortly."

"Right." Con sighed and stretched. "I need to use a phone, then. I'm expecting a message at the hotel."

"Don't worry," Davies said with a smug grin. "We picked that one up for you. From Neve, I presume?" He pulled a piece of paper from his shirt pocket and dropped it on the rickety desk.

The day he saw Davies either dead or in prison could not come soon enough.

Con opened the paper and read the note.

FROM: HERSELF. MESSAGE: MISSING YOU.

Time stopped.

Con stared at the paper and read it again. He was so exhausted, he had to review his memory of his conversation with the White House answering service several times before he could trust that he was taking the correct meaning from the message.

Things had not gone to plan.

Neve is not safe.

"What, it's not from Neve?" Davies teased, flirting with death. "In that case, you're going to be in hot water when you get home, my friend!"

His friend? A dark fantasy of throttling Davies until his eyes popped out of his head sped to the forefront of Con's thoughts. But he couldn't allow his temper to get the better of him. Not now. Not yet.

Shite and onions. He was going to have to do the goddamned surgery after all. *Thank God for Banshee,* he thought as he reached into his pocket, reassuring himself that his special cigarette lighter was still there. "Don't worry about me," he told Davies. "It's from Neve. Just wanted to make sure her trip was all right."

"Of course."

If Davies didn't stop grinning at him…. Con needed to be in a different room from this man. "I need a smoke before we get started."

That wiped the smile from Davies's face. Amazing that the man had no trouble with trafficking people and their organs but disapproved of a fellow doctor smoking cigarettes. "I didn't know you smoked."

In fact, Con didn't smoke anymore. He'd done so as a teen, but not since. Now seemed like an excellent time to start up again, though. "Only on occasion." Con took out the pack he had purchased earlier and tapped it against his palm, packing the tobacco at the tips. "I find it calming."

"Oh." He could see Davies doing some mental calculations before concluding that it was also in his best interest for Con to remain calm. "No problem. Whenever you're ready."

"Five more minutes to review. Then I'll be down."

Davies nodded. "Sounds good."

When he was alone once again, Con's mind raced. Where could Neve be? What had happened? Banai didn't strike him as the type to drop the ball. If the plane had been delayed for some reason, no doubt he would have put her on another one—wouldn't he? Unless she had fallen ill suddenly. Was she all right? How could he find out?

Con cursed himself. He couldn't ring her, or ring anyone else to ask after her, because his phone was still being monitored. Davies believed she'd flown home, at least, and Con wanted to keep Brickhaven under that impression for as long as possible. He raked his fingernails over his scalp. Where the hell could she be?

Jaysus wept. He would have to do this damn surgery, then get away as quickly as possible and find Neve. Then he would contact Banai so they could both get back to the US and he could turn in the evidence he was about to gather on Brickhaven before anything else went sideways.

Con took a few more moments to collect himself. It was time to focus. Then he made his way down the stairs, where Davies met him.

"The donor is here. These gentlemen need a smoke break as well." Davies nodded at the two security guards approaching. "They'll show you where to go."

He followed them outside into the night air. A

light drizzle had begun to fall. He turned his face upward and allowed the rain to cool his skin. Con took his time opening his pack, looking around to get his bearings. The lights illuminated the skyline of the city to their left. In front of them, the river was wide with a building in the middle, so there was an island. Across the water, there was a wall of lights that dimmed as they rose, indicating a large hill. They must be on the south side of Cork Harbour, then, near Kennedy Quay if not on it.

"You smokin' or what?" one of the security guards asked.

Con pulled a cigarette out of the pack and set it between his lips. Then he held up his special lighter, flicking it a few times before a flame appeared. *It's on,* he thought as he held the flame to the tip and sucked a bit of smoke into his mouth. He tried to make it look like he was inhaling without actually doing so, but some of the smoke made it down into his lungs anyway, prompting a bout of coughing.

Con smiled at the security guards. "It's been a while."

Thankfully, they laughed at him, loosening up a bit.

He puffed away until about half the cigarette was gone, then followed the others in dropping it on the ground and stubbing it out with his heel. A dirty way to dispose of a cigarette, but he was more concerned with blending in.

Inside, a woman wearing a blue paper apron was helping Davies scrub up in the sink under the staircase. Wistfully, Con recalled his now-defunct escape plan.

"Con, this is Nadia. She's one of our nurses. The patient is being prepped."

Con nodded at her, and she nodded back, expressionless. He couldn't help wondering if she was here against her will, just as he was. He waited his turn, then accepted Nadia's help scrubbing up, leaving off his sling so it wouldn't get in his way.

He followed Nadia inside the surgical suite. Sure enough, their patient was there, lying on the gurney with a large oxygen mask over his face, already out cold.

The sight shocked Con to his core. The patient's body was bare but for his briefs, which were pulled down low on his hips. He was emaciated and must have been freezing, but no one had covered him with so much as a sheet. As though nothing was amiss, another nurse was checking the patient's IV while Davies looked over the surgical tools, which were laid out on a tray.

The deep anger that had been festering inside Con ever since Davies first put him in this situation began to roil. He stepped close to Davies, working hard to rein in his temper. "What the hell is this?"

Davies glanced at him, surprised at first. Then he took in Con's expression and shook his head. "I know it's not what you're used to."

Con took a step back so he wouldn't stab Davies with a scalpel. "That's one hell of an understatement."

In a voice heavy with sarcasm, Davies asked, "Tell me, Dr. O'Brien, what is not to your satisfaction?"

Now they had drawn the attention of both nurses. *You must keep Neve safe,* Con reminded himself as he took a beat to calm down. As he thought through every aspect of this sick situation and how horrific it was, he realized Brickhaven simply didn't give a damn about anything but their own agenda. Still, he would list the problems he saw for the benefit of the recording. "It's bad enough that you're forcing me to harvest organs from a human trafficking victim—"

"I've told you, we don't like to use that term—"

"—but you didn't tell me the man was starving. It might not be safe to operate."

"I looked over his blood work myself. He's perfectly fine."

"And not only are we in unsanitary conditions here, but it's freezing, and you haven't even given the man a sheet or the dignity of covering him up. Besides which, he's already out, so I can't talk to him—"

"And why would you want to talk to him, Con?" Davies's expression began to harden. "To establish consent? Trust me, that's not something you need to worry about."

Con reckoned he had gathered enough damning information. If he pushed further, he might raise suspicions. "Fuck you, Davies."

"Ah," Davies said casually as he turned back to the tray, "speaking from the amygdala. That's fine; probably good to release those emotions before you operate. Just be sure to get back into your prefrontal cortex by the time we begin."

He was trapped, well and truly cornered. Nothing left to do but admit it. Now he had to do the best he could for the poor bastard on the gurney. Pushing back a cresting wave of worries about what had happened to Neve, Con walked over to examine the patient.

Just when he thought it wasn't possible to be more horrified….

"What the…!" He stepped back, bumping into

Davies. Starting on the patient's left lower abdomen and angling up toward his back was the telltale scar of a previous nephrectomy.

"What is it now?" Davies snapped, joining him at the bedside.

Con turned to stare murder at his so-called colleague. "This man only has one kidney!"

Wearing the same long-suffering look he'd given Liam so often the night before, Davies shook his head. "Again, not our concern."

"Not our *concern*?" He took another step back as rage pumped through him. "You're asking me to kill a man!"

"Don't be dramatic." Davies waved a dismissive hand. "He could live for decades on dialysis."

"You're asking me to believe that having bought his freedom with his remaining kidney and returned to his home country, this man will somehow find the means to pay for decades of dialysis—provided he even makes it back alive?"

Davies rolled his eyes heavenward. "Con, this is not the time—"

"No, this is not what we agreed!" Con thundered. "Your whole pitch was that we'd be saving two lives, not taking one. Get out of my operating room!" he shouted at the security guard who had poked his head inside their space.

Davies nodded, and the guard withdrew. Evidently unaware of the peril he faced, Davies stepped closer to Con. In a conspiratorial tone, he murmured, "Whatever was said last night, the reality is this: If you play ball, you can pay off your debt and Neve's. If you fail, though, it's open season on you both." Then he took a step back and held his hands up in surrender. "I don't like to be crass, but I think it's only fair to you that we're a hundred percent clear about the stakes here."

Con stared at Davies, trying with all his might to refrain from strangling the man, when suddenly they heard shouting. It sounded like two men's voices, and a woman's.

His heart tumbled. *Wait, is that…?*

Davies's eyes widened. "What the hell is going on?"

"Neve?" Con called out.

"Con!"

It was her. It was definitely her.

The jolt of joy Con felt at hearing her voice, knowing she was alive, was quickly overshadowed by a dark cloud of dread.

He had to get her the hell out of here.

CHAPTER 16
CON

Con pushed Davies aside as he bolted out of the surgical suite. He got about twenty feet in the direction of Neve's voice before he was grabbed by two security guards. He dragged them along ten feet more before two more guards caught up to them. The four of them held him in place as he shouted again, "Neve, are you all right?"

Now the people around him were also shouting, scrambling. He strained to hear Neve's voice through the din. He didn't have long to wait, though. Soon, two other security guards appeared, holding Neve between them.

She looked angry, confused, and terrified—but unharmed, thank God.

She's okay, he thought, looking her over. *Jaysus, my heart.*

Davies caught up and inserted himself between them. "I ask again, what the hell is going on?"

There was a circle of security guards around them now. Con's thoughts whirred. How and why was Neve here? Judging from the shock on Davies's face, her presence wasn't Brickhaven's doing. Why wasn't she on a plane, then?

And why was she dressed like a ninja? Neve's hair was pulled back in a ponytail, and she wore all black, including her runners. Her clothes were so close-fitting that he could make out the shape of her phone in the waistband of her leggings.

"Get these arseholes off us," Con demanded.

Davies must have done the math and concluded the two of them posed no threat. "Let them go," he barked, and the security guards released them.

Con gave Davies a nod and walked up to Neve. As they gaped at each other, he couldn't stop himself from touching her, just to be certain she was here and she was whole. He placed his hand gently on her shoulder, sliding it down until her hand was in his. Meeting her eyes, he tried to communicate the gravity of the question as he asked, "Neve, what are you doing here? I thought you'd gone home."

She stared at him, then flicked her gaze toward Davies and back again. He could nearly hear the wheels turning as she searched for words. Finally, she settled on "I changed my mind. I decided to"—she glanced at the security guards on either side of her—"join a tour group so I could see more of the city." Neve finished off her explanation with an apologetic smile.

That couldn't be true. Could it? No, it couldn't. Neve wouldn't have promised him she was going home only to turn around and….

Con's mind flashed back to their trip to Galway. He had tried to leave her at his parents' house, but halfway to Killarney, he discovered Neve had decided to come with him after all, stowing away in the back of his SUV.

They had talked about that, though. She'd promised not to do anything like that again, and he'd believed her. They had also agreed to talk through any disagreements in future—although he had certainly dropped the ball on that this morning. Still, she had agreed to give him a "freebie," as she'd put it. He trusted Neve enough to know that something else must be going on. Whatever it was, he would help her by playing along.

Con squeezed her hand. "If you wanted to stay,

you should have called me."

Neve flashed him a grateful look, telling him she knew what he was doing. "Yeah, but you would have objected, so…." She smiled and shrugged.

A red-faced Davies tried to speak, but Con held his hand up. "Hang on." He turned back to Neve. "But why are you here? As in *here*?" He pointed at the ground.

"Oh! Well." She laughed lightly. "Funny story. Everyone else in the tour group wanted to go to bed early, but I slipped away to go on a pub crawl. I was looking for that brewery you told me about—Calfwood, isn't it? It's around here, right? But I got lost and was wandering around when, um, Keto and Ace here found me outside and agreed to help me find my way back to the main road."

Keto and Ace looked as surprised by Neve's innocent description of their involvement as Con was, but he gave them an appreciative nod. "Thank you, gentlemen."

"Indeed, thank you," Davies said. Ace and Keto gave him thumbs-up gestures, verifying Neve's story. Davies smiled at her with jarring warmth. "I'm sorry to hear about your troubles this evening. It sounds like you've had quite an adventure."

"You could say that." She smiled back. "But what

are *you* doing here?" Having spun her tall tale, Neve directed her inquiry at both Con and Davies.

"A fair question," Davies replied as he nodded at Con, shooting him a subtle but sharp look. He was leaving it in Con's hands, then.

Everything Con did from that moment on had to be geared toward one goal: getting them both out of here. He had no idea what had brought her to the warehouse, but now Neve had seen it. She knew where it was located, and who knew what else she might have seen or overheard? She was too much of a liability now for Brickhaven to simply let her go. Con knew that whatever Davies might say, Neve wouldn't be out of danger until he took her to safety himself.

The bones of a plan began to click into place. "Well," he began, "Davies here runs a humanitarian clinic." With a sweep of his arm, Con indicated the paper aprons he and Davies were wearing, as well as the surgical suite behind them. "It's busy this week, so he asked for my help."

"Oh!" Neve looked around her. She had enough cop-on not to appear skeptical about the existence of a humanitarian clinic located in a warehouse populated largely by security guards. "Why didn't you tell me?"

It was Con's turn to look grateful. "It's a secret clinic," he freewheeled. "They treat vulnerable people who need their identities protected. That's why I wasn't free to explain earlier. But now that you know...." He held a finger up to his lips.

"Oh, of course," she said, the picture of sincerity. To Davies, she promised, "Your secret's safe with me."

"Much appreciated, Neve," Davies replied.

They were all playacting now.

"Well," Davies said, "if we're all done here, Con and I have patients to see, don't we, Con? Neve, I'm sure Ace and Keto here would be more than happy to take you back to your hotel."

The last thing he wanted was to leave Neve in the hands of those goons. But if they took her outside, Con could follow and steal her away from them. Two goons, he could handle.

Nodding to indicate the desired reply, he asked her, "Does that suit?"

She chewed on her lip for a moment, considering. "Um, sure, yes. Although, I changed hotels, so...."

That revelation threatened to disrupt Con's composure. Had she intended to conceal her presence in the city from him? "You're welcome to stay with me."

Whatever she was feeling, she covered it with a bright smile. "Okay, then!"

"Glad that's settled!" Davies clapped his hands together. "Keto and Ace, will you please take Miss Keane to the place where she'll be staying?"

The two men nodded, their expressions deadly serious. Something in Davies's tone told Con that "the place where she'll be staying" was code for somewhere else, somewhere Brickhaven could hold her.

"Look after her," Con instructed them. "Neve, I'll see you at the hotel later."

"Okay." She waved and smiled, walking with the two guards toward the exit at the front of the warehouse. "Sorry for intruding!"

The security guards disbanded, returning to their posts, as Davies turned to Con. "It's unfortunate that you have so much trouble controlling your woman, my friend."

Con knew the next step would be Davies telling him Brickhaven would control Neve *for* him, and he had no desire to hear what that might entail. He needed to get out the door to her quickly. "Can we get on with it, please?"

As they walked back toward the surgical suite, Davies asked, "No more objections to removing the kidney, then?"

Con huffed. "Not as long as you let me scrub up again. On the off chance the patient makes it home and gets on dialysis, I'll be damned if I'll be the reason he dies from infection."

With a sick laugh, Davies clapped him on the back. "All right, Dr. O'Brien, have it your way. Nadia?" he called.

The nurse popped her head out from between the walls of the surgical suite, but Con waved her off. "I can wash my own damn hands!"

"All right, all right. See you in there."

The second Davies stepped inside the curtain walls and out of sight, Con pushed his mind into laser-like focus. First, he turned on the sink. Tearing off his paper apron, he draped it over the faucet so it fell into the stream of water, creating an irregular flow so it would sound more like hands were being washed.

Then he looked around for something to use as a weapon. A stack of steel rods of the type used to construct the frame of the surgical suite were piled against the wall. He found one about three feet in length and painstakingly pulled it out so as not to send the rest of the rods rolling across the floor. Then he pulled out his phone and tucked it behind the stack. *Track this, you bastards.*

With the sink running and a weapon in hand, he

went to the door under the staircase and slipped outside.

He heard Neve before he saw her. Con headed toward the sound of her voice at the front of the warehouse, where she seemed to be having an argument with Ace and Keto.

"...I don't see why, when I can call a taxi," she said.

"Just come with us, please," one of the men replied. "The boss told us to take you."

It sounded like the two men were trying hard to get her into their car without making a scene. No doubt Davies wanted them to get Neve off the premises without further upsetting Con so he would complete the surgery. Then Brickhaven would have their "collateral" on him and be able to control them both.

"But if you just direct me to the road, a taxi can take me the rest of the way," Neve said. "I'm sure driving people around the city is below your pay grade."

That's my girl, Con thought as he peered around the corner where they stood in front of a gray sedan. One of the men had his back to Con, and the other was off to one side. Neve was facing Con, but if she saw him, her expression didn't betray the fact.

There was no time to waste. He had to drop both of these feckers, and he had to do it on the first hit, before they had a chance to raise the alarm.

Tapping into the rage that had been building inside him for the past twenty-four hours, Con raised the steel rod. Using his good arm for power and his injured one for stability, he whacked the first man on the back of the head as hard as he could. The blow made a satisfying cracking noise, and the man crumpled to the ground. As Neve's mouth dropped open, the other guard put together what was happening and began to reach for the handgun strapped to his side. He didn't move quickly enough, though, and Con had the advantage of surprise. By the time the man's hand reached his weapon, Con had already slammed him across the temple with the rod. The guard listed to the side and fell hard.

That left Con and Neve alone on the street, but only for the moment. They had to get away quickly, before someone came out to check on them. The quickest option would be to take the sedan, but knowing Brickhaven, it likely had a tracker installed. It would be safer to start out on foot.

Once they were discovered to be missing, the Brickhaven crowd would no doubt expect them to head toward the main road leading into the city. Con grabbed a wide-eyed Neve by the hand and pulled her down the alley in the opposite direction, toward the river.

Once she recovered from her shock, Neve's gait matched his and she ran alongside. They ducked in and out of the shadows and managed to put three more warehouses between themselves and the goons before they heard shouts behind them.

Having reached the river, they rounded the corner of the last building, and Con pulled Neve into a blackened doorway. He held her against him, listening to the shouts in the distance, the gush of the river flowing, and the jagged sounds of their breaths.

Neve clung to him. Their chests heaved together as they panted, then slowed as their breathing began to normalize. They heard the growl of engines as a couple of vehicles drove from the warehouse they had fled in the direction of the city and away from them.

Thank Christ.

Con felt Neve's heart beating against his rib cage. She was alive, and she was okay.

The sound of the river rushing along had a soothing quality, and the lights of the city danced on the water. The iconic Port of Cork sign was lit up like a welcome at the end of Custom House Quay. Clouds rushed across the swollen moon as though they were late for something. If they had taken a tour of the brewery, this could have been quite a romantic spot to spend the rest of the evening—if their lives weren't in danger, that was.

Goddamned Davies.

Suddenly, Neve began to shake like a leaf. The adrenaline was leaving her body. Con gave her arms and shoulders a series of brisk rubs. "You all right?"

Brave as always, she nodded. "Yeah, I've just never…. Keep doing that, please…. I mean, you hit those guys really hard." Her next whispered question drifted up to his ears. "Who were they?"

No reason to hide the truth from her now. She needed to know what they were up against. "Brickhaven," he whispered back.

"Oh," she gasped.

He tightened his arms around her. "So, if you're asking if I killed them, I don't know, and frankly I don't care."

Neve nodded again. Slowly, the intensity of her shaking lessened. "Why were you wearing that apron?"

"They wanted me to remove a kidney. They're selling organs on the black market. The donors are supplied by a trafficking ring."

"Good God!" Neve melted against him in horror.

He pulled her even closer. Con knew well how strong she was, but that didn't stop him from wanting to shield her from every ugly, evil thing on earth. "Why were *you* really there?"

"Same thing, sort of. I found out Ghost Girl was killed by human traffickers—probably the same ones, since I tracked them to a warehouse next to the one you were in. My God, what are the odds?"

That must be why she stayed. Con should have known Neve would have only broken her promise to him because she was trying to save someone, or in this case, a group of someones. "Pretty high, I would hope, given the size of Cork," he pointed out. "If it's home to more than one major human trafficking outfit, then the city's in more trouble than I thought."

She shuddered. "Con, there were *dozens*...." Her voice melted into tears.

Con leaned down and kissed a line across her forehead. "We'll do what we can for them."

Sniffling, she said, "Okay."

Although he already had the gist, he asked, "So, this is why you didn't fly home?"

Neve nodded, fisting his shirt. "I had to stop Kayla from investigating on her own."

Of course. Those two were far too much alike. "Is she all right?"

"Yeah."

Con placed a firm but gentle kiss on the top of her head. "And you?"

"I am now." He felt her smile against his chest. "How about you?"

"I will be, once we get out of here."

Neve pulled away slightly, creating a couple of inches of air between them. "I have the number of a taxi we can call."

But before Con could consider that option, they heard more shouts—this time closer to where they were hiding. Neve's whole body tensed.

"We can't go to the main road," he concluded. "They'll be looking for us there. I have an idea, though. Follow me."

They crept along the buildings by the wharf. Neve stayed just behind him, holding on to the back of his shirt. He was reassured by the tug, by feeling her here with him.

Two long buildings later, they stood in front of a tall cement structure, painted white with a prominent sign near the roof that read "Calfwood Brewery."

Neve peered up. "Eamonn's place?"

Con nodded. "Let's go."

They went to the far end of the building and turned the corner. Con found a side door and began pounding on it. He was determined to either draw someone to them or break the door down trying.

Finally, the door swung open from the inside. Their hands flew up to protect their eyes from the powerful flashlight shining in their faces.

"Who are you?" a man's voice demanded.

"Drop the fecking light!"

The man did as asked, pointing it toward the ground. He was dressed casually, more like a regular employee than a security guard.

"I'm Eamonn O'Brien's brother, Con, and this is my girlfriend, Neve," Con explained, keeping his voice low. "Can you let us in?"

"Of course." The man opened the door wider, allowing Neve to step inside. He squinted at Con. "Eamonn told us to expect you, but I'm afraid it won't be much of a tour at this hour."

"We're not here for a tour," Con said, eyes darting around as they heard more shouts. "We need help."

The man straightened up, eyes sharpening. "Tell me."

He was ready for action, and with no questions asked. This was a friend of Eamonn's for sure.

Con did a quick calculation. He could hide in the brewery with Neve. It would be the last place on the docks Brickhaven would look, since they wouldn't expect them to hide out in a spot Neve had said she'd planned to visit. But look they would, and they would find them eventually. His best hope of keeping her safe would be to stash her in the brewery and lead them away. And if they caught him, he could misdirect them about Neve's whereabouts, buying her time.

He also needed to do everything he could to make sure the surgery didn't go forward. Although Con had never spoken to the man on the gurney, he still thought of him as his own patient. If not legally, then morally and ethically, he felt the weight of a duty of care.

From where he still stood outside the door, Con grabbed the man by the arm. "Hide her," he commanded. "Keep her hidden no matter what. You didn't see us. Call Eamonn; you can give her to him."

To his credit, the man didn't even flinch. With grim determination, he replied, "Sure thing."

"And call 999, tell them there's a huge fire at the warehouses. Neve will tell you where they are." Even if the people who responded to the call were in Brickhaven's pocket, they would jump to attention when they heard the warehouses were at risk of destruction. If nothing else, fire trucks, gardaí, and a crowd of first responders would descend on the place. It was even possible the victims would be rescued, but at the very least, the chaos would ensure the surgery didn't go forward. It would buy the patient some time, at least.

"No bother."

Neve watched their exchange, confusion etched across her face.

"Call Banai," Con told her. "Tell him what's going on, and tell him not to trust the gardaí. Until he can get someone to you, do what this man says, or Eamonn. Got it?"

"Wait, what?" She reached for him. "Where are you—"

But he couldn't wait around and explain it to her. The shouts were getting closer.

Cursing his life, Con pulled the door closed, shutting out the sound of Neve's voice, and ran.

CHAPTER 17
NEVE

Eamonn's office inside the brewery had an industrial function-over-form feel to it, but it was comfortable. I curled up on the couch with my phone while Alex, a brewmaster at Calfwood, sat at the desk and monitored security cameras on the computer. Nursing coffees, we stewed quietly in our sullen détente.

After he met us at the door and then locked me inside once Con left, Alex and I had exchanged words. But he had proven to be as stubborn as I was —why, I had no idea, since he didn't know Con and me from Adam. I realized he was just trying to help, though, and he did make a good point: If Con was trying to evade someone, his chances would be better if he were alone. He would be more nimble on his own, and it would be easier for him to find adequate places to hide.

That didn't stop my stomach from churning, though. I told myself to wait, hang on, keep the faith. But the more time that passed without spotting Con on the cameras or hearing him at the door, the more despair nipped at my spirits.

After making the 999 call Con had requested and reporting "massive fires" at the warehouses, Alex had called Eamonn. I could tell by the way they talked that they were close. That at least explained why Alex had been so determined to follow Con's directions. I spoke to Eamonn as well, and once I started talking, information came spilling out of me at an alarming rate. Eventually, he stopped me and told me to wait and tell him the rest when he arrived. He was in Sligo, where he and his fiancée, Ciara, were taking a few days away, so it would be about four hours before he could reach us. I hated that they had to break up their vacation after all they'd gone through lately with Mad Max, but I was also grateful to know he was on his way. It would be good to see a familiar face, and to be with someone who loved Con as much as I did—someone who wouldn't give up until he was safe.

After that, I did everything else I could think of to get help. First, I called Agent Banai and filled him in as much as I could on what was happening. He said he would reach out to the US government's contacts in Ireland to request help on the ground. He suggested they could send me some protection and support first responders at the warehouses at the same time, hopefully saving Con's patient and the other victims before it was too late. He also promised to get help finding Con, but he pointed out that human traffickers were experts at keeping themselves and their cargo hidden. In the event that they caught Con and took him anywhere other than the warehouse, he warned me that it might take time to find him and advised me to be patient.

That was the very last thing I wanted to hear, as was his offer to put a private jet on standby at Cork Airport to fly me back to the US. I told him I wasn't leaving without Con. He sounded disappointed but not surprised, then asked if I thought Kayla was at risk. I told him she wasn't before, but since she knew Con and me and we had just pissed off some very serious criminals, I couldn't be certain anymore. Agent Banai said he would activate a protective detail for her and consult with President Duran about the possibility of bringing her home.

My next call was to Banshee. Alex raised his eyebrows when I greeted her by name but quickly went back to monitoring cameras when I launched into yet another explanation of the trouble we were in. Chipper and resourceful even in the dead of night, Banshee asked me for the locations of the warehouses. Alex chipped in then, having already reported their exact whereabouts to the emergency response line.

Banshee said she could scan the videos I'd sent her for any other information she might need to muck up the warehouses' electricity and Wi-Fi. She also said she would try to listen in on their devices for any news about Con. Since she had the license plate number of the Gang of Four's vehicle, she offered to disable their van as well. I told her to do her worst.

Those phone calls only took up the first hour, though, and waiting around was doing my head in. I asked Alex if I could wander around the brewery, and he agreed. He took me on a mini tour of the staff kitchen, the pub, and the tasting room—all areas with no windows. After reminding me that only *he* could operate the outer door locks and making me repeat back to him how to return to Eamonn's office, Alex left me on my own.

Under such distressing circumstances, Alex's stern, no-nonsense approach rubbed me the wrong way. But it also reminded me of Con, so I couldn't really bring myself to dislike the guy.

I had settled into the pub, a spacious room with an enormous bar. The floor was peppered with tall tables and stools, and leather booths lined the walls. I poured myself a ginger ale, sat in one of the booths, and stared at my phone, waiting for someone to call with news.

When boredom got the better of me, I started scrolling through my phone. The photos I'd taken of Thomas and his taxi almost made me smile. I began watching the videos I had taken at the warehouse, but it proved too upsetting in the context of my current powerlessness.

Then the sharp corner of something poked my finger. The business card from Rose, the psychic medium, was falling out of my phone case. I looked it over for a long time, considering. Given the comforting information Con had shared with my drunken self in our hotel room the other night, I felt a bit more ready to hear whatever message Rose wanted to give me about my medical tests.

Before I lost my courage, I shot off a text to her, then jumped when she replied right away. Rose said that she was a night owl, too, and offered to talk.

Figuring it would be a good distraction if nothing else, I called her.

"Neve, it's lovely to hear from you!" She did sound wide awake.

"You really are a night owl? I didn't disturb you?"

"Not at all! I'm delighted to talk to someone. This is usually a lonely time of day to be up and about."

Her voice was as warm and sincere as I remembered.

"Well, I was just calling because you said you had received a message for me."

"Yes, I did, about your medical tests. I wrote it down as soon as I got home from the coffee shop so I wouldn't forget anything. Can you hold on a moment?"

"Of course."

While she was away from the phone, I couldn't help laughing at myself. Here I was in Cork, Ireland, hiding from human traffickers in a brewery while Con was out God knew where, running from them. The Secret Service was organizing multiple rescues for everyone involved, Con's brother was driving down from Sligo, and what was I doing? Calling a psychic about my biopsy. The absurdity of it struck me all at once, and I was still laughing when Rose got back to the phone.

"Neve, are you okay?"

"Yes, I'm fine." I pulled myself back into the moment and tried to relax. "There's just a lot going on over here."

"Anything I can help with?"

"Ha!" I wished. "You could tell me everything's going to be all right."

She laughed lightly. "'Everything' is a bit broad, but if you narrow it down…."

Part of me wanted to ask her about Con. Maybe because he didn't believe in psychic phenomena, though, it just felt inappropriate. "Thanks, but maybe you should give me the other message first."

"Sure. Let's see." I heard the crinkling of paper. "Here's what I wrote down that night. A woman came through, connected to you on your father's side. She had an *E* name, and I picked up that she crossed herself over—that usually means a suicide. She showed herself to me holding you as a baby. Does that make sense?"

I felt the pressure of tears forming behind my eyes. Did it make sense? No, it didn't make sense to me at all that a woman who knew nothing about me was talking about my aunt Esther, my father's sister, who had died by suicide before I was a year old. It was my desire to save other families from such tragedies that had inspired me to pursue a career in mental health. I had only spoken about Aunt Esther with my family, Con, and Rosanna. Never had I written or posted about her on social media—nothing Rose could have stumbled across.

One of the details she shared, or even two or three, might be universal. Everyone had a father and at least one woman on their father's side of the family. Even *E* names were common enough. But suicide? And someone who held me as a baby? All those pieces of information, and all put together like that…. It couldn't possibly be a coincidence, or even a lucky guess.

So no, it didn't make sense. In fact, it defied all the rules of reason and logic. Despite that—or maybe because of it—I believed her. I blinked, and tears slid down my cheeks. "Yes, it makes sense."

"Okay," she said, "good to know we're on the right track."

"Is… is she okay?"

"She is. She's happy, and she's at peace. Those things that troubled her in life, she has released."

I swallowed hard, trying to contain the bubble of emotions swelling in my chest. "Thank you for that."

"Of course," she said gently. "So, the next thing I saw was a little boy, maybe three years old."

All at once, disappointment slammed down on me. There were no three-year-old boys in my life, nor had there ever been. And I certainly wasn't going to be having one of my own. Maybe this had been a mistake after all.

Before I had a chance to object, though, Rose continued.

"I wrote down that he was translucent—I could see through him. That usually means it wasn't a spirit but rather a symbol for something. The boy ran in and out of my field of vision, too, which means he represents a possibility, something that may or may not happen. I asked for clarification. That's when the woman told me about your medical tests."

I was officially invested in the reading again. I braced myself, unsure what to expect.

"She said something about infertility, but she said if you want to be a parent, you will have the chance to become one in a nontraditional way. I took that to mean adoption or fostering. But she told me that if you choose that road, it will be long, and there will be multiple obstacles to overcome. It won't be easy, but if you choose to, you can do it. Is this still making sense?"

I swallowed hard. *Infertility: check. Already talked to Con about the possibility of adoption or fostering, including potential difficulties: check.* Barely able to speak, I managed, "Yes."

"Okay. So, with the boy flitting in and out, the spirit was showing me that whether you become a parent is up to you. She was saying you shouldn't feel under pressure to choose one way or the other."

So many feelings were overwhelming me, I could barely think straight. Rose had just touched upon one of my deepest fears: if I didn't become a parent, would I miss out on some crucial aspect of life or fail to fulfill an important part of my destiny? Lessons learned growing up in church still echoed in my subconscious, things like, "Motherhood is a woman's highest calling" and "You can never know real love until you have a child." On top of that, I had always been highly conscientious and worried about making the right choices in life. So there was something profoundly comforting about hearing that this particular choice was being left entirely up to me. That meant no matter what I decided, it would be impossible for me to screw it up. The sense of relief that possibility gave me was enormous—provided Aunt Esther could be believed, that was.

"She also showed me that you're a healer," Rose said. "Is that right?"

"Uh, I don't know. I'm a therapist. I work in psychiatry."

"Right. So, you're a healer, and she said no matter what you choose, your life will be a story of love. All kinds of love. Great love."

Con. As I thought of him, the falling tears turned into a flood.

"The last thing she showed me was a jigsaw puzzle with the final piece being snapped into place. That's how spirits show me that everything in your life lately has happened for a reason, but you might not be able to see the full picture yet. She wants you to trust that there's a bigger purpose, some larger plan at work. That was the last thing she showed me before she pulled her energy back."

Rose must have been used to people crying during her readings, because she waited patiently while I bawled my eyes out. Slowly, I pulled myself together. "I'm sorry."

"Please, don't be."

I took a deep breath and let it go. "What you just told me… it was very emotional. It all resonated with me. It's just going to take me some time to process it, I think."

"Of course. That was a lot."

"Yes. It was great, but a lot. And it got me thinking about my boyfriend, Con. He's gone missing, and I don't know...." The rest of that sentence was too terrifying to articulate.

Fortunately, Rose picked up my thought. "Oh, I'm so sorry. Would you like me to see if Spirit has any insights to share?"

At that point, not only was I completely convinced of Rose's gifts, but I was willing to take advice from anyone, anywhere if it would help me find Con. "Sure, absolutely. Thanks."

I waited on pins and needles, listening to the silence on the other end of the line. After a few minutes, Rose finally spoke. "It's the same woman coming through again, the one with the *E* name. I guess she heard us talking about her!"

We laughed, and it was nice to share a light moment after all the heaviness. "Tell her I said hello!"

"You know you can tell her yourself, right? You can talk to her anytime. She'll hear you."

My hand flew to cover my fluttering heart. "No, I didn't know that. Okay, then. Hi, Aunt Esther!"

"Esther, so that's her name! Well, she says you'll find your boyfriend from above. She's showing me… it looks like she's in the sky, looking down on the lights of the city." She paused for a long moment. "Sorry, Neve, that's all Esther had for me. She's pulled her energy back again."

What the heck, Aunt Esther? "What do you think it means?"

"Honestly, I don't know. It just seemed like she was floating above the city, looking down."

"Which city? Cork?"

"Among the lights I did see the Port of Cork sign lit up, so yes, it must be."

We'll find Con from above? I squeezed my eyes shut, willing my brain to solve the riddle. A random idea sparked. "Was she floating in one place or moving around?"

"She was moving. It was like she was flying."

"How far above the city was she? Are we talking helicopter, airplane, space shuttle?"

"Not that far. Helicopter, maybe."

"And you said she could see the lights of the city, so it was at night?"

"Yes, it was dark. Not completely black, though. Twilight, maybe."

"Good to know. That might help. I'll take it on board." Excitement bubbled through me as my brain began to storm. "Rose, thank you so much. I can't tell you how much this meant to me. You have an incredible gift."

"So do you," she replied. "We all have gifts. I just hope I don't need yours anytime soon!"

I wasn't used to thinking of myself as having a gift. My work had always felt like a calling, not just a job. But Rose was the first person who had ever referred to me as a healer. Meanwhile, her own unique line of work had to be quite challenging. I certainly wished her good mental health. "You and me both."

"And you're most welcome. It was my pleasure. Let me know when you find him?"

"Of course. Thanks again!"

After we said our goodbyes, I leaned back, closed my eyes, and tried to absorb the new feeling I was having. Something light and bright was washing over me, feeding the hopeful part of me—the part where faith still lived.

The messages Rose had given me related to my infertility were complex, and I would have to sort through them later. But the meaning I took for the moment was that I didn't have to put myself under pressure—whatever choice I made, it would turn out okay. That was enough for me to hold on to while I returned to my most urgent task: finding Con.

I did have an idea where to start, but I needed to share it with someone who would help, who *could* help, and who would do so without asking any questions.

Once again, I picked up the phone and dialed Banshee.

CHAPTER 18
CON

Think, think, think. Sitting with his elbows on his knees, head bowed, Con pressed the heels of his palms into his temples as though the pressure might force his brain to find a way out of his predicament.

Thank God the moon was full, or nearly. Otherwise, he wouldn't be able to see anything in the attic of The Close where Liam and crew had stashed him. It was a sizable room with a gable roof that was eight feet high at the center, so he was able to straighten up and move around a bit. Doing so hurt, of course, but everything hurt at this point.

He had managed to lead the Brickhaven boys quite far south of the brewery, but they knew the area better than he did—including the best places to hide, evidently. They had been far from gentle when they finally nabbed him and threw him in the back of a passenger van. But his relief at having shifted them off Neve's trail had numbed the pain, and when they drove him past the warehouses, hearing the sirens and seeing the cascade of lights from first responder vehicles gave him a deep sense of satisfaction. At least they had succeeded in ruining Brickhaven's plans for the night.

After the goons dragged him into the back door of the pub and forced him up the stairs, the pure and visceral desire to see Liam, Davies, and the rest of them *really* die in a fire energized him as he tried to find a way out. There was a single door, and it was solid, as were the floors, the walls, and everything else, he discovered with a grudging sense of respect for whoever built the place. In the middle of the attic, the original roof had been replaced with fixed skylights—made of plexiglass, not glass, unfortunately, as he had discovered in one of his breakout attempts. At least it allowed in the moonlight, and he could even see some stars, including Neve's favorite constellation. Orion hung there in the sky, taunting him.

She was safe, at least. He had to believe that, and from the frustrated conversations he'd overheard between the goons in the van, he had every reason to be hopeful. Con hung on to his instinct that the man who had let them into the brewery was solid, and the knowledge that Neve knew how to handle herself in a crisis. God knew she had more than risen to the occasion in the bizarre situations they'd faced lately. But even back on the psych unit, she was the person her colleagues turned to when a situation became intense and a cool head and gentle hands were required. Even after the stabbing and the anxiety issues that had followed from it, Neve pulled herself together when required, only allowing herself to fall apart later. He hated that she needed to do that, now or ever, but he was grateful for her ability all the same.

When his first round of escape attempts proved futile, he turned to searching the piles of clutter in the attic. It seemed to be a storage space for party supplies, costumes for parades, and holiday decorations—nothing helpful like a crowbar or a brick of C-4. The goons had robbed him of his cigarettes and lighter, so not only had he lost his secret recording, he couldn't even set the place to flame.

At least Con had found one semi-useful thing: a box of glow sticks. He pulled one out and cracked it, tucking the blue light into his shirt pocket as he sat down on a box holding artificial Christmas garlands.

The small light was more of a comfort than anything, but still he was grateful for it.

Think, think, think. By now, Neve would have spoken to Banai, so the cavalry would be on the way. While he hoped Banai would convince her to return to the US and enter protective custody until Brickhaven was well and truly dealt with, knowing Neve, she might refuse to leave Ireland without Con. Maybe once Eamonn arrived, he could talk her into going home, convince her there was nothing she could do for Con that his brother wouldn't also.

Well, by morning, the argument would be moot. If Con didn't get out of that attic, his body would be found somewhere very public. Liam and the other thugs in the van had taken great pleasure in informing Con that since he had proven himself useless to their organization, they had been given the green light not only to kill him by sunrise but to make an example of him. Among those who were in the know, his death would be a warning to those who might think about crossing Brickhaven in the future. To keep any official investigations to a minimum, however, they had been ordered to make it look like a suicide. Liam had nearly salivated as they brainstormed possible methods.

It wasn't in Con's nature to give up, nor was he a

pessimist. He was a realist, however, and the situation was looking fairly grim. For even a splinter of a chance to be with Neve, he would fight tooth and nail to stay alive. But if he failed, at least once he was dead, she would have no reason to stay in Ireland. Banai would finally be able to swoop in and take her out of harm's way.

In the meantime, though, he was going to fight, so he had to figure out what he was working with. Con gave himself a moment to take stock, dropping the walls he normally kept built up around his physical pain and allowing himself to feel everything. With the barest touch, he ran his fingertips over his face, the part of his body that had absorbed most of the blows when Liam and crew finally found him. There wasn't much pain yet—his face felt numb for the most part—but it was already swollen and misshapen, and he definitely had a split lip and an open cut above his eye. He could still open and close one eye, though, so he'd had worse.

Con moved around slowly, checking for other injuries. There would definitely be some bruises and painful ribs from where they'd kicked him when he was down, but no other obvious broken bones, and no additional damage to his gunshot wound or his bad leg. He was fairly lucky on the whole—for now, anyway. As angry as his captors had been about the emergency vehicles showing up at the warehouse, he wouldn't be surprised if they decided to have a bit more fun with him before finishing him off. On the other hand, if they wanted to make it look like a suicide, he supposed they couldn't inflict too much grievous bodily harm before killing him. Unless they planned to drop him from a height; then the fall damage would cover up any preexisting injuries.

When he started to mentally catalog buildings tall enough to facilitate such a drop, Con shook himself. It had been nearly two days since he'd slept, and pain and exhaustion were starting to overtake him. He needed to change focus.

Con couldn't find a way out of the attic, and if he didn't get out before sunrise, they were going to try to kill him. He might be able to fight his way free of them at some stage, but for now he was stuck. Meanwhile, he knew Neve would be doing everything she could to find him, including getting help from Banai, Eamonn, and anyone else she could think of. If he could help her with nothing else right now, he could at least try to find a way to help her with that.

The skylight—that was something, at least. He thought about gathering all the strings of Christmas lights, piling them up in the middle of the room, and lighting them. That would look strange, at least, from the perspective of a search and rescue helicopter, and possibly draw some attention. But that plan died when he realized there were no electrical outlets in the attic—not to mention how unlikely it was that a helicopter would find him in time. They weren't exactly thick on the ground, and even if Neve did manage to convince someone to send a helicopter out, the chances were very slim that they'd do so before morning.

The final problem was of his own making, and it made Con want to kick himself. In all his conversations in the past twenty-four hours, he hadn't thought to tell anyone about The Close. They would have no idea where to start looking for him, and the extreme unlikelihood that they would coincidentally decide to search the Shandon area took the odds of his rescue from slim to none. An emotion dangerously close to despair rose into his throat, threatening to choke him.

Stop it, he ordered himself. *Neve deserves better than this.*

It was settled, then. When Liam's crew came for him, he would just have to fight his way free. And if he died trying, he was determined to take Liam out with him at the very least—Davies, too, if he was lucky.

It had been a while since he'd done any fighting

to speak of, or even played rugby. As a young man, trouble seemed to find him often enough. But Con had hoped he'd left that behind him when he qualified as a physician, and especially when he moved to the US. Over the last few months, however, he had been required to resurrect the part of himself that had a capacity for violence. He had no regrets about that since his motivation had been to keep Neve safe, something he would do at any cost. Now that he had someone to protect, he'd have to find a way to let the "civilized" and "dog rough" sides of himself coexist. It was time to accept that he couldn't simply bury an entire aspect of himself, especially when he might need to call upon it at any moment. Of course, his intention would be to create a life for Neve that was safe and free from threats so they never had to worry. But at the moment, that goal seemed a long way off—and to reach it, he'd first have to survive the night.

To refresh his rusty memory, Con began running different fight scenarios in his head.

Even with that mental activity going on, though, thoughts of Neve remained in the forefront of his mind. On the off chance that he didn't survive this fecking ordeal, he wanted to leave something behind for her, some sort of message. Something to let her know that right up to the last moments of his life, he was thinking of her, loving her.

In that moment, the night sky provided Con with a stroke of inspiration. There it was, almost directly overhead: the constellation Orion. And the glow stick in Con's pocket projected the same cold light as the stars.

As bone-tired and sore as he was, the idea of leaving a love note for Neve galvanized him. With a renewed sense of purpose, Con rooted around in the boxes until he found a roll of brown packing tape. He grabbed the box of glow sticks and cracked a few. Then he worked his way around, mapping the constellation by taping a cluster of glow sticks to the skylight in the same configuration as the stars.

He remembered the night at Neve's parents' house when she had first shown him the constellation. Over dinner, her mother had told the story of how as a child, Neve had regularly talked to the man in the stars. When she was a teenager, those conversations had transformed into prayers for Orion to bring her the man of her dreams. If Con hadn't already been head-over-heels in love with Neve, that single revelation would have done him in.

Outside after dinner, he had asked Neve to point out Orion for him. Although embarrassed about her secret relationship with the mythical hunter, Neve had played along, pointing out the two bright stars for Orion's shoulders, two for his knees, three for his belt, and the dimmer string of stars indicating his sword. It had also been the night of their first kiss….

Lost in his daydream, Con completed his work of art. In truth, he was pretty proud of how closely the configuration he'd created resembled the actual constellation. He supposed the only thing left was to sign it. A bit of tape and a few glow sticks later, he had "CON" written across the skylight where Orion's feet would have been if the heavens hadn't run out of stars.

Grand, he thought, pleased with the final product. He didn't know how long glow sticks lasted, but maybe a helicopter would spot them before they went dark. Or maybe one day, the guards would raid The Close, find the arrangement on the skylight, and tell Neve about it. Then she would understand what he'd been trying to say to her.

That hope would just have to be good enough for now.

Con sat back down on the box of garlands, not to rest but to lie in wait.

CHAPTER 19
NEVE

Dear God, please bring him back to me, please. Amen.

Over and over, I repeated the words in my head, sending them up to heaven. It became a chant, a constant refrain behind all my other thoughts, the words I spoke, and the words that were spoken to me. Mentally, I played it on a loop as I filled Eamonn in, made Alex tea, and fielded calls from Agent Banai. *Please bring him back to me, please.* For the first time, I understood what was meant by the biblical instruction to "pray without ceasing."

Exhausted though I was, I still had enough energy to remain tense. Every part of my body hurt, but none as much as my heart—raw, mangled, and bruised. Even one second of not knowing where Con was or whether he was safe had been too long. Now hours had passed, multiple, entire hours. At least there were three of us here now, sharing the burden of worry. Eamonn had been a bit stunned by my revelations about what Con and I had been up to back in DC, making friends in the White House and enemies of Brickhaven. After he had a chance to absorb it, though, he just shook his head and said he would "give out to Con later" for not calling him over to the US to help. Eamonn's certainty that he would soon get the opportunity to yell at his brother boosted my confidence.

The first call we got from Banshee nearly threw me into a tailspin. She had been listening in on communications at the warehouses. Most of the chatter was between emergency responders, but she kept trying to get news about Con. Finally, she overheard a snippet of a cell phone conversation that was potentially relevant: "We got the doctor. He's not going anywhere." Context clues from the rest of the conversation suggested the people on the line were part of Brickhaven's crew.

While it was a huge relief to hear what sounded like confirmation that Con was still alive and they planned to keep him that way for a while at least, the news also snuffed out our hope that he had escaped somehow. He had been caught by those evil, sick monsters, and what they were doing to him or planned to do was anyone's guess.

But whenever my mind moved in the direction of what Con might be going through or what would happen if we didn't find him, pain whooshed through me like a back draft and threatened to throw me into a state of panicked paralysis. And I couldn't afford to panic. Not now. Not until I had Con next to me, safe and sound. So I pushed those thoughts away and allowed my chanted prayer to drown them out as much as possible while we focused on finding him.

In light of Con's admonition to me not to trust the gardaí, Eamonn decided to call in his own reinforcements: two men he had grown up with who owned a local weightlifting gym and a pair of twins who worked at the brewery and "could handle themselves." As his friends trickled in over the next hour, each new arrival gave our spirits another lift.

It was the second call from Banshee, however, that really pumped life back into my veins. Alex, Eamonn, and I were sitting in the office when my phone rang.

"Hey, Neve!" Banshee chirped. "We found something strange. Might be Con."

"What? You found him?" I heard a clatter around

me as I flew off the couch, knocking something over. "Where is he?"

"Put it on speaker," Eamonn said as he grabbed a notebook and pen.

"Can't be sure, but you said to look out for anything odd, and this is odd all right. So, the skaters sent their drones up—"

Eamonn and Alex exchanged baffled looks.

"She knows a lot of skateboarders," I explained. "A whole group of them have another hobby operating camera drones."

"Right," Banshee said. "They hang out evenings on the Grand Parade. My buddy Foley dropped by and explained the situation to them, so they activated the drone army and started searching for anomalies. One of them just spotted something strange in the Shandon area near the Four-Faced Liar."

I shot Eamonn a desperate look, and he nodded. "I know where she means."

"They saw something odd in a skylight," Banshee continued. "Not sure what the light source is, but I have a still image from the footage. I'm sending it over now."

I clicked into my text messages. The photo she'd sent was an overhead image of rooftops along short, narrow streets with a large building nearby that appeared to be a church with a tall tower. Because it was night and most of the roofs were black, there wasn't much contrast in the image. But there was one rooftop that seemed to have glowing dots of whitish blue on it. I pinch-zoomed into that part of the image, enlarging it a few times until I could see it clearly.

"Orion," I whispered, nearly dropping the phone.

Eamonn's hand cradled mine from beneath to keep the phone from falling. "What?"

"A constellation," Banshee said. "It does look like Orion, but the proportions are a bit off. Zoom into the bottom there, though."

Sure enough, there were a few more lights where Orion's feet should be. I zoomed in farther. Clear as day, the small arrangement spelled out three letters: C-O-N.

"Oh my God, it's him!" I dropped the phone into Eamonn's hand as my whole body began to tremble. "It's him! It's definitely him!"

Eamonn didn't need any more convincing. "What's the address?"

How can it possibly take this long? Somehow, I managed to keep that thought to myself as we drove through the city streets just under the speed limit. Alex's solid point that we didn't want to be delayed by getting pulled over for speeding did nothing to cool the burn of impatience searing through my body.

Our now-large group had piled into one of Calfwood Brewery's white panel vans. Alex drove with Eamonn in the passenger seat. I rode in the back of the van with "the lads," as Eamonn called them.

At first, Eamonn and Alex had decided I should stay behind, but even I was startled by how frenzied my voice sounded as I shook my fists and screamed, "Have you *met* me, Eamonn?" A look passed between them as though they feared if they left me alone in the brewery, I might destroy the place. They agreed to bring me along under the condition that I stayed out of sight until they had Con and the situation was contained. I had to admit that made sense, since Brickhaven knew what I looked like and were out to get me as well. Besides, Eamonn claimed that if he allowed me to be put in harm's way, Con would kill him stone-dead. While we both knew Con would protect his brother with his life, I still took his point.

With that decided, I had called Agent Banai to fill him in on our plan. He strongly advised us to stay where we were and let him work on getting local resources to check out the address. But when he admitted that might take an hour or more, Eamonn simply continued gathering supplies. I thanked Agent Banai and accepted his offer to send backup but made it clear that we were already on our way. We had no idea what Brickhaven's plans were for Con, but since we knew they were comfortable with murder, there was no way we were going to sit around and wait to find out.

Now, "the lads" and I swayed and jolted in the back of the van. In a kind attempt to keep my mind occupied, Eamonn explained that the Four-Faced Liar Banshee had referred to was the four-sided clock tower of Saint Anne's Church, located just near our destination. It was called the Four-Faced Liar because all four clocks never kept the same time. Alex added that the tower also housed the famous Bells of Shandon, which I could play myself if I visited in the daytime.

Given the church's proximity to a Brickhaven-friendly establishment, I didn't think I would be visiting it anytime soon. But learning a little bit of Cork history did serve as a helpful distraction as we rode through the city.

Although Eamonn had made everyone aware of the gravity of the situation, that didn't stop the group of guys from joking around all the way to Shandon.

They were so at ease together, it was obvious they had known one another long enough to develop trust and loyalty between them. They were also so hell-bent on rescuing Con, it made me smile for the first time in ages.

We had crossed the river and were heading up a hill—a fairly steep one, I guessed, since we had to cling to one another to keep from sliding toward the back doors. The van took a few turns. Then we slowed and Alex and Eamonn leaned forward, talking as they looked out the window.

"I think that's it," Eamonn said.

"The pub?"

"Yeah, that's the address."

I crept up in between their seats and raised my head just enough so I could peer over the dashboard. Alex pointed out a two-story building down a side street. Sitting amid a row of houses was a dark green storefront facade with tall windows and the words "The Close" painted in gold over the door. It appeared to be closed, but the entrance was still dimly lit, and we could see from the windows that there were still lights on inside.

"Look at the roof!" I whispered in awe. The blue-white light of the glow sticks was barely visible from where we were but undeniable all the same. "That's it, definitely!"

I only became aware that I had turned and lunged toward the back doors of the van when several sets of arms caught me and pulled me back.

"Neve!" Eamonn stage-whispered. "You're staying here, or have you forgotten?"

I *had* forgotten. Nothing could have prepared me for how impossible it would be to be so close to Con but unable to run to him. I forced myself to sit back down. "Of course. I'm sorry."

"Don't apologize. Believe me, I get why you want to rush in there, guns blazing."

"Where should we park?" Alex asked.

"Maybe on the main road, across from Saint Anne's," Eamonn suggested. "Then we're close but out of sight."

Alex eased the van to the curb, turned off the headlights, and switched the engine off. Across the street to the right, a wide stone staircase led up to the doors of a church with a bell tower so high, we couldn't see the top of it from inside the van.

"What now?" Alex asked.

What now, indeed. My heart thumped so powerfully, it felt like it was pushing my lungs out of the way.

"Choose your weapons," Eamonn said. "Something you can keep hidden but will do some damage. We'll go to the pub, pretend we're plastered, and bang on the place until they open up to tell us to feck off. Then we'll force our way in."

"Got it," the men muttered as their earlier good humor evaporated. Suddenly all business, they sorted through the hammers, crowbars, wrenches, and other objects in the back of the van and tucked them under their shirts.

"I'll leave the key in the ignition in case you need to make a quick escape," Alex told me once they were geared up and ready to go. "Right, Eamonn. Let's go get your brother."

Eamonn reached back and squeezed my shoulder. "Don't worry. We'll be back soon."

"Good luck!" My heart surged with hope as the men piled out of the van. I knew how evil Brickhaven was, but our group looked fairly intimidating as well, and they had surprise on their side.

I watched in the side mirror as they marched down the street and rounded the corner. God willing, this was it, and before long they'd return to the van, bringing Con with them.

I brought the chanted prayer from the back of my mind to the forefront, whispering the words aloud and wrapping my arms around my shoulders. The temperature outside was dropping, and the van didn't have much insulation. I convinced myself that was the reason I was shivering even though I was wearing a hoodie Alex had loaned me.

After rocking back and forth for a few minutes, my brain began to drift to terrifying places. To distract myself, I crawled into the front seat and lay across the seats, staring up at the church bell tower and trying to see the top. But no matter how I contorted myself, the tower was simply too tall. After scanning the street to be sure there wasn't a soul in sight, I rolled down the window just enough to put my head out and look up. From that angle, I could finally make out the top of the tower against the sky as it brightened with the pre-sunrise twilight.

I slumped down in the passenger seat, pulling the hood of my sweatshirt over my face so on the off chance someone walked by, they wouldn't be able to make out my features in the dark. I left the window half down, letting the chilly air touch my skin, the discomfort a reminder that I was still alive, and Con was still alive.

I nearly jumped out of my skin when a loud *bang* and sudden movement at the front door of the church grabbed my attention. It looked like someone was trying unsuccessfully to pull the door open from the inside. Through the half-open window, I heard men's voices shouting. It sounded like they were having an intense argument. One angry voice yelled, "Hold him, goddammit!" Just as the door to the church slammed shut, another voice roared as if in pain.

That roar.

I froze. I couldn't move or breathe. Goose bumps raced across my skin.

It was Con's voice.

He wasn't in the pub anymore. He was in the church. And from the sound of it, he was fighting for his life.

With that realization, my body flared into motion. Compelled by pure instinct, I pulled the keys from the ignition, yanked open the van door, and jumped out into the street.

CHAPTER 20
CON

IT WAS LIAM WHO HAD GOTTEN THE BRIGHT IDEA TO fake Con's suicide by throwing him off the clock tower at Saint Anne's Church. Someone had ordered them to get the job done before the sun rose and the neighbors started to wake, and that tower was the only spot that was both close enough and high enough to serve all purposes.

After they managed to drag Con from the attic, Liam and the three goons who had brought him over from the warehouse gagged him, tore off his leg brace, and bound his hands and feet. Then they rolled him up in a rug and carried him to the church, where one of the men made quick work of the front door lock. Once inside, however, another member of the crew observed that the stairway in the tower had too many tight turns; they couldn't carry Con up inside the rug. Instead, they had been forced to unroll him and untie his feet.

Con took immediate advantage of the situation, spitting out his gag and getting in a few good kicks. He even made it to the church door, turned around, and used his bound hands to open it a few inches before one of the feckers stabbed him in the thigh with something. It hurt like hell, but at least the cut didn't feel deep. *Better a knife than a bullet,* he thought. Although all four men wore gun belts, they seemed to favor more traditional methods of violence —perhaps because the sound of gunshots would draw a good deal of attention.

The goons were in foul humor by the time they forced him up the first flight of stairs and into a small room with high ceilings and a tall, arched window. Twilight brightened the room a bit, and he could see a metal frame fixed on one wall with a row of thick ropes running vertically through it. Next to the frame was an ornate stand holding sheet music. Con remembered the room from his childhood trip. It was the spot where you could ring the Bells of Shandon.

That would be one way of waking up the neighborhood, Con thought, but Liam must have guessed his intent. He ordered the goons to walk Con around the side of the room opposite the bell ropes.

Once they made their way around to the next set of stairs, though, another problem became evident. The old stone passageway was so narrow and the ceiling so short that even if Con had wanted to climb the tower, it would have been a struggle given his size. Unwilling and with four other men in tow, it looked next to impossible.

Liam took a few steps up the stairs and peered around the corner, stroking his jaw like he was trying to work out a complex equation.

"Can't we just shoot him?" one of the men suggested.

"We could dump him from the boat," another chimed in.

Liam, who was a proud man for reasons Con had yet to ascertain, was unwilling to consider any plan other than his own. "We're going up!"

"It would seem you boys haven't thought this out." Con knew it was probably unwise to bait the men who were trying to kill him, but the situation was so absurd, he couldn't help himself.

"Shut up!" Liam barked. "Shut him up!"

The blow that landed on his jaw didn't hurt as much as it would have were the men not already getting tired. It had been a long night for everyone, and Con certainly hadn't made it any easier on them.

Better to keep making things difficult, he thought, lurching to one side to throw the men holding him off-balance.

As they struggled to get him back under control, Liam cursed a blue streak. "Just get him up there! I don't care how you do it!"

The men were scrappy; Con had to give them that. Bulky figures all, they figured out they needed to leave behind their jackets and gun belts to get through the space—and to be sure their contortions didn't lead to accidental friendly fire. Then they began shoving him up the stairs. Con only managed to send one tumbling down the steps with a swift kick to the head. The two remaining men gave the impression that they had experience maneuvering livestock, as with some finesse, in spite of his struggling, they managed to force him up the remaining stairs.

All breathing heavily, they spilled out onto the next landing. It was a narrow walkway with plexiglass walls on both sides and windows at each end. Con could see from the dim outline of the buildings outside that they were about halfway up the tower at that point. He would have to start finding new ways to disable the rest of the men before they got much farther.

Or maybe he wouldn't have to do anything at all. Suddenly, a cacophony of sound blasted their eardrums. Someone was ringing the bells, and judging from the noise they were making, they definitely weren't following the sheet music. Instead, it sounded like the bells were brawling with each other.

Con's hands were still tied, but the rest of the men raised their hands to cover their ears. As his head reverberated with the bells' vibrations, Con turned around, bent down, and ran at the men standing behind him, using his head as a battering ram. One of them fell into the other, but the narrowness of the passageway worked to their advantage this time. Instead of going down the stairs, they were able to brace themselves against the walls. Meanwhile, Liam kicked Con's bad knee from behind, and a bolt of pain shot through his body. It knocked the wind from him, and he fell against the wall. In the time it took Con to find his feet again, Liam and the other men were on him.

"Stop the fucking bells!" Liam screamed over the deafening gongs.

The man closest to the stairs turned to go down, but before he did so, the bells finally stopped. There was a muffled high-pitched scream and sounds of a scuffle. Then came the triumphant shout up the stairs: "I got her!"

Con wanted to kiss whatever madwoman had snuck into the church to ring the bells in the wee hours of the morning. The whole neighborhood would have to be awake by now. If he could just delay Liam and crew a bit longer, their plan to stage his suicide would be ruined.

"Thank Christ," Liam muttered.

"You won't believe who it is," the man yelled from below.

In that moment, everything stopped. The earth stopped turning. Con's heart stopped beating in his chest.

It wasn't possible. It couldn't be….

"Let go of me!" Neve's scream echoed off the stone walls of the staircase.

Liam's expression began to transform into a look of glee just as Con turned and saw Neve being pushed out onto the walkway. The man he had kicked in the head had one hand wrapped around the back of her neck while the other held her wrists behind her.

"Con!"

The sound of Neve's voice calling out his name cut right through him, and the sight of her…. He finally knew for certain that he was damned to hell, because in that glimpse of her face, his traitorous heart leapt with joy.

In the next moment, though, his gut quavered. Her face was a mask of terror, then horror as she took in the state of him. Con must have looked pretty rough, but before he could reassure her, Liam barked out a laugh.

"Oh, perfect!" he cried out. "Leverage—just what we needed to get you to behave yourself." He twisted the ropes around Con's wrists until they cut into his skin. "Now you're climbing the tower willingly, Mr. Good Guy, or we're making you watch while we throw your pretty girlfriend from the belfry. Let's go, c'mon!"

This time, Con allowed himself to be pushed along toward the next set of steps as he called over his shoulder, "Neve, are you all right?"

"Just… pissed… *off*!"

Con could tell by the sound of her voice that she was struggling mightily with her captor.

"Sean, are you all right?" Liam yelled back with mock concern.

To Con's surprise, the man holding Neve replied, "That bitch stabbed me with a key!"

"Well done, Neve," Con shouted behind him, his chest swelling with pride.

"Shut up, Sean!" Liam spat. His eyes widened as he looked up the stairs.

Con leaned in for a look. This passageway was all stone—the steps, walls, and ceiling. A small bit of moonlight shone in through a tiny, narrow window and glinted off the water leaking down the walls. That explained the smell of damp. But this space was so tight, Con couldn't imagine how he could make it through. "I won't fit. Do the math."

"Oh, yes you will," Liam sneered. "Even if we have to cut you into pieces!"

"That would throw a wrench in your suicide story," Con pointed out. "Not to mention, Neve woke the neighbors. We're not going to be alone here for much longer."

"Everybody, shut the fuck up!" Liam took the first few steps, then reached down, grabbed Con's shirt, and yanked. "Get up here, or we kill the girl!"

After doing a quick mental calculation, Con decided it would be wise to humor Liam until the bells did their work and more help arrived. Still skeptical about his ability to fit through, he ducked his head and stepped up into the passageway. Before he had climbed two steps, however, his shoulders became wedged between the walls on either side. Screaming a string of curses, Liam ordered Con back down onto the walkway.

The determination was made that the only way they would get Con through the passage would be to free his hands so he could reach his arms up and twist his body between the walls. But before they untied him, Liam announced that he'd go up first with Neve to give Con "the necessary incentive."

Con fought and cursed, but Liam and the two other men managed to hold him against the wall as Neve's captor pushed her through, kicking and struggling. She only stopped resisting for the two seconds she was directly in front of Con. In that moment, his gaze locked onto hers, and he saw everything: her oceanic love, volcanic rage, razor-sharp fear—and a lifetime of promises.

All of those things gave him courage, feeding his determination and strength. But what broke his heart was the deep well of forgiveness in her eyes—preemptive forgiveness, regardless of what might happen next. It was forgiveness he would never be worthy of, and never deserve, if he allowed anything to happen to her.

She was shoved past him, and Liam grabbed her arm, yanking her up the passageway behind him.

"Untie me!" Con commanded, and the goons obeyed. Now that Liam had Neve, Con couldn't waste another second dealing with these pathetic gobsheens. He raised his arms and dove up the stairwell after her.

At the top of the stairs was a tiny wooden platform enclosed by a metal gate. Beyond it was open air with a long drop down. The space was crisscrossed with thick wooden beams and the enormous mechanisms of the clocks.

He only realized the thugs hadn't followed him when he heard shouting coming from down below. Someone who heard the bells must have finally arrived. If the Brickhaven crew was otherwise occupied, that meant he was free to go get Neve—by any means necessary.

Con saw her foot disappearing up a short ladder that he guessed must lead up to the final staircase. It took him several seconds to figure out how to contort himself under a protruding beam—precious seconds he couldn't afford to lose. Finally, he managed to squeeze his way up onto the stairs, just in time to see Liam open the door to the outside viewing platform, disappear through it, and pull Neve behind him.

The shouts and cries of pain coming from below intensified, but they sounded more distant, as though the fighting was moving down the tower. Someone was definitely slowing down the goons. Feeling lighter, Con raced up the final flight of stairs and threw open the door.

The cold night air smacked him in the face as he exploded onto the viewing walkway—then stopped dead. Liam was ahead of him, facing him and panting against the railing. Behind Liam stood Neve, eyes wide. And just behind her, with one hand clutching her shoulder and the other pressing the barrel of a revolver to her head, was fecking Davies.

A malevolent smile spread across Davies's face. "Took you long enough to get here," he said smoothly, as though Con had just arrived late to a meeting in a conference room. "I thought I might have to come down myself. I warned Liam it would be a struggle to get you up here, and I can see I was right. But all is forgiven." His eyes darted in Neve's direction. "After all, he brought me a gift."

Davies's words just washed over Con, however. They were meaningless background noise, a prelude to the vigorously premeditated murders he was about to commit. He locked eyes with Neve, relieved to find as much rage as fear there. "Don't be afraid," he said, and he was glad to see the tension in her body soften a touch.

"You sound very confident," Davies mocked. "Though Neve's a smart girl, aren't you, Neve? I think she knows that standing on a high tower with a gun to her head, it's quite reasonable to be afraid."

"It would be," Con said, moving his gaze over to Davies, "if she thought any harm would come to her."

This time, Davies laughed—then stopped abruptly when no one else joined him. "News flash, Con. You fucked up tonight, and so did she." Speaking directly into her ear, he said, "I mean, ringing those bells? Neve, you managed to do the wrong thing, in the wrong place, and at the wrong time." He then sealed his fate by giving Neve an air kiss that only Con could see. "Needless to say, O'Brien, any deals we made for your safety and for hers? They're now null and void."

But Con wasn't listening to his needling. Rather, he was busy making a mental note that Davies held the revolver with delicacy, as though it was a precious object, not a tool he was accustomed to using.

Meanwhile, a flash of nerves crossed Liam's face. Keeping his eyes fixed on Con, he turned his head in Davies's direction and murmured, "They should be here by now."

"Your friends aren't coming," Con announced, then smiled at Neve. "Good job on the bells there."

Neve blinked at him twice in rapid succession—a silent acknowledgment.

Con sensed the change in energy when the penny finally dropped and both Liam and Davies realized no one was coming to back them up—at least not quickly enough to prevent any mayhem he could potentially cause. The Adam's apple in Davies's throat bobbed up and down as he swallowed.

"If you give her to me, I won't kill you." Con wasn't sure whether he would stick to his word on that or not. He would decide once Neve was safe.

"I'm the only one holding a gun, asshole," Davies hissed, sliding his hand from Neve's shoulder to grip the back of her neck. She winced, and Con decided all bets were off.

"You also brought us to the top of this tower," Con pointed out. "Maybe not a great choice given that a long fall can also be a deadly weapon."

Liam wiped perspiration from his brow and glanced down at the wide abyss below them. When he looked back up, his eyes began darting around, searching for a way out of the situation that didn't involve going over the railing.

With Liam preoccupied with his own survival, Con slowly extended his good arm toward Davies. "Give her to me."

Since Davies was a cowardly shitehawk, Con knew there were only a few actions he was likely to take. When a shift in the man's stance signaled his next move, Con was ready. Davies lurched forward and shoved Neve in Con's direction, trying to throw them both off-balance. Instead, Con caught her on his arm, allowing the momentum to turn him so his body shielded hers as Davies pointed his gun and pulled the trigger.

A stream of lava burned across Con's back. In one fluid motion, he lowered Neve to the ground and rounded on the two men before Davies got a chance to aim and fire again. Con dove headfirst at Liam, knocking him over and Davies behind him like a pair of dominos. The fall threw Davies's revolver out of his hand, and it skittered around the corner of the walkway. Liam being closer and the bigger threat physically, Con set about pummeling the man.

Davies tried to scramble into a standing position, holding on to Liam's belt and using his body as a shield from Con's fists. But when Liam tucked his head in an attempt to dodge Con's next blow, the punch landed squarely on Davies's jaw.

Davies caterwauled as he lost his balance, fell sideways, and tumbled over the railing. Still clutching Liam's belt, he pulled the other man over with him.

Liam screamed, managing to catch the railing with both hands as he went over.

As Con stood there, hunched over the two men hanging, there was a split second—maybe an entire second, in fairness—in which he considered turning around, grabbing Neve, and taking her to safety without doing another damned thing. He felt under zero obligation to save these two men from plummeting to their deaths. In fact, not only would he be doing the world a favor by leaving them to their fate, but he suspected he would find it immensely satisfying. They had hurt Neve, threatened to kill her. These were the wages of that sin.

The problem was, he could feel Neve's eyes on him. She had already seen him attack two men that day. It was one thing for her to know he had roughed up a few people, most of them in his youth. But he remembered vividly the way she had shaken in his arms earlier in the evening after watching him knock out the two thugs who'd been holding her. If he let *these* two die, she might never stop shaking.

Con hoped Neve hadn't noticed the moment it took for him to choose to act against his better judgment and help these arseholes—not because he thought it was the right thing to do but because he loved her. It was all right with him if she knew there was a part of him that wanted to murder Liam and Davies six ways to Sunday. But if he gave in to that part, she might never forgive him. And if that happened, he would never be able to live with himself.

He stepped forward, bracing his feet against the short wall beneath the railing. Leaning forward, he tried to grab Liam's arms, but the man kept thrashing around.

"Keep still, dammit," Con yelled. "I'm trying to help you!"

But Liam wasn't paying any attention to Con. He was trying to shake off Davies, screaming, "Let go of me!"

Davies still had one hand wrapped around Liam's belt, but his grip was slipping. He wore an expression of abject terror. It was the look of a man who had lived a regrettable life and was now facing impending death. Con had seen that look before a handful of times, working in the hospital. Now his former colleague stared up at him with pleading eyes.

"Help—"

But his plea was cut short. Liam was kicking, and his heel connected with the other man's ribs. Davies lost his grip on the belt and fell, disappearing into the darkness. His bone-chilling scream was quickly cut short by a sickening thud.

"Help!" Liam yelled. In the struggle, one of his hands had slipped off the railing.

Con dropped his arm over the side and tried to catch Liam's flailing hand. "Grab hold!"

At first, Liam just hung there, as though he didn't believe Con would really help him.

"Goddammit, Liam, grab it!"

Finally, the man flung his arm upward. On his third attempt, his hand found Con's.

Con moaned as he worked to pull the fecker up. It was an arduous process just getting his head and arms atop the railing. But his lower body held most of his weight, and his legs were swinging. Liam was trying, but fear and exhaustion had weakened him, so Con had to do most of the work.

He felt Neve come up behind him and wrap her arms around his waist. As she leaned back, her body provided him with an anchor. Con managed to grasp and grab until he finally got a hold of Liam's belt. With a few more maneuvers and one final, mighty pull, he hauled the man up and over the railing. Liam flopped onto the walkway, panting.

Con snaked his arm behind him and held Neve against his back. They lowered themselves to the ground. All three of them sat there for a few moments, catching their breath.

Neve was with him, and she was okay. He could feel her warmth against his body, her lungs rising and falling, and her heart beating. That was all that mattered.

After several minutes, Liam stirred. He pushed up onto his elbows, then turned to face Con. The few brain cells Con reckoned the man had were firing on all cylinders, trying to work out why they had saved him and what would happen next.

When Liam finally opened his mouth to speak, Con knew that whatever the man had to say, it wasn't anything he wanted to hear. Neve was safe. He didn't want to think about anything else. So before a single word could be uttered, Con hauled back and punched the man in the temple, knocking him out cold.

"*Con!*"

"Con!"

Two voices called his name, overlapping with each other. One was Neve's, no doubt objecting to him throwing that punch. But the other voice, calling up to him from inside the staircase....

Slowly he turned to the side, catching Neve's eye. "Is that... Eamonn?"

She nodded, smiling. "He brought me here, along with 'the lads.'"

"He brought you here?" Con wrapped his arms around her and pulled her body against his. Ignoring his split lip, he kissed the top of her head and muttered, "I'll kill him stone-dead."

But the way she threw her arms around him and buried her face in his neck told him she understood what he really meant: *Thank God.*

CHAPTER 21
NEVE

The Atlantic smelled different in West Cork.

It was a subtle change from oceanfront Maryland, where my family and I had spent so many summer vacations. But from where I sat, the scent was softer somehow, less poignant. Maybe it was down to variations in the types of seaweed or plankton.... I allowed my mind to drift out onto the water.

Eyes still closed, I inhaled the fresh, briny air as a soft breeze lifted the warmth of the sun from my face. I counted the beats between whooshing sounds as small waves stroked the beach, then receded in preparation for their next approach. The weight of my body pressed down into the earth, sending wetness seeping up into the seat of my jeans. My toes wriggled against the packed sand like the tiny flippers of baby sea turtles making their way toward the sea—making their way home.

My reverie was interrupted by the jingling of tags against a collar. Within seconds, the small white dog was upon me, wriggling in my lap and jumping up to lick my chin.

"Polo, leave her alone!" Della called after him, but he joyfully ignored her as I laughed, accepting the loving assault.

By the time Della reached us, Polo had finished greeting me and was running in large circles in the sand. "Sorry," she said, but we both grinned as she sat down next to me. "There's no stopping him when he likes someone."

"So Con has discovered!" It was our second morning at Della and Gabe's seaside bed-and-breakfast, and watching Con try to fend off the dog's advances while recovering from his injuries had been our main source of entertainment.

The couple were FBI agents in semiretirement running a safe house on the stunning Dingle Peninsula. Della's first career had been in nursing, and one of their rooms had been converted into a mini medical suite. Agent Banai had thought it safer to send Con here than to a regular hospital, at least until the gardaí had a chance to demolish Brickhaven's

Irish operations and bring any of their local allies to justice.

"That dog adores him," Della mused. "He doesn't seem to care that Con is one giant bruise."

It felt so good to laugh, and to do so freely, without any underlying worries. Well, there were some worries, of course, but they had to do with the future. I was taking full advantage of the few protected days we had to live in the moment. "Why is Polo out here instead of shadowing Con anyway?"

"He's in the shower."

"Oh, wow! That's progress." Since we'd arrived, Con had been making do washing up in the bathroom sink. If he felt able to take a shower, that was a sign of improvement.

"Too soon if you ask me." She tutted. "He's a terrible patient."

"Oh, I know. The worst." Getting him to stick to doctor's orders after his gunshot wound had been like engaging in endless negotiations with an oppositional rhinoceros.

"Breakfast is ready, by the way." Della stood back up and brushed the sand off her legs. "A dozen ham, egg, and cheese sandwiches, so I hope you're hungry."

Gabe's first career had been as a cook in the Navy,

and he seemed confident that large quantities of good food would improve Con's health and both of our spirits.

After Eamonn found us on top of the bell tower, I had breathed a sigh of relief, thinking the chaos was finally over, but in reality, it had just begun. Leaving Liam where he lay, we made our way back down to the church foyer to find "the lads" watching over the Brickhaven thugs. Having discovered the discarded gun belts, Eamonn's friends were using the weapons to hold the bad guys until the authorities arrived. All the men, both friend and foe, were sporting cuts and bruises, but our crew was grinning ear to ear as though they'd never been to a better party.

Meanwhile, the reinforcements Agent Banai had called in were beginning to arrive. Con and I left the church to find an official-looking blue-and-yellow SUV pulling up in front of us. One of the gardaí got out and handed Con a cell phone. Agent Banai was on the other end of the line, reassuring us that they were friends, and that he had sent them to take us somewhere safe. After confirming that Eamonn was happy to handle things at the church, we climbed inside. As we were driven away, we saw the blue lights of other gardaí vehicles flashing from the side street near The Close.

Con and I called Agent Banai back on the way to Dingle and gave him as many details as we could about what we had witnessed. I sent him the pictures and videos from my phone as well, and he agreed to pass everything along to local law enforcement.

I didn't know where Con was finding the strength to talk, though. My heart ached every time I looked at him, knowing that the visible cuts, swollen red areas, and bruises represented only a fraction of his injuries. He was bleeding through a tear in his shirt on the back of the same shoulder that had been injured before, but he refused to let me examine it, saying it wasn't serious and it could wait. He kept telling me he was fine, not to worry, and it looked worse than it was, but I knew he was lying to help me focus on the task at hand.

That proved difficult at first because I couldn't stop shaking. Con unbuckled my seat belt and drew me closer to him, pulling my head against his chest. But when I closed my eyes and pictured the people we had left behind in the warehouses, outrage energized me. Brickhaven and their accomplices had killed Megan, Declan, and who knew how many other people. They had tried to kill Con and hurt him badly in the process. And they had committed untold atrocities and profited from abusing other human beings in the most horrific ways. Tapping into the deep well of anger inside me made it easier to concentrate as we told Agent Banai everything we knew.

Out of an abundance of caution, Agent Banai said the decision had been made to bring Kayla back to the States. She was already in the air. He advised us to get some rest, since there would be more questions coming.

Next, I called Banshee to thank her and update her on events. Since she had tapped into emergency responder communications, she already knew we'd been rescued, but she was happy to hear it from the horse's mouth. I also asked her to extend our gratitude to the skateboarders, without whom the night might have ended very differently. Con appeared confused throughout that conversation, but the only question he asked was by way of a raised eyebrow. Unsure how I would even begin to explain how his rescue had been facilitated by a psychic medium and a skater drone army, I promised to fill him in later.

Then we called Eamonn to check in. Thankfully, bar a few cuts and bruises, he and his friends were all fine. They had gone back to the brewery to celebrate, and Con observed that by the time we called, they sounded pretty "well lubricated."

Finally, I sent a brief text to Rose:

> We found Con from above. All is well. Thank you—for everything.

Despite the early hour, the bed-and-breakfast had been fully lit when we arrived. As we walked in the front door, Polo greeted us with enthusiasm while Gabe announced that a hot breakfast was on the table. Gabe and Della were natural hosts, making us feel at home right away even under the bizarre circumstances.

That first night, Con let me sit in as Della tended to his wounds—for my benefit, not his. Having nearly lost him just hours before, I wasn't ready for us to be in separate rooms just yet. It turned out Con had been shot *again*, something he'd failed to mention on our car ride over. His shirt had been torn by Davies's bullet, which grazed his shoulder, leaving an angry red trail three inches long where it had melted away the skin. Della tended to the wound, then examined his older gunshot wound as well. We were relieved to hear it was healing up well enough in spite of Con's recent exertions.

When she moved on to the cut on Con's leg, they discussed how lucky he was that it was shallow, and how it was probably made by a box cutter. At that point, I began to swoon, prompting Della to look me over as well. She asked me to remove the shirt I was wearing over my tank top. When I took it off, Con nearly knocked over a standing lamp as he surged forward to examine the red marks on my arms. I hadn't even known they were there.

"I'm fine," I insisted, anxious for him to relax. "It's just from being pushed and pulled around a bit."

"A *bit*?" One by one, Con took my wrists between his fingers and turned my arms gently, his face darkening like a storm cloud. "I should have let him fall," he rasped.

He was talking about Liam. I started to say, "You don't mean that," but hesitated when the look on his face told me otherwise.

Della gave stern instructions for Con to sit back down and let her work. To my surprise, he did as asked. Then she hooked me up to a bag of IV fluids before moving back to Con, carefully cleaning and dressing the multiple abrasions on his body.

Confronted with the full extent of his injuries, I blinked back tears.

"Calm yourself," Con said, reaching over to give my leg a squeeze. "It was just a tight fit getting me up that tower, like a cork in a bottle."

With scissors in one hand and gauze in the other,

Della held up her arms. "Look, tough guy, if you don't sit still, we're going to be here all night!"

Con's quick obedience and contrite expression earned him a smile from Della. Once she'd finished taking care of his wounds, she gave us each a bag of gummy candies. We agreed that they tasted ridiculously good in that moment.

We had a little time to relax before the gardaí called us with more questions. They had made quick progress, arresting over twenty people so far in a sweep of the Brickhaven and Blackbird crowds, using the photos and videos I had taken to help identify the criminals. One of them was the man with the hand tattoos. He had quickly agreed to a plea deal, telling the authorities where to find the hurleys that had been used to kill Megan and Declan. The murder weapons had already been collected from the Blackbird for DNA testing. Meanwhile, the trafficking victims in the warehouses had been rescued, including the man whose kidney had nearly been taken. They were all safe and being looked after under the protection of the Irish government.

Con told them we'd had to fight our way out of the warehouse and asked if they had found anyone injured. The gardaí said they had brought in two men with bumps on their heads, but both were expected to be fine, and neither had said a word about what happened to them. One of the gardaí explained that in the unlikely event that any complaints were filed against Con or me, in this case their procedure would be to liaise with the Secret Service. At that news, Con looked as relieved as I felt. Agent Banai had already given us reassurances that the White House would handle any legal fallout from the night's events.

As we talked to the gardaí, Della kept checking Con's vitals and rotating his ice packs while Gabe brought in fresh rounds of refreshments. Meanwhile, Polo had decided Con was the person most in need of comfort and refused to leave his side. Con took it in stride, stroking the dog as though they'd been friends for years.

By the time the gardaí finished questioning us, Con looked like he could sleep for weeks, and I had to work hard to keep my eyelids from shutting against my will. Della set us up in a guest room that had a bed for me and an overstuffed leather recliner for Con. With his bruised ribs, she said he should sleep in a semi-upright position for the first couple of nights to prevent a buildup of fluid in the lungs. As soon as Con pushed out the recliner, the little dog curled up beneath his footrest. As bone-tired as I was, once in the bed, I still couldn't fall asleep until I heard Con's breathing even out and slow.

It was afternoon on that first day when I awoke to find neither Con nor Polo had moved. I managed to coax the little dog away from his post long enough to go for a walk on the beach. When we returned, he sprinted back up to the guest room. I followed him, lying on my side on the bed so I could watch Con sleep.

The swelling on his face had decreased overnight, but his bruises were darkening. It hurt just to look at him, especially knowing from the examination the night before that his whole body was covered with such marks.

There in the quiet, I unlatched the tight lid I had been keeping on my emotions. When they emerged, the feelings I had were so powerful and jumbled together, I couldn't distinguish them from one another. All I knew was that people had hurt Con and almost taken him from me. The same people had forced all those innocent victims into a living nightmare and killed two brave souls who tried to stop them. It was too much, far too much. It spilled out of me in a river of silent tears that flowed across my face and soaked the pillowcase.

It was another couple of hours before Con awoke,

"just in time for supper," Gabe observed. Agent Banai had arranged for our luggage to be packed up and delivered, and it felt outrageously good to get into my own fresh, clean clothes. After gorging ourselves on a gourmet meal of leg of lamb and roasted potatoes, we retreated to a room that served as a library and reading nook. Con perused the newspapers Gabe got delivered daily from around the world while I looked through a coffee table book about the Dingle Peninsula. Della and Gabe must have sensed that we needed some space, because they left us alone—unlike the dog. But even he was undemanding, sleeping on the floor next to Con's chair.

Most of our time over the two previous days had been spent apart, with each of us engaged in different adventures. We had a lot to tell each other, and we couldn't be sure how soon another chance might present itself.

To make the most of the time we had, we decided to lay down some ground rules. Con suggested we go chronologically, dividing the days into three parts—morning, afternoon and evening—and then take turns filling each other in on what happened during each time period. I proposed that we only ask each other factual questions, leaving comments and judgments at the door, just as we would if reporting on patients in hospital rounds. We both knew powerful feelings might come up, so Con agreed with me that we should shelve any emotional content and process it later.

"And no touching," I added.

Con seemed puzzled by that one. "Why is that?"

"To avoid distractions." The more specific reason was that if Con started stroking my hair, or the palm of my hand, or anything, really, he could easily lull me into a relaxed state where I might accidentally share more than intended.

Amusement flashed across his face, but he quickly schooled his features. "Fair enough."

And so we began, telling each other all that had happened, starting with the afternoon following our lunch with Kayla at the Hotel Dabrona.

We both did a good job of sticking to our ground rules, sometimes even in the face of strong provocation. That said, we couldn't fully control our body language and facial expressions. Those spoke volumes and gave us both previews of what "processing the emotional content later" might involve.

For example, I couldn't help glowering as Con told me what was going through his head the night he returned to the hotel, called Agent Banai behind my back, and had a whole entire conversation with me without telling me what had happened at The Close. I tried to keep my face neutral as he filled me in on his thought process at our lunch together, but I probably still came across as frosty.

Meanwhile, Con leaned forward, elbows on his knees, looking for all the world like a detective playing "bad cop" while I explained why I didn't get on the plane after he left me at the airport. At that point in the conversation, the little dog must have felt sorry for me, because he left Con's side and jumped into my lap. I was glad to have Polo to look at rather than Con's raised eyebrows as I described how I'd recruited Thomas to take me to the Blackbird and stake out Megan's murderers.

In spite of the peril we'd been in at the time, I felt a surge of happiness when I talked about the moment I heard Con's voice in the warehouse. Whatever unpleasant feelings may have emerged during our conversation up to that point, they were pushed aside by the memory of the profound relief and joy we'd both felt upon seeing each other.

After that, the retellings became almost reverent, the emotions even more powerful. Hearing about what led Con to create the Orion constellation on the roof of the pub flooded my heart. He appeared equally overwhelmed when I explained how his glow stick art had led us to him and described how we'd launched our rescue attempt.

Con didn't tell me anything about the violence he'd suffered, but I could see it all over his body. And I didn't tell him about the terror I'd gone through, but I knew he was reading between the lines. Finally, our stories intersected for the final time: the moment he appeared on top of the tower. Since then, we'd been together, so there was nothing more to say.

I lifted the dog from my lap, placed him on the floor, and joined Con on the couch. Sliding close to him, I rested my head on his chest. With one hand, he reached up and palmed my cheek while he slid his other arm around my shoulders. In turn, I draped my arm across his waist. We sat silently in that moment of transformation, breathing together as our love for each other wrapped around us, bringing with it a new, deeper level of connection than we'd ever known before.

After several minutes, Polo decided he wanted in on the love and jumped on Con's lap to join us. Con sucked air in through his teeth as tiny paws landed on a tender bruise. He still welcomed the little guy, though, creating an opening in his arms. A cold, wet nose wriggled its way into our embrace. We laughed and wrapped our arms around the dog and each other until all we could see of Polo was his white tail sticking out from beneath, wagging. Eventually, the dog had his fill and jumped back onto the floor.

"Lie down," Con said, guiding me onto the parts of his lap that were the least painful. Then he began to stroke my hair, and just as I had known would happen, everything inside me began to melt. "Since we finished debriefing, I'm assuming touching is back on the table."

Grinning, I said, "Della and Gabe could walk in at any minute."

"Noted. Hair stroking only."

"As though you need anything else to bend me to your will."

"Hmm. Also noted."

Careful not to move too much for fear of hitting a bruise, I snuggled in closer. "You know, everything we talked about, all the bizarre things that have happened lately?"

"Yes?"

"Well, in the reading Rose gave me, Aunt Esther said it's all been happening for a reason, and we just can't see it yet."

There was an almost-imperceptible pause in Con's hair stroking. "That so?"

"Well, if you think about it, everything we've

gone through has led to the dismantling of a human trafficking operation. Maybe without realizing it, we have been part of a larger plan."

Con stopped stroking altogether and laid his hand on my shoulder.

"What?"

"Well, I would tell you what I think, but I don't want to disrespect your aunt Esther."

"Please tell me. I want to know. Just because she's passed doesn't mean she's right about everything."

He smiled. "All right, then. Personally, I don't find the idea that 'everything happens for a reason' to be either comforting or useful. If it's true that all the events in our lives are part of a divine plan, but we never get to know what the plan is, we're still just getting buffeted about by a God who has shown himself to be capricious—and that's being generous."

I couldn't argue with the "capricious" part. It *had* felt like we'd been the victims of unpredictable forces recently. "Rather than '*everything* happens for a reason,' then, what about '*some* things'?"

"Well, *some* things, certainly." He leaned down and gently kissed my temple. "You, for example, are evidence that the divine is also capable of extreme beneficence. But we've already established that you're a miracle."

I smiled, my heart fluttering like a hummingbird's wings. "We have?"

"Mm-hmm." He resumed stroking my hair. "As for the rest of creation, rather than trying to figure out whether or not things happen for a reason, I prefer to think of it this way: everything has a use."

"Meaning?"

"Meaning we've gone through some hellish things lately, but because of how we chose to respond, we made use of them. Fortunately, good things resulted."

In my mind, I ran through recent events, trying to see them through Con's eyes. "Everything has a use. I can work with that."

His body moved against mine as he chuckled softly. "Glad you approve."

"I mean it," I said. "Thanks for telling me what you really think."

"And what do *you* think?"

"I don't know yet." I shrugged and smiled up at him. "I'll let you know after I run everything by Aunt Esther."

"Right, so." Con sighed heavily. "Yet *another* family member I have to win over."

CHAPTER 22
NEVE

As so often happened during our time in Ireland, Con and I found ourselves in a place apart. We were enjoying our first lunch of freedom after our stay at the safe house.

Not that our stay there had been a hardship in the least; Della and Gabe had seen to that. On our second day there, the weather was dry and bright, so they had taken us on their speedboat to see the Skellig Islands. The otherworldly rock formations rose out of the ocean like giant, craggy mountain peaks while white seabirds with black-tipped wings soared overhead. Pods of dolphins joined us on our journey as well, and Gabe caught some mackerel for dinner. It had been an idyllic day, and just the change of scenery we needed to release the stress of recent events.

On the morning of our third day, following a good night's sleep and another massive breakfast, Agent Banai had called to tell us any threat posed by Brickhaven had been neutralized, at least in Ireland. He said it might take another week or so to tie up all loose ends in DC, but he offered to give us protection details if we wanted to come back home.

Della examined Con and said he was healing up well, and Con was satisfied with the state of my bruises, which were fading and no longer tender. With no lingering health worries, we decided that what we really wanted was to go back to Cork City and enjoy the rest of the vacation we'd been looking forward to when all hell broke loose. Con said before we left Ireland, he also needed to go back to his parents' home to pick up something. We made a couple of calls to Capitol Hill General to make sure we could take a little more time off. Dr. Kamali said he would be happy to continue covering for Con, and Rosanna gave me her enthusiastic blessing. We gave the news to Agent Banai, who sent a car to pick us up and confirmed reservations for us at the Hotel Gairdín.

Now we were in a restaurant downtown called The Grotto, an all-glass room with a waterfall cascading down one wall, flowing into a pool that wound its way through the room. Palm trees and ferns surrounded our table, and it felt like we might be the only people for miles.

In terms of cuisine, The Grotto had a little bit of everything. I decided to try the Irish version of my favorite Thai dish, red curry, while Con jumped at the opportunity to have fish and chips prepared just the way he liked them. We kept the conversation light, talking about our boat trip the day before, enjoying our food, and taking our time.

The feeling of being relaxed and having no worries was so unfamiliar, it took a little time for it to sink in. For me, a pint of cider helped, as did a Guinness for Con. But while we were waiting for dessert, I began to shift in my seat. There was something I had left out of the conversation in Gabe and Della's library when we were catching each other up, and it had been rattling around in my mind ever since.

Con must have noticed something was off, because he reached his hand across the table. "What is it, love?"

I took his hand and squeezed. "It's just... I want our communication with each other to be complete, and there's something I didn't tell you back in the safe house. Something about my reading from the psychic medium, Rose."

In mild surprise, his eyebrows lifted. "Something *else*?"

"Yeah." I smiled to signal that it wasn't anything bad.

Con just waited patiently, eyes locked onto mine as he stroked the back of my hand with his thumb.

"The reason she gave me her business card in the first place was because she told me she'd received a message for me from Spirit about my medical tests."

"Oh, I see." The shift in Con's expression reflected the gravity of the topic, putting my mind at ease. He might not believe in psychic phenomena, but that didn't stop him from being there for me in every sense.

"When I called her from the brewery," I continued, "it was to get that message from her, to distract myself from how worried I was. After she gave it to me, I asked her for help finding you. That's when she told me we would find you from above."

Con brought his other hand up and cradled mine between his palms. He seemed to sense I needed encouragement. Gently, he asked, "And what was the message?"

I proceeded to fill Con in on everything Rose had told me and describe the emotions her message had taken me through. As I spoke, my feelings were reflected in his expression. Just as I'd hoped, Con was walking through the experience with me, right beside me every step of the way.

One thing I didn't see on his face was skepticism. That surprised me. Doubt crept in, and I wondered if he had been humoring me. Tentatively, I pulled my hand back and asked, "So, what do you think about all that?"

He clasped his hands on the table. "Well, I agree with Rose."

I blinked. "What?"

As he spoke, not even a drop of doubt clouded his sincerity. "I think she's right. You are a healer, and knowing you as I do, I can say your life is already a story of love. As long as I'm around, I'm going to see to it that it's a story of *great* love too."

The power behind his words struck me square in the chest, rendering me speechless.

"And you know that I'll support you fully whether you decide we should become parents or not. So yes, I agree with Rose. I think she's spot-on."

I shook my head in disbelief. This couldn't be real. I couldn't possibly be lucky enough to have this man. And my confirmed nonbeliever of a boyfriend definitely couldn't be sitting in front of me, telling me that he agreed with a psychic. "I thought you would say it was too 'woo-woo.' I mean, you don't believe...."

"Neve," he said after my voice faded out, "I don't claim to know or understand everything, and I can't say how Rose knew to tell you to look for me from above. But she was clearly insightful about you, and the advice she gave you on how to find me may well have saved my life. Whether or not I believe, at the very least, I owe her a drink."

I wondered if a time would ever come when Con would stop surprising me. It didn't seem likely.

My smile stretched from ear to ear as I lifted my pint glass. Con followed suit, and as our glasses clinked, he said, "To Rose."

"To Rose," I replied. After we each sipped our drinks, I asked, "So, are you going to call her now to get your own reading?"

"Ah, now," he said, shaking his head, "take it easy on me. That might be a 'woo' too far."

As I laughed, Con cleared his throat. "In the spirit of our communication being complete, there is something I haven't told you as well. It's hardly monumental, but I know how you like to be kept abreast of developments."

Good grief. What else had he been keeping from me? I tried not to show my frustration since he had just been so supportive about my conversation with Rose. "Yes, I do. Please tell me."

"Remember, I said that after we're done here in Cork, we have to go back to my parents' house to pick something up?"

"Yes?"

"That's because I got a message from Una. The ring's arrived."

None of the statements he had just made were connecting to one another in my head. "What ring? What are you talking about?"

"Your engagement ring."

He took a sip of his pint as shock forced my jaw to drop. Although he was acting casual, I saw a bead of perspiration near his hairline.

"I wanted to get you something from Ireland," he continued, "and Una knew of a fine designer in Dublin. It's waiting for us in Kilshannig."

The acute surge of adoration I felt for Con was so sharp and strong, it paralyzed me for a few seconds, my eyes and mouth frozen in wide-open positions.

"Neve?" Con asked, then started slightly as I got up, walked around the table, leaned down, and wrapped my arms around him. He tugged me into his lap, and I nuzzled him, kissing a bruise-free spot where his neck and shoulder met.

Tilting my mouth up to his earlobe, I whispered, "That's the most romantic thing I've ever heard. Thank you."

His posture relaxed a bit. "I'm glad. Of course, if you don't like it, we can change it."

"There is zero chance of that happening." I pulled away just far enough so he could see me smiling at him. Of course, part of my brain was whirring with questions, wondering what the ring looked like and how he had chosen it. But I held back from asking, because more than wanting to know, I wanted to enjoy the surprise, and to let him enjoy surprising me. I wasn't at all worried about whether I'd like the ring. First of all, he'd had the good sense to get Una's help, and she had wonderful taste. But most importantly, Con had picked out the ring with me in mind, and our lifetime together. Something about it reminded him of me, and for the rest of our lives, it would remind me of him. For that reason alone, I loved it already.

I would have been happy to sit there forever with Con, but our desserts arrived. The waiter was a pro; he just smiled and waited patiently as I disentangled myself from Con and returned to my own seat.

By the time we were standing outside the restaurant waiting for our taxi, my heart felt truly light and joyful for the first time in ages. Con stood behind me with his arms wrapped around my shoulders. He leaned down and whispered in my ear, "Feeling good?"

"Mm-hmm." I nodded, pressing my earlobe closer to his mouth.

He pulled away slightly and murmured, "How good?"

The subtle change in his tone reminded me that our next stop would be our hotel room. It sounded as though, in spite of his injuries, he had very definite plans for us.

Hit by a sudden rush of nervous anticipation, I asked, "What do you mean?"

Con kissed my neck softly, making me shiver. "This morning, Della said I was medically cleared to engage in 'strenuous physical activity.'"

I yanked myself forward and twisted around to look him in the eye. Con's wounds were still healing, and he was covered in awful-looking bruises. "She did not!"

"She did—within reason, of course, and depending on how I feel. And right now, I'm feeling good."

I bit my lip as my face began to heat—and redden, no doubt, like a burner on an electric stove. Was this finally about to happen? Could I really dare to hope…?

"That said," Con said as our taxi pulled up to the curb, "when we get back to the hotel, we do have a few issues to sort out."

With that ominous concept rattling around in my head, I climbed into the cab. Con closed my door and got in on the other side, asking the driver to take us to the Hotel Gairdín.

"What issues?" I asked as we rode through the streets of Cork.

"Issues arising from our conversation in the library."

"Oh." My heart sank a bit. That entire conversation had been deadly serious, and "sorting out issues" didn't sound like much of a prelude to intimacy.

I forced myself to temper my disappointment, however. He said he felt good, but Con must still be exhausted and sore all over. In truth, I hadn't expected anything to happen between us for another week at least, so further delay wouldn't come as a surprise.

To reassure him I was fine with waiting, I said, "Okay, that sounds fine. Let's do that."

Then my cell phone rang. Agent Banai was calling with an update. The gardaí had begun the search for Declan's body in the river near the Blackbird. They thought it unlikely they would find anything since so much time had passed, but they were looking, nonetheless. In the meantime, using the CCTV footage from the pawnbroker and DNA from blood found on one of the hurleys they'd recovered, they had been able to rule Declan's disappearance a homicide and remove him from the list of suspects in Megan's murder. Agent Banai said he had shared the news with Kayla, and she had asked him to express her thanks to Con and me for our help.

Before he signed off, Agent Banai said, "I have one more request. Would you both be kind enough to stay out of trouble for the remainder of your time in Cork?"

Con sighed heavily as I suppressed a laugh. "I will, of course," he replied, "but I can't make any guarantees about *herself*."

"Understood." Agent Banai's tone of resignation made me laugh in earnest. "Do your best."

"Goodbye!" I said, hanging up the phone and turning to face Con. "You can't make any guarantees about *herself*?"

We pulled up to the hotel entrance. As the doorman took care of our bags, Con replied, "As I said, we have issues to sort out, and we're sorting them out today."

Although his words were serious, there was something sly about his demeanor. Maybe he wasn't dead set on killing the mood after all. "Today, as in now?"

"Yes," he said, holding the door open for me as we entered the hotel.

"It can't wait?"

"Until when?"

"I don't know, maybe—" I shrugged as we walked through the lobby. "—*after* some strenuous physical activity?"

Con steered me toward the elevator doors. "You misunderstand," he said, hitting the Up arrow button. "Strenuous physical activity is going to be a key part of the conversation."

As we entered the elevator, I had the disquieting feeling that I had missed something crucial. "You're right. I don't get it."

When the doors closed, Con turned toward me and leaned in, pressing his hand against the wall behind my head as he looked down at me. With the fire of determination burning in his eyes, he explained, "I'll see to it that our strenuous physical activity leaves you so boneless with pleasure that you can't get out of the bed. Then I won't have to worry about you fleeing airports, hiding out in hotels, staking out murderers, spying on human trafficking warehouses, or drawing gunfire."

I swallowed hard, and loudly enough that he must have heard it too. Between Con hovering over me and his promise to render me boneless, my body had already begun to melt like an ice cream cone dropped on a hot sidewalk.

Still, I couldn't believe he was bringing up things I had freely shared in our library conversation and using them as ammunition against me. With rising indignation, I asked, "And what about *you*? You lied to me too—repeatedly, might I add! You called the Secret Service behind my back, set up an extradition flight, made a deal for my safety without my agreement, and had whole conversations with me without telling me what the hell was going on. Not to mention, you threw yourself in the line of gunfire *on purpose!*"

I realized my last point wasn't as strong as it sounded in my head only after the elevator door opened and Con didn't move. He just peered down at me, eyebrows slowly rising as the elevator door closed again.

"Okay, scratch that last part." I sucked in my cheeks. "Thank you, by the way," I mumbled, "for pushing me out of the way and, you know... *really* taking a bullet for me."

"Anytime." Finally, he stepped back and I could breathe again. Con pressed the Door Open button and said, "In any case, the things I did are different from the things you did."

Now he was being absurd. "And how are they different, exactly?"

Con took me by the elbow and steered me into the hallway. "Because if anything ever happened to you, the world would end," he said matter-of-factly.

Was he seriously trying to argue that his pain if I got hurt would be greater than my pain if he got hurt? With everything I had gone through, worrying about him, trying to save him....

I whipped my elbow out of his grasp and stopped in the middle of the hallway. "And what if something happens to *you*?"

He frowned down at me. "Nothing will happen to me."

I threw my hands in the air. "How can you say that? Multiple things have *already* happened to you!"

"Yet here I am," he said with infuriating calm. "As I've pointed out before, my skin is so thick with scars, I'm indestructible at this point. And while you are quite extraordinary and highly capable in many ways, physically, there are relevant differences between us."

I glanced down at my chest to make the point that I understood the concept of physical differences, but Con's face didn't even twitch. "Relevant how, exactly?" I knew very well what he meant, but I wanted him to spell it out so I could debate him point by point.

He held out his hand, and I allowed him to take my arm. As we once again walked toward our room, he explained, "Relevant in situations where we might find ourselves in physical danger and need to protect ourselves from harm."

So, he *was* referring to his size and strength, knowing how to fight, etc. But I had also proven myself useful in dangerous situations—ringing the Bells of Shandon, for example, to bring people to our aid, and using my weight to help him pull Liam over the railing atop the tower—although I knew Con might not be too appreciative of the second part. I suspected he would have been just as happy to watch the man fall, but given all that had happened, I couldn't hold that against him. After all, in the end, he'd chosen to save the man's life.

As we turned down another hallway, he added, "The fact is, there are certain things I can do that you can't, and in such situations, those things make all the difference."

I stopped again and turned around to face him, hands perched on my hips. "Like what?" Once again, I knew the obvious answers. But if I got him to state specific examples, it would be easier to make a counterargument.

Then Con confused me by suddenly bending over.

"What, you can tie your shoelaces? Hey!" I yelped as he tucked his good shoulder against my hips. With a grunt of pain, he stood up, lifting me onto his shoulder like a big bag of flour.

"Like this," he said as he locked his arm around the back of my knees.

"What the…?" I curled my arm around his neck so my torso wouldn't be completely upside down. "Con, what are you doing? You're going to pull a stitch!"

He reached up and took my wrist, wrapping my upper body around him like a shawl. "Worth it," he declared and proceeded down the hallway.

"Put me down!" I clutched at his shirt as my body bounced helplessly. I wanted to wriggle off him, but from where I was, it looked like quite a long way down.

"Not until we reach the bed."

The bed? The bed! I froze. Not only was this happening, it was happening *right now*—and it seemed Con had a very specific agenda in mind. I had thought I was ready, but was I ready for *this*? "What exactly do you think you're doing?"

His voice grew deeper, rougher. "Processing emotional content."

"Ha!" Now he really was using my words against me. "For your information, that requires talking!"

"And we'll resume talking once your muscles have turned to jelly."

His words and the low vibration of his voice rumbling through me lit a pilot light deep in my core. My whole body began to squirm, trying desperately to release the rising heat. "Wait… but that's not… I mean, you can't…," I sputtered, struggling to find the words.

Con tightened his arm around my legs. "Don't worry," he soothed, "I remember what you told me. You're nervous about undressing in front of me—"

As a scorching fire rushed through me, I rued the moment I'd shared that little tidbit.

"—and I've decided I'll save you the trouble by taking your clothes off for you. Very slowly, of course, and not until you beg."

Did he really just say...? No, he couldn't have. I must have been growing lightheaded from being carried around. "What?"

Con stopped as we reached the door to our room. "I said, I won't take your clothes off until you beg. That way, we'll both be certain you're ready. Meanwhile, I'll focus on helping you forget all about your insecurities—and everything outside of our room, for that matter."

Oh hell no. Con had "tortured" me with pleasure before when we were in Galway, and then we had only been kissing. There was no way I'd be able to endure that again, not with flames of desire already licking my body. But expecting me to *beg*? That was a step too far. "You're just mad at me because I didn't get on that plane! Well, guess what? I'm mad at you too!"

"Angry and begging at the same time?" He had the nerve to sound amused. "I'll admit, I like the sound of that. But look, if you don't know how to beg, just say the word. I'll be happy to give you some lessons."

All I really wanted in that moment was for Con to

stop talking and take me inside. I was already so worked up that my skin felt hot, tight, and supersensitive, like I had a full-body sunburn. But although desire clawed at me, my pride was still hanging on—if only by a thread. "It'll be a cold day in hell before I beg you for anything, so you can just give up on that idea right now!"

Con replied, "You mean, 'give up on that idea, *please*.'" There was a telltale beep as he inserted the key card into the door handle.

"Stop being an ass and put me down immediately," I half ordered, half pleaded, but even I could hear the conviction in my voice waning.

"It's 'put me down, *I beg you*,'" he cheerfully corrected, and I heard a click as he pushed the door handle down, opening the latch.

It didn't even matter to me that other guests might hear my deep-throated moan of frustration. Any insecurity, uncertainty, or hesitation I'd felt before was being utterly destroyed by the searing conflagration of desire Con was igniting within me. "If you don't let me go right now, I swear to Go—*oooh!*"

I grabbed his shirt tightly as Con kicked the door open and spun us both inside. Then he slammed it shut behind us.

"Ah, love, you haven't got the hang of this

begging thing at all," Con declared with roguish vigor as he marched me toward the bed. "Don't worry, I'm here to help. Time for lesson one!"

THE END

AUTHOR'S NOTE

Thank you so much for reading *Dead Late*, Book Three in the Things Unseen series! I certainly hope you enjoyed it. If you'd like to help other readers find this book, please consider telling a friend, or taking a few minutes to leave a review on your favorite book website. The entire Things Unseen trilogy is now available on all platforms, including audiobook for those who prefer to listen. Happy reading!

ABOUT THE AUTHOR

Anise Eden is the psychotherapist-turned-author of the acclaimed Healing Edge paranormal romantic suspense series and Things Unseen thriller series. Anise's novels have garnered numerous awards, with her most recent book, *Dead Keen*, the winner of a New England Reader's Choice Award and finalist for the prestigious Daphne du Maurier Award for Excellence in Mystery/Suspense.

After studying at New York University and working for over a decade in mental health, Anise is now an educator and advocate. She can often be found sipping coffee while writing songs about dogs, messily sketching in charcoal, or visiting ancient historic sites. Originally from the US, she now lives with her Irish husband in County Cork, where she keeps several analog devices on hand in case of apocalypse. She is a member of International Thriller Writers, the Romantic Novelists' Association, and the Irish Writers Centre.

Keep in touch with Anise via her website: https://AniseEden.com

- facebook.com/authoraniseeden
- x.com/aniseeden
- bookbub.com/profile/anise-eden

RESOURCES

If you or someone you know is dealing with mental health issues, intimate partner abuse, or is a victim of human trafficking, please know that help is available. Contact your local emergency services or crisis hotline for assistance.

HelpGuide.org is a source of information and resources for mental health support. You can visit their website here:

HTTPS://WWW.HELPGUIDE.ORG/FIND-HELP.HTM

Hot Peaches Pages provides a list of international agencies for victims of domestic violence. Here is their website:

HTTPS://WWW.HOTPEACHPAGES.NET/A/COUNTRIES.HTML

The Alliance against Trafficking in Persons is a

broad international forum geared toward combating human trafficking. Learn more here:

HTTPS://WWW.OSCE.ORG/SECRETARIAT/107221

For members of the CNBC (Childless Not By Choice) community, the World Childless Week website has a list of supportive resources:

HTTPS://WORLDCHILDLESSWEEK.NET

ACKNOWLEDGMENTS

I would first like to thank my brilliant readers for all the love you have given the Things Unseen series. I sincerely hope you enjoyed this final installment of Neve and Con's story! You breathe life into my books by reading them, and for that, I am forever grateful.

Many thanks to my amazing editor, Kristin Scearce, my fabulous publisher, Rebecca Johnson, and to the team at Tangled Tree for peerless administration and marketing support, talented and sharp-eyed beta readers, and wonderful covers by Book-Smith Design. You have provided me with such tremendous support in every way. Thank you for making this series possible!

Sincere gratitude as well to Lisa Kay, the gifted and intuitive narrator of the audiobook versions of this series. Thank you for lending your voice and talents to make these books available to a whole new audience of readers!

I would like to express my gratitude to the following individuals for their special contributions to this volume:

My dear friend Rose O'Driscoll for all the laughs, and for "authenticity checking" the psychic medium scenes featuring her namesake character.

My *anam cara* Lisa Fahy for generously providing early feedback, for sharing her knowledge of exorcism waiting lists, and for all manner of solidarity throughout the writing process.

My writing bestie Rosanna Leo for giving this volume an early read, and for her invaluable feedback, friendship, and support. Next time, it's Niagara Falls or bust!

My neighbor Maureen, who suggested the title for this book—but who, in addition to being an amazing baker, gardener, and friend, is never late for anything.

Bubz at Lux Ink Tattoo and Beauty in Mallow for generously sharing her insider knowledge of Cork City.

John Foley of Foley's Express Food Store in Mallow for sharing his insights about Shandon and inspiring his namesake character in this book.

Marissa at Saint Anne's Church for answering my questions about the church and the tower, and for keeping an eye on me so I didn't get trapped up there!

Michael at the Hayfield Manor Hotel in Cork City for generously showing me around their gorgeous establishment, which inspired the Hotel Gairdín in this book.

As the Things Unseen trilogy draws to a close, I would also like to give my heartfelt thanks to the following for their support of the series:

The Mallow Scribes for their ongoing friendship and encouragement, and the Mallow Arts Festival for demonstrating such steadfast support with the Irish launches of *Dead Sound* and *Dead Keen*. Special thanks to Mecca Barrett, Tim Casey, and Paul Murphy, and to my fellow Suspicious of Scones sisters Lisa Barrett and Joanna Foley-Carroll.

My heart-sister Sarina Prabasi, Elias Gurmu, and the incredible Buunni Coffee family for hosting "Book Therapy: Saving the World Through Fiction," and to the wonderful LaQuette for participating with us. What a fabulous event, for which I am deeply grateful!

All the booksellers, libraries, reviewers, members of the media, writing contests, book clubs, and bloggers who have made the series available, read it, talked or written about it, and generally spread the word. Special thanks to Briggs on Books, the Cork

County Council Library & Art Service, the Paw Paw Book Club, Philip's Bookshop, The Ripped Bodice, and Word Up Community Bookshop.

Members of both the virtual and in-person writing communities who are always there with a share or a like, a word of encouragement, and offers to read or boost, shout-out or support. You keep me going in so many ways, and you have my heartfelt thanks.

I would also like to express my deep gratitude to my friends, who keep me company on this giant blue-green ball floating through space. I know I haven't seen many of you in person for quite some time, as we've scattered to the four winds. But regardless of time or distance, you are very precious to me and bring so much warmth and joy to my life. Special thanks for writerly solidarity to Kathy Cottle and Shannon Rowan.

My deepest gratitude I give to my own Irish hero and genius "plot doctor" of a husband, and to Mom, Dad, Amy, Sam, Gail, Carol, Navy, Barb, Helen, Adrian, and all of my other family members whose unconditional love and unwavering belief in me are my lifeblood, every moment of every day. You are all so busy living full lives and engaging in meaningful activities; it touches me deeply that you find the time to read my books and offer such encouraging words and meaningful support. I hold you in my heart always.

To my wonderful goddaughter and new favorite author, Olivia Liao: SUPER-congratulations on your fabulous debut novel, and I wish you all the fun and creativity you can handle in your first year of college!

Finally, thank you to all the beautiful souls from Cork City to Springfield who reached out with condolences on the loss of our dog, Polo, my little sweet pea and canine writing companion. He was the heartbeat of our home, and I was so happy to immortalize him in this book. Your kindness is very much appreciated.

ABOUT THE PUBLISHER

Tangled Tree Publishing loves all things tangled and aims to bring darker, twisted, and more mind-boggling books to its readers. Publishing adult and new adult fiction, TTPubs are all about diverse reads in mystery, suspense, thrillers, and crime.

For more details, head to WWW.TANGLEDTREEPUBLISHING.COM

- facebook.com/tangledtreepublishing
- x.com/ttpubs
- instagram.com/hottreepublishing
- tiktok.com/@hottreepublishing